About Melvyn Barnes

Melvyn has spent the whole of his care   ublic libraries. He began as a school   en occupied posts of incre   e, Manchester, Newc   & Chelsea and West eighteen years as Di   es for the City of London.

He has served as Pr   ent of both The Library Association and the International Association of Metropolitan City Libraries, and acted as an advisor on various bodies relating to government cultural policies and the British Library. In 1990 he was awarded the O.B.E. for services to public libraries.

His fascination with crime fiction began as a schoolboy with radio thrillers and paperback copies of Agatha Christie, and has continued ever since. This led to his books *Best Detective Fiction* (1975), *Murder in Print* (1986) and *Dick Francis* (1986), and his many contributions to periodicals in the genre and reference books including *Twentieth Century Crime & Mystery Writers* (four editions, 1980-96), *Scribner's Mystery and Suspense Writers* (1998) and *The Oxford Companion to Crime & Mystery Writing* (1999). From 1977 to 1982 he selected and edited *Remploy's "Deerstalker"* series of Golden Age detective fiction reprints.

In 2015 his book *Francis Durbridge: a Centenary Appreciation* was self-published with a limited print run, but such was the international interest that he was encouraged to pursue further research and to solve the many puzzles surrounding Durbridge's career. The result is the revised and vastly expanded *Francis Durbridge: The Complete Guide.*

FRANCIS DURBRIDGE

THE COMPLETE GUIDE

Melvyn Barnes

WITH AN ANNOTATED LISTING OF HIS NOVELS AND HIS WORKS FOR RADIO, TELEVISION, THE STAGE AND THE CINEMA

Copyright © Melvyn Barnes

This edition published in 2018 by Williams & Whiting

All rights reserved

No part of this publication may be reproduced, stored in a retrieval system, or transmitted, in any form or by any means without the prior permission in writing of the publisher, nor be otherwise circulated in any form of binding or cover other than that in which it is published and without a similar condition including this condition being imposed on the subsequent purchaser.

Cover photographs by courtesy of

Stephen and Nicholas Durbridge

ISBN 9781912582198

Williams & Whiting (Publishers)

15 Chestnut Grove, Hurstpierpoint,

West Sussex, BN6 9SS

CONTENTS

INTRODUCTION BY NICHOLAS DURBRIDGE   p 1

AUTHOR'S FOREWORD   p 7

FRANCIS DURBRIDGE 1912-1998   p 13

FRANCIS DURBRIDGE - A SURVEY   p 18

NOVELS   p 43

WORKS FOR RADIO   p 60

WORKS FOR TELEVISION   p 134

STAGE PLAYS   p 175

CINEMA FILMS   p 195

THE PAUL TEMPLE COMIC STRIP   p 207

FRANCIS DURBRIDGE - SOME OTHER WRITINGS   p 217

SOME OTHER REFERENCES   p 223

CHRONOLOGY - PAUL TEMPLE RADIO PRODUCTIONS   p 231

INTRODUCTION

BY NICHOLAS DURBRIDGE

From the 1930s to the 1990s my father Francis Durbridge was a household name in the United Kingdom, Germany and other parts of Europe, renowned for his radio, television and stage thrillers with frequent plot twists and cliff-hanger endings.

Born in 1912, he grew up in a home where reading was encouraged and throughout his life he was a voracious reader. From an early age he declared that he wanted to be a writer, particularly of thrillers, and this was common knowledge amongst his school friends. Once when a class teacher at Bradford Grammar asked him what he wanted to be, a friend jumped in and answered for him – "He's going to be the next Edgar Wallace, sir!" – as Edgar Wallace was a particular favourite of his at the time. Whilst at Birmingham University he joined the university theatrical club and started writing and appearing in revue sketches, and it was there that he was "discovered" in 1932 by a BBC radio producer called Martyn C. Webster who noted that his acting was terrible but that he rather liked the sketches that were credited to him in the theatre programme.

The early work of my father was enormously varied, ranging from radio sketches for variety shows to children's programmes, short stories and even lyrics for musical numbers. Sadly little of this survives due to a fire in a storage depository in the mid-1970s, where he had stored all his early work written before his creation of the radio detective Paul Temple which made him famous. His earliest surviving work from this period is a radio drama with incidental music called *Murder in the Embassy* which was broadcast in August 1937, a recording of which on old 78s I found last year at the back of a cupboard when having a clear out. These records also included *The Melody Man*, produced in December 1937, another musical drama specially written by him for the popular singer Leslie Hutchinson who was known to listeners as "Hutch". Both of these recordings were unknown to the BBC, but are now part of their early sound archive.

One of the startling facts about my father's writing career was how long it spanned, and in his early years he was extraordinarily prolific. Although he focused on Paul Temple from 1938 onwards, he continued to write variety and other material for several years. The early Temple serials were of course broadcast live, and to maintain the suspense the cast were not given the script of the last episode until the day of rehearsal and broadcast so they did not know who the villain among them would be. It is conjecture though as to whether even my father knew how the mystery would be solved at the outset of writing a serial. My mother once recalled to me that the broadcast of an eight part Temple serial had already commenced when he had not at that point written the final episode. When she expressed concern, he simply told her not to worry as it would all be fine!

Without doubt the success of Paul Temple opened many doors and opportunities. Paul Temple radio serials became novels and were then made into feature films. A Paul Temple newspaper strip appeared in the London *Evening News* from December 1950 and ran until 1971. My father used to joke that my brother Stephen and I were educated by a strip cartoon as it paid for our school fees, and it is therefore somewhat ironic that my subsequent career should be spent merchandising and exploiting successful characters amongst them Paddington Bear and Peter Rabbit.

With the advent of television broadcasting he carefully picked his moment, having stayed with radio whilst some of the early lessons of television were worked out. When he was ready he presented the head of BBC Drama with the first television serial *The Broken Horseshoe*, which was televised in 1952 and was the first of seventeen separate television serials which were produced and broadcast by the BBC up until 1980. These proved extremely popular with viewers, not only because of their trademark complicated plots but also because of the particular cliff-hanger endings, some of which with television could be visual in nature. One episode of *A Man Called Harry Brent* ended with the hero in his sports car pulling out into the road behind a laundry van, which the viewers recognise as having been used in a shooting earlier in the serial. Was the rear door going to open, revealing a man with a machine gun as before? Just as the viewer was tensing for action the credits began to roll up the screen, and he or she would have to wait until next week's episode to find out.

But aside from the twists and turns of his plots and his cliff-hanging endings which were unique in this period, what was perhaps most unusual about my father's television work lay in his understanding of intellectual property rights. In the early days of television writers normally granted the BBC world broadcast rights, and the resulting programmes would be sold by the BBC around the world and particularly to the British Commonwealth. The fees paid to writers by the BBC for these sales were small, if they existed at all. Due to his popularity and the keenness of the BBC to retain his services against the growing competition of the commercial ITV network, he negotiated a position whereby the BBC only acquired English language production and distribution rights. This left him free to license his television work to be made into local productions in Germany, Holland, Sweden, Finland, France and Italy, deriving a fee for every production.

The German productions of his serials in particular were hugely successful, many produced by the WDR television network, and often cast with the most popular leading television actors of the day. Such was their success that the German parliament on one occasion adjourned a debate at the request of members so they could go home to watch the final episode of a Durbridge serial. A phrase was even coined for him. He was referred to as the *straßenfeger* or street sweeper, as German streets, stations, shops and cinemas were noticeably quieter on the nights when a Durbridge serial was being broadcast. As with his radio serials he also licensed novelisations of each of his television serials, many of which were published internationally as well as in the UK. Identifying all these overseas productions has been a challenge as the titles were always changed, and he also often agreed to change the character names and on occasion even the identity of the villain so that journalists could not disclose the dénouement of a serial based on the earlier BBC production.

In the early 1970s he began to turn his attention to his great interest - the theatre. Throughout his life he read and collected stage plays and was fascinated by the technical challenges that a stage play presented, especially in more recent times when cast numbers and stage sets had to be kept low and simple for cost reasons. Whereas with radio he could move the drama around to conjure up an image for the listener through sound, and with television one could film on location albeit with some cost restraints, on the stage the drama had to unfold perhaps within a single room. As my father remarked, the greatest challenge was to get the characters on and off stage. There was a limit to how many times a phone or doorbell could ring!

Lost to family memory until recently was his first stage play, which was based on *Send for Paul Temple* and produced at the Alexandra Theatre Birmingham in 1943. We are indebted to Melvyn Barnes for having discovered details of this production. Fortunately all theatre productions had to be licensed in 1943 and the Lord Chamberlain, who was responsible for theatre censorship, always kept a copy of the scripts. The Lord Chamberlain's archive is now housed as part of the British Library and so, when an enquiry was made there recently a copy of the script was discovered, unseen for over seventy years, as my father's copy was not among his papers having no doubt been destroyed in the fire that consumed much of his early work.

His career spanned sixty hugely productive years and was unusual for its sustained popularity, and for its movement from one dramatic medium to another. Many writers might focus on a career as a novelist or write for television or film and may occasionally stray into other media. My father however had a consistently varied career writing for radio, television and film often simultaneously and then later for the theatre, all the while also working with others on turning his scripts into novels, movies, strip cartoons or writing short stories for magazines to meet the continual demand for new Durbridge material, particularly featuring Paul Temple.

Throughout his career my father constantly sought to fine tune plots and to hone dialogue and search for that perfect character name. Sometimes changes were made between a radio serial and its publication in book or some other form. All of this has made the researching of this guide by Melvyn Barnes a particularly complicated task. In a hand written cash book, which was found after my mother's death in 2017, my father recorded all his income but often against working titles that were later changed, and of course like any writer he had a fair number of ideas or plot outlines that were never commissioned or saw the light of day for one reason or another. The research and sleuthing required of Melvyn Barnes in identifying so much of my father's work has been phenomenal and worthy of Paul Temple himself, by Timothy! My brother Stephen and I are extremely grateful to him for undertaking this task so diligently and successfully.

Nicholas Durbridge
January 2018

FOREWORD by MELVYN BARNES

Francis Durbridge was a prominent name in popular culture for half a century from the 1930s, and in recent years his reputation has been revived by reprints of his novels and the release of new CDs and DVDs of his radio and television thrillers. It is therefore timely to produce this updated and greatly expanded edition of my book *Francis Durbridge: A Centenary Appreciation*, particularly because further research has enabled me to add much previously unrecorded information about many aspects of his writing career. It is even more timely, given that 2018 sees the twentieth anniversary of Durbridge's passing (11 April 1998) and the eightieth anniversary of the first radio appearance of his best-known creation Paul Temple (8 April 1938).

It has also proved appropriate to introduce an international dimension, as my earlier book concentrated upon the original UK versions of Durbridge's novels and his works for radio, television, the stage and the cinema. Little coverage was given to his impact overseas, but subsequent discussions with Durbridge enthusiasts beyond the UK has brought home to me the true extent of his popularity throughout Europe in particular. While I always knew that his novels had been widely translated and that versions of his radio and television serials had regularly gripped enormous audiences abroad, I now have no doubt that a phenomenon that might be called "EuroDurbridge" must be properly recognised. Indeed, to give a significant example of something that might surprise even the most ardent Durbridge fan, my section on his stage plays now reveals that his success in the theatre world was achieved in Germany long before his first play opened in London.

Any bibliography of Francis Durbridge remains a minefield for those seeking to identify all his works. An online search for "Francis Durbridge" produces many thousands of results, which reassuringly confirms that his name is not forgotten. The downside, however, is that such saturated coverage means that errors on one website are repeated on numerous other websites and thereby acquire an authenticity that is both spurious and permanent.

To highlight one of the most regular Durbridge errors that has been repeated over many years, his name is still frequently linked with the 1956 film *Town on Trial* starring John Mills and in particular with the suggestion that it was adapted from his novella *The Nylon Murders*, but this film made no mention of Durbridge in its credits. Another problem concerns the origin of the 1963 German film *Piccadilly Null Uhr Zwölf*, which is legitimately included in my filmography because Durbridge's name appeared in the credits and on the posters. In respect of four other Internet references to Durbridge titles that were never used – television serials called *The Brass Candlestick* and *Stupid like a Fox* and stage plays called *Murder Diary* and *The Grandma Game* – I have now been able to demystify them in the relevant sections of this book. In other words, in these cases and many others my research results have corrected inaccurate references to Francis Durbridge, but sadly it must be accepted that such false information is likely to remain in the ether forever.

The Brass Candlestick is a particularly interesting case, in view of the many assertions that a Durbridge television serial with that title gave rise to the 1957 film *The Vicious Circle* starring John Mills. Indeed, whenever this film is shown on television, press listings can always be relied upon to perpetuate the myth. There is no doubt that the film *The Vicious Circle* was based on Durbridge's 1956 television serial *My Friend Charles*, which admittedly had a brass candlestick as the murder weapon and also as the motif of a criminal gang. So perhaps *The Brass Candlestick* was Durbridge's original working title that was changed in the course of production, as so often happens. I can also now reveal that when the film *The Vicious Circle* was released in some Spanish-speaking countries, one of its titles was *El Candelabro de bronce* – so no prizes for guessing the English translation!

I can only add a further amusing comment, as I discovered in *The Times* theatre column dated 1 January 1951 that a play called *The Brass Candlestick* was about to open at a fringe London theatre. Could this be it, I wondered, and might Durbridge have written a stage play with this title? But no, because a first night critic then revealed that it was a melodrama on a Jack the Ripper theme written by E.R.S. Blythe and Telford Field. Such are the highs and lows of the research process.

When looking at Durbridge's body of work, a major complication arises from his penchant for recycling his plots. By this I am not referring to the many straightforward cases where one of his novels or films was openly acknowledged to be an adaptation of one of his radio or television serials, even if the title was changed. Instead I refer specifically to the fact that he occasionally wrote "new" works that were actually recycled versions of earlier works, often with changes of character names and revamped plots. For example, his 1938 novel *Send for Paul Temple* was re-written to become his 1951 novel *Beware of Johnny Washington*. On radio, his 1934 play *Murder in the Midlands* became his 1945 play *Over My Dead Body*, his 1935 play *Crash* became his 1938 play *Information Received* and his 1945 serial *Send for Paul Temple Again* became his 1968 serial *Paul Temple and the Alex Affair*. The one example on television occurred when he transformed his 1959 serial *The Scarf* much later into his final television serial *Breakaway: The Local Affair* in 1980.

There were even instances when Durbridge unaccountably removed his popular characters Paul and Steve Temple from novelisations of his radio serials - with *Paul Temple and the Gregory Affair* (1946), *Paul Temple and the Jonathan Mystery* (1951) and *Paul Temple and the Gilbert Case* (1954) appearing in print as *Design for Murder* (1951), *Dead to the World* (1967) and *Another Woman's Shoes* (1965) respectively. But surely the longest chain of recycling began when his 1946 radio play *The Caspary Affair* was much later re-written as an Italian radio play called *Preludio al Delitto* (1960), and then re-appeared on the German theatrical stage as *Zaradin 4* (1988) before it was finally presented to British theatregoers as Durbridge's "new" stage play *Sweet Revenge* in 1993.

It has therefore been a challenge to confirm that "this was a new version of that", but I can confidently state that several years' research has enabled me to compile the most accurate and comprehensive listing in existence, together with a numbering system that links related items. Throughout this process I have valued the interest and support of many people, but first and foremost I must thank Stephen and Nicholas Durbridge for copying to me their father's original financial records and other documents – thus helping me to solve many mysteries and providing new lines of investigation – as well as for their patience in replying to my frequent questions.

In spite of my comments above, digital websites are important sources of information – particularly in the present case The Times Digital Archive, The Guardian and Observer Digital Archive, ukpressonline, the British Film Institute online database, IMDb (formerly Internet Movie Database) and the BBC Genome Project. Turning to hard copy, the collections of the British Library have been invaluable, as have been the resources and staff of the BBC Written Archives Centre at Caversham. Patrick Rayner, the producer of the BBC Radio 4 re-creations of the "lost" Paul Temple serials, has been most helpful. In seeking to identify the theme music for each of the Durbridge television serials, I have relied heavily upon research by Alexander Gleason of *filmusicuk*. Crime fiction aficionados Tony Medawar, Barry Pike, Peter Lovesey, Martin Edwards and Liz Gilbey have provided useful information, and in preparing this new and expanded edition I have benefitted greatly from the extensive "EuroDurbridge" knowledge of Dr. Georg Pagitz in Austria and Antonio Scaglioni in Italy. To summarise, therefore, I offer warm thanks and acknowledgements to all of those mentioned above.

In respect of Durbridge's novels and stage plays, my own collection of first editions has provided the necessary facts - to which, after searching British Library hard copies and microfilms, I have been able to add details of his novels that appeared as newspaper or magazine serials but not as books. The book trade bibliographies in the British Library have further confirmed publication data, and ensured that there are no published novels or stage plays that previously escaped my attention. To list his main body of work, his radio and television productions, I have accumulated a vast amount of information from websites and recordings, but to ensure accuracy it has been necessary to search the original copies of the *Radio Times* as well as scouring the BBC Written Archives. This was a pleasure in itself because, Durbridge apart, the reminders of so many other programmes were joyously nostalgic!

Rather than rely entirely upon websites for details of Durbridge's work for the cinema, I have viewed the actual films. To compile the first ever comprehensive list of his Paul Temple comic strips, I have consulted the original copies of the London *Evening News*.

In most cases there is a plot summary under the first appearance of a Durbridge plot, albeit deliberately brief rather than a "spoiler".

So to summarise my personal feelings, I sincerely hope that this book will help to perpetuate the name of Francis Durbridge as a key figure in the history of broadcasting and crime fiction. Few writers on popular culture have ever accorded him the recognition he deserves, but irrespective of this his legion of fans throughout the world will doubtless continue to enjoy his work for many years to come.

FRANCIS DURBRIDGE
1912-1998

Francis Henry Durbridge was born into a relatively prosperous middle-class family in Kingston upon Hull on 25 November 1912, which is a fact that sadly remained one of that city's best kept secrets when Hull celebrated 2017 as the UK City of Culture. His parents were Francis and Gertrude Durbridge, his father being a Woolworths store manager who rose to control the store's Midland region. He married Norah Elizabeth Lawley in 1940 and they had two sons, Stephen (who became a literary agent) and Nicholas (who became a specialist in copyright law and product licensing).

Durbridge was educated at Bradford Grammar School, Wylde Green College and Birmingham University, and as an undergraduate he determined to pursue his schoolboy ambition to become a writer. Already, as a teenager, he had written a play called *The Great Dutton* which was performed for charity. The bug had clearly bitten, and although he spent a brief period in a stockbroker's office his career as a full-time writer was launched by the British Broadcasting Corporation in the early 1930s with his children's stories, comedy plays, musical libretti and numerous short sketches. His first radio dramas *Promotion* and *Murder in the Midlands* indicated the direction he was ultimately to follow, but his earliest airing was a play called *The Three-Cornered Hat* in *The Children's Hour* on the BBC Midland Region on 25 July 1933.

In 1938 he established himself as a crime writer in particular, several months before his twenty-sixth birthday, when the BBC Midland Region broadcast his serial *Send for Paul Temple*. The listening public submitted over 7,000 requests for more, and he rapidly became one of the foremost writers of radio thrillers. His output was prolific, and increased even more by his use of the pseudonyms Frank Cromwell, Nicholas Vane and Lewis Middleton Harvey. To place him in context, in the mid-twentieth century his closest comparators were Edward J. Mason and Lester Powell (both coincidentally born the same year as Durbridge), together with Ernest Dudley, Alan Stranks and Philip Levene.

The early Paul Temple radio serials were soon adapted as books, but Durbridge's first five novelisations were collaborations with another author because he was essentially a writer of dialogue, a playwright rather than a novelist. This was, however, just the beginning of a long career that saw him dominate the airwaves and the television screen, as well as writing stage plays, novels, film scripts and a long-running newspaper strip – thus displaying a versatility that made him a rare example of a truly multi-media writer.

Francis Durbridge died on 11 April 1998 in Barnes, the leafy area outside London that had been his home and the type of background he had used in many of his plots. In response, the BBC did little to mark the passing of a writer who had been prominent in its radio and television schedules for half a century. While the Corporation posted a brief tribute on its BBC News website within hours of his death (albeit with a photograph of the wrong man), a more fitting recognition would have been a repeat of one of his radio or television serials or even more appropriately a special programme surveying the wide range of his work over the decades. In direct contrast, radio and television stations in Germany were glowing in their obituaries and in their praise for his work. Describing his serials as unforgettable masterpieces, they recalled the days when Durbridge cliff-hangers resulted in deserted German streets because over 80% of the population insisted on staying at home, glued to their radios and television sets.

A few years earlier, the BBC had shown greater appreciation of Durbridge's role in the history of radio drama by repeating his serial *Paul Temple and the Spencer Affair* (29 October – 17 December 1992) to celebrate his 80th birthday, thirty-five years after its original broadcast. Yet this still prompted *The Times* (5 November 1992) to comment: "The BBC publicity machine … has been strangely reticent." From this it seems that *The Times* thought this broadcast should have been given a higher profile, and few will have disagreed with their critic's assessment that "The serial carries its years lightly. The crisp editing and cliff-hanging fade-outs of the Durbridge thrillers, plus their refusal to sacrifice dialogue for sock-in-the-jaw action, made them models of their kind."

More recently the BBC has awoken to the fact that Durbridge remains a significant figure in British popular culture and still has a substantial fanbase, as well as potentially attracting a whole new audience. Revivals of some of the "lost" Paul Temple radio serials have been broadcast and released on CDs; surviving recordings of his original serials continue to be repeated on Radio 4 Extra and marketed on CDs; DVDs of many of his television serials have become available; and today's audiences have the opportunity to buy CD readings and audio downloads of his novels. In short, Durbridge has become big business again.

As an aside, here is a piece of trivia that provides further evidence of Durbridge's continuing appeal. In 2008 Edward Viita, the manager of the Artesian Bar in London's famous Langham Hotel near Broadcasting House, created a new cocktail to celebrate the 70th anniversary of the first Paul Temple radio serial. He called it "the Paul Temple", and given one of the detective's favourite tipples it was appropriately whisky-based.

So what sort of a man was Francis Durbridge, who in his *Who's Who* entry listed his interests simply as his family, reading and travel? On 8 July 1968 he was the guest on the radio programme *Desert Island Discs*, and revealed an eclectic taste. His eight record choices were Jill Haworth singing the title song from the Kander and Ebb musical *Cabaret*; Artur Rubinstein playing a Chopin nocturne; Sammy Davis Jnr singing Rodgers and Sondheim's "Do I Hear a Waltz?"; Mickey Rooney singing Rodgers and Hart's "Manhattan"; part of Rimsky-Korsakov's *Scheherazade* suite (very appropriate, as this was the original signature tune for his Paul Temple radio serials); Noël Coward singing his own song "Nina"; Jack Cassidy singing "Ilona" from the Bock and Harnick musical *She Loves Me*; and as his favourite choice, Wilhelm Kempff playing Beethoven's piano concerto no. 5, the "Emperor". His chosen book was George Bernard Shaw's *Plays and Prefaces*, and his luxury item was the Henri Matisse painting "Still Life with Oriental Rug".

Durbridge's interview on *Desert Island Discs* showed him to be a man who eschewed pretentiousness, and we are left unsurprised that this also typified his writing. Whatever the literati might say, he sought only to give pleasure to millions and he continues to do so long after his passing.

FRANCIS DURBRIDGE
A SURVEY

Crime fiction historian Jack Adrian opened his obituary of Francis Durbridge in *The Independent* (13 April 1998) with the statement: "To children of the 1940s and 1950s, who grew up in the radio age, Francis Durbridge is the sound of *Coronation Scot*, that most compelling of pieces by Vivian Ellis which invariably heralded yet another Paul Temple serial."

Although Durbridge made numerous contributions to BBC radio in various genres, Jack Adrian was perfectly correct in acknowledging that he will primarily be associated with his serials featuring the novelist-detective Paul Temple and his wife Steve, of Bramley Lodge near Evesham and fashionable Eaton Square in London. They were played firstly by Hugh Morton and Bernadette Hodgson (three times), but later and definitively by Peter Coke and Marjorie Westbury (eleven times). In between, they were played successively by Carl Bernard and Thea Holme (once); Carl Bernard and Bernadette Hodgson (once); Richard Williams and Lucille Lisle (once); Barry Morse and Marjorie Westbury (once); Howard Marion-Crawford and Marjorie Westbury (once); and Kim Peacock and Marjorie Westbury (nine times, plus the 1949 spoof play *The Night of the Twenty-Seventh* by Edward J. Mason). The Radio 4 re-creations of Paul Temple serials, which began in 2006 and of which there have been five so far, have starred Crawford Logan and Gerda Stevenson. From these figures, it can be seen that the definitive duo scored eleven for Peter Coke as Paul Temple and a resounding twenty-three for Marjorie Westbury as Steve.

It will be evident from the above that Kim Peacock was associated with the role of Paul Temple for a long period, and consequently became the epitome of Temple to the listening public. It is hardly surprising, therefore, that throughout Peacock's tenure there were numerous press reports of his personal appearances as "Paul Temple" at publicity and charity events. Indeed it seems that Peacock felt that he had become Temple and that he would remain permanently in the role, which explains his understandable resentment when supplanted by Peter Coke (as mentioned in various Coke radio interviews).

It is also worth mentioning Sir Graham Forbes, the top Scotland Yard man who always relied upon the Temples to assist him with his latest investigation and who featured in every case except *Paul Temple and the Geneva Mystery*. In this role the actor Lester Mudditt reigned supreme, appearing from the initial *Send for Paul Temple* in 1938 and on a total of nineteen occasions until the final episode of *Paul Temple and the Spencer Affair* on 1 January 1958. During Muddit's tenure he was replaced only twice - by Cecil Trouncer for the one-hour abridged version of *Send for Paul Temple* in 1941, and by Laidman Browne for the one-hour abridged version of *News of Paul Temple* in 1944. Lester Muddit was succeeded as Sir Graham by Richard Williams (who appeared in three serials in 1959), then James Thomason (who also appeared in three serials, 1961-68), and finally by Gareth Thomas in the re-creations from 2006 to 2013.

While the early Paul Temple serials were somewhat blood-and-thundery, they grew in sophistication. In fact Durbridge himself, in an article entitled "Talking of Serials" (*Radio Times*, 8 November 1957), confirmed that "looking back at the first Paul Temple serials I find that they were much more violent and straightforward than they are today." This was even reflected in the signature tune, with the menacing extract from Rimsky-Korsakov's *Scheherazade* suite making way in December 1947 for the melodic strains of Vivian Ellis's *Coronation Scot*.

There can be no doubt that the Paul Temple serials became a national institution. They were particularly championed by "Collie Knox" of the *Daily Mail* during the 1940s and 1950s, when the columnist could always be relied upon to trail the latest Temple case. Their comfortable regularity in the BBC's radio schedules for thirty years was also demonstrated by the fact that Martyn C. Webster was the only producer for their entire run.

Webster was a BBC stalwart who joined its variety department in Glasgow in 1926, later worked as a producer in the Midlands and nationally, and also broadcast as an actor and singer under the name Gerald Martin. He is, however, chiefly remembered as the producer of numerous radio dramas that dominated his career until his retirement in 1967, which in addition to the Paul Temple serials included John Dickson Carr's series *Appointment with Fear*, the Philip Odell serials by Lester Powell, original radio plays by Agatha Christie, and a wide range of *Saturday Night Theatre* productions. Although the Temple serials were his most memorable association with Durbridge, he was responsible for many other Durbridge radio programmes. He also directed Durbridge's first two television serials in the early 1950s, *The Broken Horseshoe* and *Operation Diplomat*, and the cinema film version of *The Broken Horseshoe*.

In fact Martyn C. Webster might accurately be described as the man who discovered Francis Durbridge, because he recognised Durbridge's writing skills when he attended a Birmingham University revue in the early 1930s and expressed an interest in receiving a script for broadcasting. This proved to be the beginning of several decades of professional partnership and personal friendship, which even saw Webster return to produce the radio serial *Paul Temple and the Alex Affair* in 1968 after his official retirement from the BBC in the previous year. Throughout this long association there was no doubt that Webster shared Durbridge's enthusiasm for creating mystery and suspense, including the need to withhold from the listener any inflection or nuance that might inadvertently point to the guilty party, which Webster maintained by famously refusing to disclose the identity of the murderer to members of the cast until they arrived to rehearse the very last episode of each Paul Temple serial.

But how did Paul Temple and Steve originate? It might not be coincidental that in 1934 on both sides of the Atlantic the detective duo Nick and Nora Charles achieved enormous popularity with the publication of Dashiell Hammett's novel *The Thin Man*, which led to spin-off films and radio and television programmes. Perhaps more significantly, a BBC radio adaptation of *The Thin Man* was broadcast nationally on 16 June 1936. It is therefore likely that Durbridge was aware of Nick and Nora, and although they might not have been his direct inspiration he would at least have appreciated from their success that there was scope for another husband and wife detective team. Nevertheless any comparison must end there, as Paul and

Steve were quintessentially British and their creator displayed his own style that owed little or nothing to Hammett.

Some years later, the Temple serials themselves attracted interest from American radio networks. In the *Daily Mail* (11 February 1949), under the heading "U.S. Calls for Paul Temple, Detective", a news item reported that on that day Durbridge was to sail for New York to consider offers from leading bidders. Durbridge was quoted as modestly saying: "I have always presented him as a typically British detective, probing his cases with an unhurried calm. It may be necessary to adapt the whole character of the man and his adventures to American tastes." There is no evidence, however, to suggest that Temple subsequently made an impact on US radio.

As Paul Temple was almost a real person to so many listeners, it is only right that he should have a background biography. The most reliable must surely come from Durbridge himself, and he duly provided accounts in several publications over many years. In the London *Evening News* on 27 November 1950, in an article entitled "This Man Temple", he recalled his creation of 1938. This article, incidentally, was enhanced with a portrait of Temple by Alfred Sindall, who soon became the first artist of that newspaper's daily Paul Temple comic strip. Durbridge stated that Paul Temple was born in Ontario, the son of Lt-Gen Ian Temple, and came to England at the age of ten. He was educated at Rugby and Magdalen College Oxford, afterwards writing his first of more than thirty novels at the age of twenty-two. The same article recorded that Paul Temple and Steve were married in St Mary Abbots Church in Kensington in 1938, which chronologically accords with their first meeting in *Send for Paul Temple*. Durbridge also listed Temple's interests as fishing, collecting first editions, Debussy, Beethoven, Jerome Kern, Rodgers and Hart, Cole Porter and the watercolours of Raoul Dufy – some or all of which we might assume to be among his own interests.

In that *Evening News* article concerning the origin of Paul Temple, Durbridge recalled that he had come across a fellow passenger who inspired him when taking a train from London to Birmingham. He later referred to this encounter again in an article entitled "Scripting for Suspense", published in *TV Mirror Annual* (Amalgamated Press, 1956), commenting: "I had been brooding upon the character of Paul Temple for some months ... We never spoke, but I found my mind recalling the deliberate manner he had inserted a cigarette into its unusual holder, the keen, intelligent face, the smiling eyes and shrewd mouth ... Yet I wonder if the most avid Temple fan would detect any resemblance?"

It has to be said that within the Durbridge family it is believed that this story was invented in order to deal with frequent tiresome questions about Temple's origin, although the family has never doubted that Steve Temple was based on Durbridge's wife Norah, to whom he had become engaged in 1937 and married in 1940. Nevertheless he remained consistent over many years in his recollection of the fellow traveller, as he first mentioned it in an article published at the time of the original Paul Temple serial (*Radio Times*, 22 April 1938), in which he also revealed that for his detective's name "Mark Conway" had run Temple a very close second – and it is interesting to note that "Mark Conway" was a name that reappeared subsequently in Durbridge's radio career (see **126**, **131** and **148**).

In his later article "Meet Paul Temple Again" (*Radio Times*, 10 October 1963) Durbridge repeated some of these details, but also mentioned that Temple's play *Over My Dead Body* was produced shortly after the war and ran for just seven performances. This doomed play was recalled on the radio in episode one of *Paul Temple and the Geneva Mystery* in 1965, when Temple described it as "the flop of the season" — although way back in 1946, in episode one of *A Case for Paul Temple*, he had referred to *Over My Dead Body* as a novel on which he was then working. In any case Durbridge probably had his tongue firmly in his cheek, because *Over My Dead Body* was in reality the title of his own radio play that was broadcast on 11 April 1945!

There are, however, various Internet accounts of Temple's life that supplement or even contradict Durbridge's version, although many simply repeat the information given in Durbridge's first novel *Send for Paul Temple*. Some say that Temple's career began as a reporter on a London daily newspaper, and that after writing the play *Dance Little Lady* (which closed soon after opening) he achieved success with his first mystery novel entitled appropriately *Death in the Theatre*. Maurice Wiltshire, in a *Daily Mail* article of 11 October 1949, had even more fun with his speculations when he alleged that Temple the novelist always wrote under a pen-name, and that *There Is No Mystery* was his only signed novel to date and his most successful. He described Temple as "six-feet-one-inch of brawn, and weighing 14½ stone," which is certainly not the way most fans pictured him.

The Paul Temple serials proved to be Durbridge's most enduring work for the radio, as witness the fact that "Temple, Paul" secured a place in *Brewer's Dictionary of Modern Phrase and Fable*, which is something of an accolade for a twentieth-century fictional character. Little wonder, then, that in the twenty-first century Temple and Steve have been breathing new life on the airwaves with repeats of the surviving original recordings and new productions of the "lost" serials, together with a multitude of printed books, e-books, compact discs and downloads. Today new listeners and readers can enjoy, as did previous generations, the gripping exploits of the urbane detective who was constantly threatened with bombs concealed in packages or "radiograms", who deplored violence except in self-defence, and who never used bad language but allowed himself the oath "By Timothy!" on every conceivable occasion.

Paul Temple might easily have become so closely associated with his typically English *milieu* as to have little to commend him overseas, but instead he became a worldwide attraction. A heavy crop of fan mail was received by Durbridge from as far afield as Israel, Canada, South Africa, Fiji, Hong Kong, Australia and New Zealand, but his popularity was most markedly prevalent in Europe.

From 1949 to 1968 fifteen German productions of Temple radio serials were broadcast, all faithfully translated from the Durbridge originals. Most of them featured the Luxembourg-born actor René Deltgen, and they were described as *straßenfeger* (street sweepers) because so many people stayed at home to listen to them. The same phenomenon occurred in Denmark in 1954, when

Gregory-mysteriet resulted in deserted streets to such an extent that it is still remembered today.

In the Netherlands twenty-three productions were aired from 1939 to 1969, with Temple re-named Paul Vlaanderen (Flanders) and Steve re-named Ina. Apart from the name change, these too were translations of the original Durbridge scripts. Some of them were revived much later, with new Dutch radio productions from 2004 onwards.

In addition there were three oddities among the Vlaanderen productions. Broadcast on 6 August 1947, and not based on a Durbridge original, *Paul Vlaanderen wordt onthaald* (Paul Vlaanderen Is Welcomed) was written by Bob de Haan and produced by Kommer Kleijn. It featured Jan van Ees as Vlaanderen and Nico de Jong as Sir Graham Forbes, and some of its characters were barely disguised versions of genuine crime writers including Agatha Pristie, Philips Roppeneime and Georges Dimenon. Broadcast on 14 September 1959, *Paul en Ina Vlaanderen incognito* was based on Durbridge's 1945 radio play *Over My Dead Body* (see **148**) and featured Jan van Ees and Eva Janssen. Broadcast on 5 April 1998, *Paul Vlaanderen en het media mysterie* was written by Thomas Ross and produced by Reinier Heidemann. Not based on a Durbridge original, this was a three-episode "spoof" with Erik van der Donk as Vlaanderen, Maria Lindes as Ina, Peter Aryans as Sir Graham Forbes and Donald de Marcas as Charlie.

There were also three serials in Belgium, with Nick and Ellie Holland played by Cor De Flem and Lisette T'Seyen, although these were not based on Durbridge scripts.

Broadcast in 1958, they were written by Ronald Petterson and produced by René Metzemaekers. The rather colourful titles were *Nick Holland en het Bulldog-Mysterie*, *Nick Holland en het Oldcate-Mysterie* and *Nick Holland en het Kolibri-Mysterie*.

At least ten European countries broadcast Paul Temple serials, and the international appeal of Durbridge was finally recognised in 1967 when he became the first author commissioned by the European Broadcasting Union to write a radio serial for multi-lingual broadcasting. The result, *La Boutique*, was heard throughout Europe - in Austria, Italy, Germany, Belgium, Norway, Sweden, Switzerland, Turkey, Greece and Finland – and even in Australia, New Zealand, Canada, South Africa and Japan.

While Durbridge's radio successes extended into the 1960s, television had also beckoned and from the early 1950s he had built a new and parallel reputation on the small screen. Again there was a guru, with Alan Bromly producing and directing most of the Durbridge television serials just as Martyn C. Webster had done on the radio, and perhaps inevitably these attracted a huge body of viewers that has rarely been equalled. Today his titles ring nostalgically in the mind, perpetuated by the fact that they were later novelised, including *Portrait of Alison*, *My Friend Charles*, *The Other Man*, *The Scarf*, *The World of Tim Frazer*, *Melissa*, *Bat out of Hell*, *The Passenger*, *The Doll* and *Breakaway*. None of them featured Paul Temple, but each involved a protagonist who could be described as an antihero, often an innocent suspect attempting to extricate himself from a web that enmeshed him more securely at every turn. Each episode saw this central character increasingly snarled up in a murderous plot that was masterminded by someone whose identity, needless to say, remained a mystery until the dénouement.

When Durbridge secured his niche in television in March 1952 with *The Broken Horseshoe*, television serials were a novelty. Consequently he received the distinction of a listing in *The Hutchinson Chronology of World History*, which recorded for posterity the fact that *The Broken Horseshoe* was the first thriller serial on British television. There had of course already been one-off television plays in the mystery genre, and there had also been two series (rather than serials) by Lester Powell called *The Inch Man* – featuring Robert Ayres as Stephen Inch, the house detective in a London hotel - transmitted as six thirty-minute episodes from 30 June to 4 August 1951 and eight thirty-minute episodes from 8 December 1951 to 26 January 1952. Even Sherlock Holmes had made an early television appearance, in six thirty-five minute cases adapted by C.A. Lejeune, with Alan Wheatley as Holmes and Raymond Francis as Watson, from 20 October to 1 December 1951.

By coincidence, it was also Lejeune who in her *Observer* column (23 March 1952) reviewed Durbridge's first television serial in terms that now seem strange. She wrote: "It will be interesting to see how Mr. Durbridge manages his 're-capping' from week to week, for *The Broken Horseshoe* is a true serial and not a series of associated adventures with a beginning, middle and end. The skill with which such a programme can arrange for new viewers to start viewing here, without boring old viewers or wasting time, will achieve much to do with the serial's success. But if it goes on as well as it has begun, I don't intend to miss a Saturday." From this it appears that Durbridge was regarded at the time as an innovator, although he had been doing that very thing for over ten years on the radio.

Perhaps because his television serials were presented sparingly, enabling him to retain a degree of freshness within a type of mystery he made very much his own, the appeal of Durbridge became awesome. An anonymous review of the first episode of *The Scarf* (*The Times*, 10 February 1959) commented: "When he writes a script nowadays Mr. Francis Durbridge takes full advantage of his position as undisputed master of the detective serial. Boldly stamped across the screen, his signature is less the mark of an author than a brand name, guaranteeing the quality of the goods." When *Melissa* was first screened, the leading man Tony Britton (*Radio Times*, 23 April 1964) said: "He constructs a plot like a solidly built house ... with twisting passages leading to strange rooms. He never telegraphs where the story may lead to next, and just when it seems to be taking a straightforward course you're slapped in the face with a fabulous cliffhanger." And when a new production of *Melissa* was televised, Stanley Reynolds (*The Times*, 12 December 1974) wrote: "He is plainly and simply a master of mystery ... And here it is where the men are separated from the boys, and Mr. Durbridge from the mundane writers of 'tecs and thrillers ... It has a nightmare quality, a touch of the Franz Kafkas – no wonder Durbridge is a great favourite on German telly."

Such was Durbridge's success on television that for all his serials from 1960, beginning with *The World of Tim Frazer*, the BBC gave him the unprecedented accolade of the "Francis Durbridge Presents" screen credit before the title beginning each episode. In an article in the *Daily Mail* (18 May 1964), Marshall Pugh quoted the head of BBCTV serials Donald Wilson: "Durbridge is in a class of his own. He knows to the fraction of an inch how the audience will react to everything he does." In fact in 2006, in his obituary of the Professor Quatermass creator Nigel Kneale (*The Independent*, 2 November 2006), Jack Adrian stated that: "During the 1950s and 1960s Nigel Kneale bestrode the world of British television like a colossus (and) the only writer who came anywhere near him in terms of sheer entertainment and popularity was Francis Durbridge." We know that Durbridge was himself an admirer of Nigel Kneale, as he said as much in a brief *Radio Times* column called "Speaking for Myself" (2 May 1958) – in which, to digress, he also admitted that "I'm a sucker for Sergeant Bilko" (of *The Phil Silvers Show*).

But was there a place for Durbridge's principal radio creation, Paul Temple, in the new world of television? From the outset that was unlikely, as it is generally believed that Durbridge considered Temple to be unsuitable for the small screen because for very many years he had been firmly rooted in radio and the atmosphere of Temple's cases had relied for its effectiveness on the medium of sound. Furthermore the four Paul Temple cinema films that had been adapted between 1946 and 1952 from Durbridge's radio serials could not compare in quality with the crime films produced in the USA or with many of the British films in the genre, so the likelihood of seeing Temple on television was minimal.

It has nevertheless been claimed in various articles, and indeed in Durbridge's obituary in *The Times*, that he wrote a twelve-episode Paul Temple series for television in 1968 starring John Bentley and Dinah Sheridan. This is mistaken, although admittedly Bentley appeared as Temple in three of the four cinema films and Sheridan was Steve in two of them, so these films might have been shown on television in serial form (probably on ITV).

There is in fact overwhelming evidence to refute the suggestion that Durbridge wrote an original Paul Temple series for television. For example, when Temple was eventually brought to television by other hands as described below, *The Stage and Television Today* (6 November 1969) reported that: "Among new series are Paul Temple, the detective created by Francis Durbridge, who comes to television for the first time with Francis Matthews in the title role." Malcolm Winton introduced the Francis Matthews series in the *Radio Times* (20 November 1969) with the statement: "The only thing that's surprising about Paul Temple breaking into television is that he hasn't done it before." Even more revealing are Durbridge's own words in the same article: "I wanted to hold off putting Temple on television, because I wanted to establish myself as a television writer quite apart from the character of Temple. And having done that – I'd had many offers for Paul Temple from various sources – I felt now was the time to put him on." This was later confirmed in Michael Wynn Jones' interview with Durbridge (*Radio Times*, 21 October 1971) to launch the television serial *The Passenger*, when Durbridge said: "Twenty years ago in the United States, a producer told me that I was wasting my time by not going into television. So that's what I did – I tried to build up a reputation with serials, since I'd vowed never to write a Paul Temple episode for television."

The arrival of Temple on television therefore clearly dates from 23 November 1969 with the launch of the Anglo-German films starring Francis Matthews and Ros Drinkwater, which ran for four series totalling fifty-two episodes until 1 September 1971. The first twenty-six episodes allegedly cost £630,000, then the biggest budget for a crime series in the BBC's history, and understandably viewers were wooed with a high profile *Radio Times* cover photograph of Matthews and Drinkwater (11 December 1969). For a new generation these Temple films were attractive, but an older generation brought up on the radio serials must have been slightly bemused. There were no cliff-hangers, as each episode was a separate story; no discernible Durbridge touch, as the scripts were by various other writers; no haunting post-war atmosphere, as the settings were modern and glossy; usually no "whodunit" element; and no old friends like Sir Graham Forbes and Chief Inspector Vosper and Charlie the factotum to share the investigations with Temple and Steve.

In short, these updated and colourful television exploits had to be judged on their own merits – which was fair enough, if one refrained from harking back to the bygone age of the radio serials when the Temples unmasked master criminals in the final episodes. This was reflected by James Thomas in the *Daily Express* (8 December 1969) shortly after the series began, who headed his review "Temple – An Insult To Us All" and commented: "Paul Temple has not transferred too well to television. Despite the lavish colour production, it might as well have seen out its retirement on radio ... It is almost a caricature, a throwback, a tv clanger which must make Francis Durbridge, Temple's creator, sweat a little each Sunday." Reviewing an episode in *The Stage and Television Today* (7 May 1970) under the caption "Unimaginatively Written Corn", John Lawrence's verdict was that: "At least it can now be said that the television character called Paul Temple has ceased to have even the remotest of superficial similarities to the character which was created by Francis Durbridge, although the series still carries his credit." Even later, after the first episode of the fourth series, Stanley Reynolds (*The Times*, 10 June 1971) felt that "All over Britain people will be clucking their tongues, shaking their heads, and moaning about television managing to destroy their favourite detective." But Reynolds also sought to justify the changes, by accepting that "The radio show was in its heyday in the era of post-war austerity, and Steve and Paul represented the secret world of beauty and riches," and he added: "I find television's Steve and Paul terribly glamorous ... In brief, a new generation of Temple fans is being born."

Meanwhile, as with his radio serials, Durbridge's non-Temple television serials had been attracting large audiences throughout the world. Several Commonwealth countries provided a voracious market, but to an even greater extent European viewers were afflicted with Durbridge mania aroused by translations of his television serials with their own top actors in key roles (including Albert Lieven and Hardy Krüger in Germany and Rossano Brazzi in Italy). In Germany *straßenfeger* was again the appropriate word, and even more so than in the case of the radio serials. When in January 1962 the final episode of *Das Halstuch* (*The Scarf*) was presented on German television, in order to watch Heinz Drache as the Detective Inspector reveal the solution, politicians deferred meetings, diners left restaurants and clubs empty or closed, audiences abandoned theatres and cinemas, and factory workers absented themselves from their night shifts.

The German production of *The World of Tim Frazer* prompted Norman Crossland of *The Guardian* to comment (20 January 1964): "Not until the curtain falls does life in West Germany stand a chance of returning to normal." He reported that: "From all parts of West Germany reports have been coming in of declining theatre bookings, of half-empty cinemas, and of losses by the public transport system as the bewitching hour approaches ... Most public houses have television and the landlord and his wife sit enraptured at the set, clearly resentful at the intrusion of a customer who seeks refuge in half a pint of beer." Two years later Crossland returned to the subject (*The Guardian*, 15 January 1966) regarding the German version of *Melissa* which, he said, had dominated social life in West Germany, Austria and Switzerland. Although an American news agency had disclosed the solution, which had been printed in some newspapers, the popular *Bild Zeitung* had used its front page to state that it would not spoil its readers' fun. Crossland further reported that, yet again, a marked loss of revenue had been suffered by theatres, cinemas, public houses, bowling alleys and public transport undertakings, and that many events had been cancelled. Most bizarre, however, were the newspaper reports that a family in Westphalia had been so engrossed in the second episode of *Melissa* that they had failed to notice a smell of burning, until a passer-by alerted them to the fact that their house was on fire! And according to *The Observer* on 13 March 1966, the Bavarian town of Kulmbach saw a pact between its Christian Socialist and neo-Nazi parties to suspend campaigning in order to watch *Melissa*.

The obsessive thrall of Durbridge on German television screens lasted long after his last British television serial in 1980, and IMDb details eighteen German productions from 1959 to 1988, ten Italian productions from 1963 to 1980 and five French productions from 1966 to 1975. German and Italian viewers also saw televised adaptations of some of Durbridge's stage plays, which is something that has never been done on British television.

In spite of his success on radio and television, Durbridge needed to find another string for his bow that would keep him in the public eye at a time when fashions in broadcast drama were changing. Britain in the 1970s saw television thrillers taking a new and more gritty direction, far removed from cosy middle-class settings and the crossword puzzle type of devilish guessing-game. Already in the 1960s such series as *Danger Man* and *Z Cars* had contrasted with the Durbridge style, and this escalated until such 1970s series as *The Sweeney* and *The Professionals* made his distinctive blend of sophistication and labyrinthine murder plots seem contrived and unrealistic by comparison. Durbridge nevertheless held his ground and continued to write his own brand of television serial up to 1980, but from 1971 in the UK (and even earlier in Germany) he had already turned to the theatrical stage and for some thirty years wrote cleverly crafted plays.

For his stage plays, Durbridge specialised in convoluted plots where nothing is what it seems — perhaps more Frederick Knott than Agatha Christie. Their appeal was aptly summarised by Ian Woodward (*Woman's Journal*, March 1976), who commented: "The 'theatre of reassurance' has a brand name nowadays, but when it produces a specialist as expert as this you have to salute him." It is, however, worth mentioning the little-known fact that Durbridge was not entirely a newcomer to the theatrical stage because as early as 1943 his play *Send for Paul Temple* was presented in Birmingham. Nevertheless his UK career as a stage dramatist began in earnest in the 1970s, with his West End success *Suddenly at Home* achieving a long run at the Fortune Theatre from 30 September 1971 to 16 June 1973. It also played to capacity audiences in Germany, and ran in many other countries including Belgium, Switzerland, Australia and the USA. His next play, *The Gentle Hook*, had a modest run of just four months at the Piccadilly Theatre, and his other plays were not particularly successful if judged solely by the existence or duration of West End runs — although this has proved somewhat irrelevant, as Durbridge has remained a mainstay of the professional and amateur stage to the present day.

So looking at Durbridge's body of work, how is he to be assessed? Firstly and incubitably, as stated in his obituary in *The Times*, "What Agatha Christie was to the novel, Durbridge was to the radio and television play." That is of course agreed, but he must also be recognised for his longevity - with many of his radio serials still broadcast, many of his television serials available on DVD, his novels still reprinted and released as audiobooks and e-books, and his stage plays still regularly performed. In short his name remains with us twenty years after his death, and over thirty years after he stopped writing, with an appeal that is undiminished in spite of the fact that his *milieu* of Thames houseboats, expensive flats, sports cars and dry martinis must be alien to the experience of many among his twenty-first century audience.

Thousands of new Durbridge fans are apparently prepared to suspend their disbelief and immerse themselves in his bygone world, so how is it that he still manages to attract such a sizeable audience when his offerings might conceivably be described as *passé*? The answer, surely, is that mystery fans are intelligent enough to appreciate that realism and storytelling can be two different things, and that the latter can still be highly enjoyable without the former. They recognise that Durbridge had no special message to convey, no mission to examine the springs of violence or the motivation that leads someone to murder, and seemingly no purpose other than to present one piece of craftsmanlike escapism after another. They are prepared to accept him on this basis, and they know that the same could be said about the enduring popularity of Agatha Christie after nearly a century and the longstanding success of Edgar Wallace. The latter, incidentally, was greatly admired by Durbridge, as confirmed by radio producer Martyn C. Webster (*Radio Times*, 22 February 1968) when he reminisced about the original creation of Paul Temple and quoted Durbridge as saying: "If only I could be half as good as Edgar Wallace."

While some critics might argue that Durbridge's characters were puppets and that his dialogue was stilted, or even that there was a degree of sexism or class snobbishness in his stories, he was himself totally secure in the knowledge that his legion of fans cared not a jot about such things. He knew precisely what his listeners, viewers and readers expected of him, and he worked within his own particular niche and gave them what they wanted. His characters were drawn from the gin-and-tonic set, with photographers, estate agents, car salesmen, antique dealers, psychiatrists and sinister foreigners abounding within plots involving deception and criminal intrigue. Of course there were also "low life" characters, the pawns who did the bidding of the well-concealed master criminal and were usually rewarded by meeting a sticky end.

Durbridge was undeniably one of the world's best spellbinders. Red herrings were his stock in trade, and particularly in his television serials he excelled in playing mind games as his protagonist writhed under the heinous complications inflicted by the yet-to-be-revealed murderer. His fans probably became so well acquainted with the Durbridge style that they began to find the twists and turns of his plots somewhat predictable – or at least they thought they did so, only to be confounded when he came up with yet another stunner. As a master of his craft he was always capable of springing a surprise and revealing a totally unexpected murderer, an oft-quoted summary of his golden formula being that "everybody is lying, and nothing is as it seems."

His plots were peppered with pals of the hero who often turned out to be something completely different, and his settings frequently switched from London to Thames-side locations that saw the hero lured to a cottage at Marlow or a houseboat on the river, only to find a door ajar and a corpse just beyond. Pauline Peters (*Sunday Express Colour*

Magazine, 22 November 1981) commented favourably: "There is a special place in the British psyche for a well-dressed middle-class murder story, free from pain with not too much mess and ideally within sight of a nice pair of French windows." Indeed, as *The Times* acknowledged in Durbridge's obituary: "Far from being a weakness, the cosy sameness of his settings was in fact his greatest strength."

Perhaps most memorably, there was one thing that Durbridge did more effectively than any other British crime writer. He was the master of the recurrent motif, the sort of thing for which film director Alfred Hitchcock coined the term "MacGuffin". On his side of the Atlantic, Durbridge was the one to introduce with enormous dexterity the commonplace object that assumed an increasingly sinister significance when appearing and reappearing as a plot progressed - be it a cocktail stick, a pair of spectacles, a gramophone record, a fountain pen, a cigarette lighter or a dog collar. This represented the Durbridge trademark, with his tantalising "MacGuffin" heralding the closing credits of each radio or television instalment and leaving his audience stunned and wanting more.

Turning to Durbridge's novels, many of them tend to reveal their origin as radio or television serials by their succession of cliff-hangers, frugal descriptive passages and predominance of dialogue. They indicate that his real skill was in creating scripts rather than novels, as acknowledged by Tim Heald (*The Times*, 29 April 1981): "He doesn't regard himself as a novelist any more than a novelist who has had books turned into a television series would regard himself as a screenwriter." In fact Durbridge wrote very few original books, as most of them were clearly labelled as novelisations of his radio and television serials and close examination of some of his others proves that they also came into this category. *Beware of Johnny Washington* (1951), *Design for Murder* (1951), *Another Woman's Shoes* (1965) and *Dead to the World* (1967) were all originally Paul Temple radio serials that became books with recycled plots but without the Temples. In short, the only original Durbridge novels are *Back Room Girl* (1950), *The Tyler Mystery* (1957), *The Pig-Tail Murder* (1969), *Paul Temple and the Harkdale Robbery* (1970) and *Paul Temple and the Kelby Affair* (1970), plus those that he wrote as newspaper or magazine serials in the 1950s. Nevertheless, while his novels could so easily be dismissed as inconsequential, it is worth noting that some commentators have compared him with the American master Cornell Woolrich and the Belgian legend Georges Simenon.

At this point, however, it might be appropriate to mention that there has been occasional speculation about the possible involvement of "ghost writers" in the production of Durbridge novels. While it has always been openly acknowledged that his first five novels and the two credited as "by Paul Temple" were collaborations with other writers, there remains a question mark about many of the others. Was the name Francis Durbridge a "brand name" on his books, with the actual writing largely in the hands of other writers? That would have been easily achieved in the many cases where his radio and television scripts were simply transferred (almost word for word) to the printed page, with the minimum of descriptive passages added – but even if so, given the fact that

Durbridge devised and wrote the original scripts, surely the use of his name as the author can be justified?

If there was a "ghost writer" or collaborator, the most likely person would have been James Douglas Rutherford McConnell (1915-88), who himself wrote many stylish thrillers as "Douglas Rutherford". He was Durbridge's credited co-writer of the two "by Paul Temple" novels, *The Tyler Mystery* and *East of Algiers*, as well as being a personal friend who might have been involved in the writing of other Durbridge novels. Was it simply coincidental that he died in the year that *Paul Temple and the Madison Case* was published, with no new Durbridge books appearing thereafter? There is also evidence in Durbridge's business files that several of his novels were collaborations with one Paul Townend, but whatever the truth of the matter such speculation can take nothing away from Durbridge himself because it was from his creative mind that all these novelisations sprang.

Leaving his novels aside, Durbridge was the undisputed supremo in radio and television thrillers for several decades and he undoubtedly influenced other writers in the field. In an article by H.R.F. Keating in the *Radio Times* of 28 November 1974, the acclaimed crime novelist Michael Gilbert recalled that when he was asked to write his first television serial he was advised by the producer to study Durbridge's technique, so he watched complete recordings of *My Friend Charles* and *The Scarf* in one day. In the same article, Dick Francis revealed that listening to Paul Temple radio serials as a boy had inspired him to write thrillers - and although his career as a jockey put this on hold, the rest is history.

Durbridge's particular (possibly unique) skills have been widely applauded. Tim Heald (*The Times*, 29 April 1981) wrote: "Whereas the average crime novelist twists his plot sparingly, Durbridge is almost prodigal. Innocents become villains and vice versa with a persistent unpredictability which is dazzling." Dennis Barker, in Durbridge's obituary in *The Guardian* (13 April 1998), commented: "In getting an audience's attention and keeping it, he had few peers in his generation." But perhaps the closing words of Durbridge's obituary by Jack Adrian in *The Independent* (13 April 1998) provided the sort of epitaph that such an unpretentious writer would have appreciated: "He had no other ambition but to entertain, and entertain on a generous scale he did."

NOVELS

Fourteen of Francis Durbridge's books are novelisations of his Paul Temple radio serials, including four in which he revamped the stories and replaced Paul and Steve Temple with other detectives. Sixteen of his other books are novelisations of his television serials, and five more are entirely original novels. In addition he wrote four short novels that appeared in the UK as newspaper or magazine serials – *The Nylon Murders* (**9**), *The Yellow Windmill* (**10**), *The Man Who Beat The Panel* (**11**) and *The Face of Carol West* (**15**). These novellas, by their very nature, showed a lack of embroidery and economy of words that made them fast-moving and particularly readable. It is therefore sad that they have never been published in book form in the UK, although together they would make an ideal volume collecting "lost and recovered" Durbridge mysteries. His fans can only remain hopeful.

In the following listing of his thirty-nine novels, the first edition of each is identified. If the first edition was an original paperback, this is followed by details of the first hardback edition. Audiobook versions are identified under each novel, but at the time of writing there might well be more to come.

Many of Durbridge's novels have been reprinted over the years. Most recently paperback editions and/or e-books have been produced by House of Stratus, Arcturus, Pan Macmillan Bello and HarperCollins, and some are now also available as audio downloads. Details of all these publications can easily be found online.

Durbridge novels have been translated and published throughout Europe, and to assist in identification the foreign language titles are quoted here as comprehensively as possible but without further publication details.

1. *Send for Paul Temple*. John Long, 1938 [June]. Written jointly with John Thewes (generally believed today to be a pseudonym of Charles Hatton). Novelisation of his 1938 radio serial (**112**), but see also his 1951 novel *Beware of Johnny Washington* (**7**). French title: *La Bande des oiseaux noirs*. Dutch title: *Paul Vlaanderen en de ruitenboer*.
Plot summary: See **112**.
Adapted as a stage play 1943 (**191**) and filmed 1946 (**202**). Five audiocassettes, read by Alistair McGowan, ISIS Audiobooks, 1994. Two CDs, abridged reading by Anthony Head, BBC Audio, 2007.
When this novel was published, newspaper advertisements described it as "the novel of the thriller that created a BBC fan-mail record" and it was made Book of the Month by the Crime Book Society. It was later serialised in the Birmingham *Sunday Mercury* from 19 November 1939, following that newspaper's successful serialisation of *Paul Temple and the Front Page Men*.

2. *Paul Temple and the Front Page Men*. John Long, 1939 [May]. Written jointly with Charles Hatton. Novelisation of his 1938 radio serial (**114**). German titles: *Paul Temple und die Schlagzeilenmänner* and *Paul Temple und der Klavierstimmer*. French title: *Paul Temple et les hommes de la première page*. Dutch title: *Paul Vlaanderen en de mannen van de voorpagina*.
Plot summary: See **114**.
Adapted as a stage play 1943 (**191**).

Six audiocassettes / Seven CDs, read by Tom Crowe, ISIS Audiobooks, 2000. Two CDs, abridged reading by Anthony Head, BBC Audio, 2009.

Like its predecessor *Send for Paul Temple*, this novel was made Book of the Month by the Crime Book Society. It was serialised in the Birmingham *Sunday Mercury* from 5 March 1939.

3. *News of Paul Temple*. John Long, [1940, May]. Written jointly with Charles Hatton. Novelisation of his 1939 radio serial (**123**). German title: *Paul Temple und der Fall Z*. French title: *Le Tragique Rayon d'Inverdale*. Italian title: *Ritorna Paul Temple*. Dutch title: *Paul Vlaanderen en het Z-mysterie*. Swedish title: *Dags för Paul Temple*. Finnish title: *Mitä uutta, Paul Temple?*

Plot summary: See **123**.

Filmed as *Paul Temple's Triumph* 1950 (**204**).

Six audiocassettes, read by Michael Tudor Barnes, ISIS Audiobooks, 2001. Six CDs, read by Michael Tudor Barnes, ISIS Audiobooks, 2003. Two CDs, abridged reading by Anthony Head, BBC Audio, 2008.

4. *Paul Temple Intervenes*. John Long, [1944, December]. Written jointly with Charles Hatton. Novelisation of his 1942 radio serial (**142**). French title: *La Tragique Énigme du Marquis*. Dutch title: *Paul Vlaanderen en het mysterie van de Markies*. Swedish title: *Paul Temple griper in*.

Plot summary: See **142**.

Filmed as *Paul Temple Returns* 1952 (**205**).

Five audiocassettes / Six CDs, read by Michael Tudor Barnes, ISIS Audiobooks, 2003. Six CDs, read by Toby Stephens, AudioGO, 2011.

5. *Send for Paul Temple Again!* John Long, [1948, April]. Written jointly with Charles Hatton. Novelisation of his 1945 radio serial (**151**). German title: *Paul Temple jagt Rex*. French title: *L'insaisissable Rex*. Dutch title: *Paul Vlaanderen trekt van leer*. Spanish title: *Scotland Yard llama a Paul Temple*. Swedish title: *Paul Temple kommer igen*.
Plot summary: See **151**.
Filmed as *Calling Paul Temple* 1948 (**203**).
Seven audiocassettes / Eight CDs, read by Peter Wickham, ISIS Audiobooks, 2008.

6. *Back Room Girl*. John Long, [1950, July].
Plot summary: Crime reporter Roy Benton retires to No Man's Cove in Cornwall to write his memoirs, and discovers that a disused tin-mine has become a research station for a secret project to develop a devastating weapon. He joins forces with scientist Karen Silvers and a Scotland Yard man to fight a sinister organisation intent on stealing the plans.

7. *Beware of Johnny Washington*. John Long, 1951 [April]. Novelisation of his 1938 radio serial *Send for Paul Temple* (**112**).
Plot summary: The central character of Durbridge's 1949 radio series *Johnny Washington Esquire* (**159**) is framed by a gang of criminals led by the elusive Grey Moose, and throws in his lot with the police.
This is a re-write of *Send for Paul Temple* (**1**), with all the character names changed and Washington instead of Temple joining reporter Verity instead of Steve in the hunt for her brother's killer.

8. *Design for Murder*. John Long, 1951 [November]. Novelisation of his 1946 radio serial *Paul Temple and the Gregory Affair* (**154**). German titles: *Schöne Grüße von Mister Brix* and *Mr. Rossiter empfiehlt sich*.

Plot summary: When Det. Insp. Lionel Wyatt retires to a smallholding in Kent with his wife Sally, his only regret is that he never succeeded in arresting the one person who merited the description "master criminal". A visit from his former chief convinces him that this person is again terrorising wealthy Londoners with kidnappings and murders. The latest victim is Barbara Willis, found strangled in the sea off the Devon coast, and this has been linked with the disappearance of a policewoman who worked closely with Wyatt. Then Wyatt finds the policewoman's body in his garage – and in both cases there are messages in red ink, "With the compliments of Mr. Rossiter".

In this novelisation of *Paul Temple and the Gregory Affair*, the character names are changed and the Wyatts instead of the Temples pursue Rossiter instead of Gregory. The first German version, *Schöne Grüße von Mister Brix*, was published in the magazine *Bild und Funk*, 1961-62 – with the character names changed yet again, and Insp. Richard Grant and his wife Margaret pursuing Mr. Brix. The slightly later German book version, *Mr. Rossiter empfiehlt sich*, was a straight translation of *Design for Murder* with the Wyatts pursuing Mr. Rossiter.

9. *The Nylon Murders*. A twelve-part serial in the *Sunday Dispatch*, 23 November 1952 – 8 February 1953.

Plot summary: A young actress, Andrea Lake, is found dead in the Thames with a nylon stocking around her neck. Her doctor sister investigates, ignoring the discouragement of Det. Insp. Charles Merlin, but Andrea proves to be only the first victim.

This was never published as a book in the UK, but it was published in Germany as *Kommt Zeit, kommt Mord* (Signum, 1965) and later under the same title by Goldmann in 1968. Under the title *Die Nylonmorde*, it was also included in the Durbridge omnibus *Drei berühmte Kriminalromane in einem Band* (Lingen, 1966), together with *Tim Frazer* (*The World of Tim Frazer*) and *Der Andere* (*The Other Man*). In fact it was very widely published, with rights sold to countries including Italy, Australia and South Africa.

Some websites allege that *The Nylon Murders* was the basis of the 1956 British film *Town on Trial*, which is included in the filmography section (**210**) only as a talking point because it shares no common features with Durbridge's plot.

10. *The Yellow Windmill*. An eleven-part serial in the *Sunday Dispatch*, 17 January – 28 March 1954.

Plot summary: Susan Kelford, the five-year-old daughter of Sir Cedric Kelford, is kidnapped in the street by a man who gives her a little yellow windmill. Det. Insp. Mike Houston's first potential informant is killed in a hit-and-run, and he recognises the driver as the author of the television play in which his own daughter is appearing. Matters worsen when Houston's son is found shot dead in front of his television set, which bears a crayon sketch of a yellow windmill.

This was never published as a book in the UK, but an adapted German version appeared as *Die gelbe Windmühle* in the magazine *Bild und Funk*, in eleven instalments, 1965-66.

11. *The Man Who Beat The Panel*. A six-part serial in *TV Mirror*, Vol 4 No. 16 to No. 21, 16 April - 21 May 1955.

Plot summary: Crime reporter Michael Lance and Det. Insp. Jack Gaylord are investigating the murder of Swedish film star Carel Helvin. When watching a television programme called *Guess My Birthplace* Lance recognises the man who beats the panel, Victor Vorse, as someone he saw with Carel shortly before she died. Then Carel reappears, and confirms that the murder victim was her sister Paula.

This was never published as a book in the UK, but an extended and adapted German version appeared as *Mitten ins Herz* in the magazine *Bild und Funk*, in nine instalments, 1962-63.

12. *The Tyler Mystery*. Hodder & Stoughton, 1957 [September]. Written jointly with Douglas Rutherford as "by Paul Temple". The paperback edition (Hodder, November 1960) was credited to Durbridge rather than "Temple". German title: *Vier mußten sterben*. Dutch title: *Paul Vlaanderen en het Tyler mysterie*. Spanish title: *El misterio Tyler*. Polish title: *Tajemnica Betty Tyler*. Slovenian title: *Štirje so morali umreti*.

Plot summary: Outside Oxford, police officers find a woman's body in the boot of a stolen car. Paul Temple initially has no interest, but when it transpires that the principal suspect is known to him he feels compelled to investigate and is faced with three more murders.

Five audiocassettes / Six CDs, read by Michael Tudor Barnes, ISIS Audiobooks, 2004. Two audiocassettes / Two CDs, abridged reading by Anthony Head as *Paul Temple and the Tyler Mystery*, BBC Audio, 2006. Six CDs, read by Toby Stephens as *Paul Temple and the Tyler Mystery*, AudioGO, 2012.

"Paul Temple", in an author's note in the first edition, confirmed that this story had never been broadcast.

13. *The Other Man*. Hodder & Stoughton, 1958 [October]. Novelisation of his 1956 television serial (**178**). German title: *Der Andere*. French title: *L'Autre Homme*. Italian title: *Lungo il fiume e sull'acqua*. Dutch title: *De andere man*. Spanish title: *El otro hombre*. Swedish title: *I de lugnaste vattnen*. Polish title: *Ten drugi*.
Plot summary: See **178**.

14. *East of Algiers*. Hodder & Stoughton, 1959 [February]. Written jointly with Douglas Rutherford as "by Paul Temple". The paperback edition (Hodder, January 1962) was credited to Durbridge rather than "Temple". Novelisation of his 1947/48 radio serial *Paul Temple and the Sullivan Mystery* (**157**). German title: *Die Brille*. Dutch title: *Paul Vlaanderen ten oosten van Algiers*. Portuguese title: *A Leste de Argel*. Slovenian title: *Očala*.
Plot summary: Judy Wincott asks Temple to return a pair of spectacles to David Foster when he gets to Tunis, but the mystery surrounding the spectacles involves a murder in Paris and further killings across Europe and North Africa.
Five audiocassettes / Six CDs, read by Michael Tudor Barnes as *East of Algiers* by Durbridge and Rutherford, ISIS Audiobooks, 2006. Two CDs, abridged reading by Anthony Head as *Paul Temple East of Algiers* by Durbridge, BBC Audio, 2009.
Although based on the radio serial *Paul Temple and the Sullivan Mystery*, there are changes to the plot and the character names.

15. *The Face of Carol West*. An eight-part serial in the *News of the World*, 9 August – 27 September 1959.
Plot summary: Det. Supt. Max Christian is baffled by the face of a dead girl found in the swimming-pool at a roadhouse, as he feels that he's seen her before. He later finds his own private telephone number in her diary, and it appears again on the scribbling pad of a schoolmaster who has attempted suicide.
This was never published as a book in the UK, but an adapted German version appeared as *Sie wußten zuviel* in the magazine *Bild und Funk*, in ten instalments, 1963.

16. *A Time of Day*. Hodder & Stoughton, 1959 [December]. Novelisation of his 1957 television serial (**179**). German title: *Es ist soweit*. Dutch title: *Er is een kind ontvoerd*. Spanish title: *Un momento del día*. Norwegian title: *Avgjørelsens øyeblikk*. Polish title: *W biały dzień*.
Plot summary: See **179**.
Six CDs, read by Greg Wise, AudioGo, 2013.
Magazine serialisations of novels were quite common at that time, but often they were abridged versions of novels yet to be published. In this respect *A Time of Day* was unusual, because it was after its book publication that it was serialised in the weekly magazine *Woman's Day* in eleven instalments (Vol 5 No. 91 to No. 101, 6 February – 16 April 1960). Again unusually, this serialisation used almost the full book with minimal editing, supplemented with atmospheric illustrations by John Heseltine. The first instalment was headed: "For the first time in any woman's magazine – a tensely thrilling Francis Durbridge serial".

17. *The Scarf*. Hodder & Stoughton, 1960 [October]. US, *The Case of the Twisted Scarf*, Dodd, Mead, 1961 [January]. Novelisation of his 1959 television serial (**180**). German title: *Das Halstuch*. Dutch title: *De sjaal*. Spanish title: *La bufanda*. Swedish title: *Halsduken*. Polish title: *Szal*. Slovakian title: *Šatka*. There was also a Russian translation.
Plot summary: See **180**.

18. *The World of Tim Frazer*. Hodder & Stoughton, 1962 [January]. US, Dodd, Mead, 1962 [August]. Novelisation of the first story in his 1960 television serial *The World of Tim Frazer* (**181A**). German title: *Tim Frazer*. French title: *Où est passé Harry?* Dutch title: *De wereld van Tim Frazer*.
Plot summary: See **181A**.
Eight audiocassettes / Six CDs, read by Clive Mantle, BBC Audio, 2009. Two CDs, abridged reading by Anthony Head, AudioGO, 2010.

19. *Portrait of Alison*. Hodder & Stoughton, 1962 [August]. US, Dodd, Mead, 1962 [March]. Novelisation of his 1955 television serial (**176**). German title: *Das Kennwort*. French title: *Le Portrait d'Alison*. Italian title: *Ritratto di Alison*. Dutch titles: *Portret van Alison* and *De zaak Alison*. Polish title: *Portret Alison*. Croatian title: *Alisonin Portret*.
Plot summary: See **176**.
Filmed 1955 (**209**).

20. *My Friend Charles*. Hodder & Stoughton, 1963 [September]. Novelisation of his 1956 television serial (**177**). German title: *Charlie war mein Freund*. Italian title: *…dai nemici mi guardo io*. Dutch title: *Mijn vriend Charles*.
Plot summary: See **177**.
Filmed as *The Vicious Circle* 1957 (**211**).

This novel first appeared as a *Radio Times* serial, published in ten parts from 4 July to 5 September 1963.

21. *Tim Frazer Again*. Hodder & Stoughton, 1964 [March]. Novelisation of the second story in his 1960/61 television serial *The World of Tim Frazer* (*The Salinger Affair* - **181B**). German title: *Tim Frazer und der Fall Salinger*. French title: *Le Rendez-vous de sept heures trente*. Portuguese title: *O Caso Salinger*.
Plot summary: See **181B**.
Two CDs, abridged reading by Anthony Head, AudioGO, 2011. The unabridged reading by Clive Mantle (AudioGO, 2012) is an audio download that does not appear to be available on CDs.

22. *Another Woman's Shoes*. Hodder & Stoughton, 1965 [August]. Novelisation of his 1954 radio serial *Paul Temple and the Gilbert Case* (**165**). German title: *Die Schuhe*. Italian title: *La scarpa che mancava sempre*. Dutch title: *Wie de schoen past wordt vermoord*. Spanish title: *Tres zapatos de mujer*. Polish title: *Buty modelki*.
Plot summary: Lucy Staines has apparently been murdered by her fiancé Harold Weldon, but the former crime reporter Mike Baxter investigates further. One of Lucy's shoes was missing, as is the case with the next murder victim.
In this novelisation of *Paul Temple and the Gilbert Case*, the character names are changed and the Baxters instead of the Temples pursue the killer.

23. *The Desperate People*. Hodder & Stoughton, 1966 [March]. Novelisation of his 1963 television serial (**182**). German title: *Der Schlüssel*. Italian title: *I disperati*. Dutch title: *De laatste uitweg*. Polish title: *Desperaci*.

Plot summary: See **182**.
Six CDs, read by Neil Pearson, AudioGO, 2013.
In this novelisation the name of the central character is changed from Larry Martin to Philip Holt, and his dead brother's name is changed from Philip Martin to Rex Holt.

24. *Dead to the World*. Hodder & Stoughton, 1967 [March]. Novelisation of his 1951 radio serial *Paul Temple and the Jonathan Mystery* (**163**). German title: *Der Siegelring*. French title: *Sous le signe du dollar*. Italian title: *Morto per il mondo*. Dutch title: *De zegelring*. Polish title: *Umarły dla świata*.
Plot summary: Wealthy American Robert Scranton asks Philip Holt to investigate the murder of his son at a south coast university, the only leads being a postcard from an unknown Christopher and a missing signet ring.
Six CDs, read by Neil Pearson, AudioGo, 2013.
This second book featuring photographer Philip Holt and Det. Insp. Hyde of *The Desperate People* (**23**) might appear to be an original novel, but it is clearly based on *Paul Temple and the Jonathan Mystery*, with the character names changed and the Temples replaced by Philip Holt and his secretary Ruth Sanders.

25. *My Wife Melissa*. Hodder & Stoughton, 1967 [October]. Novelisation of his 1964 television serial *Melissa* (**183**). German, French, Italian, Dutch, Norwegian and Slovenian titles: *Melissa*. Swedish title: *Vem mördade Melissa?* Polish title: *Moja żona Melissa*. Croatian title: *Moja žena Melissa*. There was also a Russian translation.
Plot summary: See **183**.
Four CDs, read by Greg Wise, AudioGO, 2013.

26. *The Pig-Tail Murder*. Hodder & Stoughton, 1969 [May]. German title: *Im Schatten von Soho*. French title: *L'Enfant au cerf-volant*. Italian title: *Mezz'ora per vivere, mezz'ora per morire*. Dutch title: *De haarvlecht*. Polish title: *Warkocz śmierci*. Slovenian title: *Papirnati zmaj*.

Plot summary: Stockbroker Mike Hilton meets a girl in a Chelsea pub that is being watched by the police. Soon her murder makes it necessary for Hilton to find the one person who can give him an alibi, but that person is being concealed by the killer.

27. *Paul Temple and the Harkdale Robbery*. Hodder & Stoughton, 1970 [July], original paperback. First hardback edition, White Lion, 1976 [April]. German title: *Paul Temple - Banküberfall in Harkdale*. Italian title: *Una strana rapina*. Dutch title: *Paul Vlaanderen en het Harkdale mysterie*. Portuguese title: *O Grande Assalto*. Czech/Slovakian title: *Harkdalská lúpež*.

Plot summary: A bank robbery goes wrong when the thieves die in a car crash. The stolen money is missing, and Temple becomes involved when their accomplice is found murdered in the garage of his country cottage.

One audiocassette, abridged reading by Francis Matthews, Pickwick Talking Books, 1973. Four audiocassettes / Four CDs, read by Peter Wickham, ISIS Audiobooks, 2002. Two CDs, abridged reading by Anthony Head, BBC Audio, 2007. Four CDs, read by Toby Stephens, AudioGO, 2012.

28. *Paul Temple and the Kelby Affair*. Hodder & Stoughton, 1970 [July], original paperback. First hardback edition, White Lion, 1973 [Dec]. German title: *Paul Temple - Der Fall Kelby*. Dutch title: *Paul Vlaanderen en de zaak Kelby*. Portuguese title: *O Diário Desaparecido*.

Danish title: *Kelby mysteriet*. Czech/Slovakian title: *Prípad Kelby*.

Plot summary: Temple is persuaded by his publisher to investigate the disappearance of historian Alfred Kelby, who has been entrusted with a sensational diary – but Kelby is then found strangled, and the diary is missing.

Four audiocassettes, read by Michael Tudor Barnes, ISIS Audiobooks, 2001. Four CDs, read by Michael Tudor Barnes, ISIS Audiobooks, 2007. Two audiocassettes / Two CDs, abridged reading by Anthony Head, BBC Audio, 2007. Four CDs, read by Toby Stephens, AudioGO, 2012.

29. *A Man Called Harry Brent*. Hodder & Stoughton, 1970 [November]. Novelisation of his 1965 television serial (**184**). German title: *Ein Mann namens Harry Brent*. Polish title: *Harry Brent*.

Plot summary: See **184**.

30. *The Geneva Mystery*. Hodder & Stoughton, 1971 [July], original paperback. First hardback edition, White Lion, 1976 [Sept]. Novelisation of his 1965 radio serial *Paul Temple and the Geneva Mystery* (**171**). German title: *Zu jung zum sterben*. French title: *Le Secret d'une actrice*. Italian title: *Il mistero di Ginevra*. Dutch title: *Paul Vlaanderen en het Genève-mysterie*.

Plot summary: See **171**.

Three audiocassettes / Four CDs, read by Michael Tudor Barnes, ISIS Audiobooks, 2004. Four CDs, read by Toby Stephens as *Paul Temple and the Geneva Mystery*, AudioGO, 2011.

31. *The Curzon Case*. Hodder & Stoughton (Coronet Books), 1972 [January], original paperback. First hardback edition, White Lion, 1976 [July]. Novelisation of his

1948/49 radio serial *Paul Temple and the Curzon Case* (**158**). German title: *Keiner kennt Curzon*.
Plot summary: See **158**.
Two audiocassettes / Two CDs, abridged reading by Anthony Head as *Paul Temple and the Curzon Case*, BBC Audio, 2006. Four audiocassettes / Four CDs, read by Laurence Kennedy, ISIS Audiobooks, 2007.

32. *Bat Out of Hell*. Hodder & Stoughton, 1972 [June]. Novelisation of his 1966 television serial (**186**). German title: *Wie ein Blitz*. French title: *Une voix d'outre-tombe*. Italian title: *Come un uragano*. Danish title: *Den der graver en grav*. Norwegian title: *Terror i mørket*. Swedish title: *Skjuten ur en kanon*. Polish title: *Jak błyskawica*.
Plot summary: See **186**.

33. *A Game of Murder*. Hodder & Stoughton, 1975 [February]. Novelisation of his 1966 television serial (**185**). German title: *Die Kette*. Italian title: *Giocando a golf una mattina*. Norwegian title: *Spillet om mord*. Polish title: *Mordercza gra*. Croatian title: *Smrtonosna igra*.
Plot summary: See **185**.
Most of the character names are changed from those in the original television serial, and in particular Det. Insp. Jack Kerry becomes Det. Insp. Harry Dawson. Interestingly these changes were also made in the German television version *Die Kette* (1977).

34. *The Passenger*. Hodder & Stoughton, 1977 [February]. Novelisation of his 1971 television serial (**188**). Danish title: *Passageren*. Norwegian title: *Passasjeren*. Polish title: *Nieznajoma*.
Plot summary: See **188**.

35. *Tim Frazer Gets the Message*. Hodder & Stoughton, 1978 [November]. Novelisation of the third story in his 1961 television serial *The World of Tim Frazer* (*The Mellin Forest Mystery* - **181C**). German title: *Tim Frazer weiß Bescheid*.
Plot summary: See **181C**.
Two CDs, abridged reading by Anthony Head, AudioGO, 2011. Six CDs, read by Clive Mantle, AudioGO, 2012.

36. *Breakaway*. Hodder & Stoughton, 1981 [July]. Novelisation of the first story in his 1980 television serial *Breakaway* (*The Family Affair* - **190A**). German title: *Wer ist Mr. Hogarth?* Italian title: *Il prezzo del tradimento*. Dutch title: *De ontsnapping*. Norwegian title: *Dobbeltspill*. Polish title: *Zmiana planów*.
Plot summary: See **190A**.

37. *The Doll*. Hodder & Stoughton, 1982 [August]. Novelisation of his 1975 television serial (**189**). German title: *Die Puppe*. Italian title: *La bambola sull'acqua*. Dutch title: *Het verdwenen portret*. Spanish title: *La muñeca*. Norwegian title: *Dukken*. Polish title: *Jaguar i lalka*.
Plot summary: See **189**.

38. *Paul Temple and the Margo Mystery*. Hodder & Stoughton, 1986 [February]. Novelisation of his 1961 radio serial (**169**). German titles: *Der Hehler* and *Paul Temple und der Fall Margo*. Italian title: *Delitto a tempo di rock*. Dutch title: *Het Margo-mysterie*. Danish title: *Margo mysteriet*. Norwegian title: *Paul Temple og Margo-mysteriet*.
Plot summary: See **169**.

Five audiocassettes, read by Michael Tudor Barnes, ISIS Audiobooks, 2002. Six CDs, read by Toby Stephens, AudioGO, 2011.

39. *Paul Temple and the Madison Case*. Hodder & Stoughton, 1988 [November]. Novelisation of his 1949 radio serial *Paul Temple and the Madison Mystery* (**160**). German title: *Paul Temple und der Fall Madison*. Dutch title: *De zaak Madison*. Danish title: *Madison mysteriet*.
Plot summary: See **160**.
Five audiocassettes / Six CDs, read by Michael Tudor Barnes, ISIS Audiobooks, 2001.

As a footnote, it is worth mentioning *Paul and Steve Temple and the Seymour Affair* (published by Meandering Currents, 2013). Written by Clifford J. Hearn, this was described as "the lost manuscript" and was allegedly based on notes found in the 1960s in the basement of BBC Broadcasting House. Although it promised more adventures of the Temples to come, it was an unauthorised use of Durbridge's characters and was withdrawn from sale after representations by the Durbridge family. It has since been republished as *The Seymour Affair*, the first in a series that does not feature Paul and Steve Temple or Sir Graham Forbes and does not purport to have any connection with Durbridge.

WORKS FOR RADIO

Paul Temple and his wife Steve were icons of the "wireless" years, but Francis Durbridge's contributions to BBC radio ranged much more widely. His earliest broadcast works were short stories and plays for children, and from his debut when he was still only twenty years old he became a prolific contributor to the airwaves who fed the BBC's voracious appetite for stories, plays, musical comedies, short sketches and one-off or serial thrillers.

His output in the 1930s and 1940s was considerable, and his list of radio credits expanded even more with his adoption of the pseudonyms Frank Cromwell, Lewis Middleton Harvey and Nicholas Vane. On the crime fiction front, in addition to Paul Temple, he created the radio detectives Anthony Sherwood, Johnny Cordell, Amanda Smith, Gail Carlton, Michael Starr, André d'Arnell and Johnny Washington, and he even wrote a serial featuring the legendary Sexton Blake.

Most of his radio productions in the 1930s were first broadcast in the BBC Midland Region, although some were also broadcast in other regions or more widely repeated soon after. Looking at his long radio career overall, however, his programmes premièred in the BBC Midland Region, various other BBC regions, the Forces Service, the National Home Service, the new Home Service and Light Programme, and the even newer BBC Radio One, Radio Two and Radio Four. Today it is BBC Radio 4 Extra that is most likely to bring to older listeners the nostalgia of a Durbridge radio serial, or indeed to whet the appetite of a new body of fans.

Herewith, therefore, a listing of the original radio works of Francis Durbridge. It is extensive, as he was so prolific as to leave present-day researchers gasping for breath. Charles Hatton made the early comment in *Radio Pictorial* (28 October 1938) that "he is one of the very few people in this country who have succeeded in making a living by writing for the BBC." The *Radio Times* of 11 February 1938, previewing his play *Information Received*, recorded that by that stage (even before Paul Temple arrived on the scene) Durbridge had written upwards of one hundred radio pieces. This is true if one includes his short sketches, over eighty of which were written between the mid-1930s and the early 1940s, many of them lasting just a few minutes and some being little more than extended jokes.

Martyn C. Webster was the producer of all the Paul Temple programmes up to 1968, so it is unnecessary to repeat this in each case. He also produced most of the radio revues and concert parties that used Durbridge sketches – including *The Radioptimists*, *The Radio Follies*, the monthly *Cocktail* series, *Mr. Mike Presents*, *Follow On*, *Everything Stops for Tea*, *Mid-Week Matinée*, *Revue in Miniature*, *Lunch Interval* and *Bye Bye Blues* – so again it would be superfluous to repeat his name in every case. Durbridge's many other radio works were produced either by Webster or by others as stated.

The inclusive dates of the original BBC broadcasts of serials are given, as are the inclusive dates of new productions, but routine repeat broadcasts are excluded. If in any case a run of dates appears to contradict the number of weekly episodes, this is because one or more episodes were deferred to accommodate another programme or conversely because episodes were broadcast more frequently than weekly.

The most comprehensive available details of cast members are listed, and it can be seen that the same names appear repeatedly. The reason for this is that the BBC for many years had its own Drama Repertory Company, which happily appears to have been revived from 2006 in spirit if not in name when one looks at the casts of Patrick Rayner's new Paul Temple productions.

Audiocassette tapes and CDs are listed under each production where appropriate, although the mentions of audiocassettes might not be comprehensive.

Numerous Durbridge radio productions have been translated in at least ten European countries, and some brief details are given about broadcasts in German, Dutch, Italian and Danish.

40. *The Three-Cornered Hat*. 25 July 1933. A play included in *The Children's Hour*.

41. *The Garden that Couldn't Grow*. 16 August 1933. A short story included in *The Children's Hour*.

42. *One-way Traffic in Golliwog Land*. 22 August 1933. A play included in *The Children's Hour*.

43. *The Word Woman*. 11 October 1933. A twenty-five minute play. Producer: Charles Brewer.
Cast: Dorinea Shirley, Gordon Bailey, Ernest Sefton and Barbara Helliwell.

Plot summary: None available, but described in the *Radio Times* as a comedy and the characters are a film actress, her brother, a scenario writer and a maid.

This was Durbridge's first adult radio play to be broadcast, and he originally planned to call it *Men Are Like That*.

44. *South of Damascus*. 7 December 1933. A play included in *The Children's Hour*.

45. *The Red Sparrow*. 23 January 1934. A dialogue story included in *The Children's Hour*.
45A. New production. 16 September 1935. Told by Barbara Helliwell in *The Children's Hour*.

46. *The Greedy Pillar Box*. 20 February 1934. A short story included in *The Children's Hour*, only on BBC Belfast.
46A. New production. 8 October 1935. Told by Valerie Larg in *The Children's Hour*.

47. *Cavalcade of Love*. 10 April 1934. A sketch included in the one-hour variety programme *Divertissement*. Producer: Martyn C. Webster.
Cast (for the whole programme, not all in the Durbridge sketch): Mabel France, Stuart Vinden, Wortley Allen, Cecily Gay, Reginald Smith, Norah Holloway, Godfrey Baseley and Marjorie Westbury.
Plot summary: The characters are Mother, Father, William and Betty, and the three scenes are listed as 1894, 1924 and 1934 – with an elopement in each year, and all accomplished in about seven minutes of broadcast time!

48. *Black Eagle: a Highwayman Play*. 24 May 1934. Included in *The Children's Hour*.

49. *Summer Showers: A Bright Interval*. 17 July 1934. A forty-five minute musical comedy, with music and lyrics by Ronald Hill. Producer: Martyn C. Webster.
Cast: John Bentley, Constance Needham, John Lang, Alma Vane, Hugh Morton, Dorothy Summers, Reginald Smith, Cecily Gay, Denis Folwell, Vera Ashe, Godfrey Baseley and Joan Daniels, with the Midland Revue Chorus and the Midland Revue Band.
Plot summary: A large seaside hotel provides the setting for two love affairs and a romantic triangle, with the story lines introduced by the hotel page calling the room numbers. This was really a series of linked sketches, one of which was the first version of *Paul Jones* (see **95**).

50. *When the Scarecrow Came to Town*. 19 July 1934. A sketch included in *The Children's Hour*.

51. *Design for Loving*, *No Refrain* and *Won't You Confess?* 12 September 1934. Three sketches included in *The Radioptimists*.
The Radioptimists was a series of forty-five minute concerts, produced by Martyn C. Webster in the Midland Region. The *Radio Times* commented: "This is a new Studio Concert Party, formed by the Regional Producer, who ran one under the same name for five years when he was at Glasgow." Webster's Midland company consisted of Alma Vane, Hugh Morton, Dorothy Summers, Marjorie Westbury, Denis Folwell, Harry Saxton and The Three Knaves (Jack Wilson, Jack Hill and Basil Hempseed).
51A. New production of *Design for Loving*. 25 October 1939. Included in *Mid-Week Matinée*.

52. *Once in a Blue Moon*. 25 September 1934. A forty-five minute musical comedy, with music and lyrics by Jack Hill. Producer: Martyn C. Webster.
Cast: Michael North, Alma Vane, Cecily Gay, Hugh Morton, John Lang, Gladys Joiner, Wortley Allen, Dorothy Summers, Mabel France, Denis Folwell, Basil Hempseed, John Bentley and Vera Ashe, with the Midland Revue Orchestra conducted by Jack Wilson.
Plot summary: Fabian works as a tourist guide at an island café called The Blue Moon, and as an accomplished pianist he is content to fill his life with music. Then he falls in love with an American visitor and pursues her to New York, only to find that she loves another – so it's back to the island and the consolation of music.
52A. New production, expanded to one hour. 5 January 1939. Producer: Martyn C. Webster.
Cast: Patrick Waddington, Dorothy Summers, Lester Mudditt, Valerie Larg, Janet Joye, Marjorie Westbury, Stuart Vinden, Leslie Bowmar, Mabel France, Hugh Morton, John Lang, Cedric Johnson, Clive Selborne, Vera Ashe and Godfrey Baseley, with the Midland Revue Orchestra conducted by Reginald Burston.

53. *Promotion*. 3 October 1934. A one-hour play. Producer: Martyn C. Webster.
Cast: John Lang, Hugh Morton, Denis Folwell, Godfrey Baseley, Raymond Smith, Vincent Curran, Mabel France, Cecily Gay, Vera Ashe, Leonard Crabtree, John Bentley, Dorothy Summers and Constance Needham.
Plot summary: Life in a large department store called Dolmans sees rivalries, jealousy, chicanery and (prophetic for Durbridge) an element of crime.
Durbridge's first "dramatic" play, this was the script originally submitted in 1933 to producer Martyn C.

Webster that resulted in Durbridge's launch on BBC radio, although it was not broadcast until the following year.

53A. New production. 12 February 1935. Producer: Martyn C. Webster.

Cast: John Lang, Hugh Morton, Denis Folwell, Godfrey Baseley, Raymond Smith, Vincent Curran, Mabel France, Cecily Gay, Vera Ashe, John Morley, John Bentley, Dorothy Summers and Constance Needham.

53B. New production. 21 June 1937. Producer: Cecil McGivern.

Cast: David Ormerod, R.G. French, Wilfred Pickles, Edith Toms, Brent Wood, Norman Partridge, John Byrne, Donald Avison, Dan Gray, E.A. Naden, Monica Marsden, Margot Webster, Doris Gambell and Mary Eastwood.

This was broadcast only in the BBC Northern Region.

54. *Did You Guess?* 9 October 1934. A sketch included in *The Radioptimists*.

54A. New production. 15 February 1936. Included in *February Cocktail*.

55. *Millionaires*, *The New News*, *100% British*, *School for Crooners* and *They Call it Love*. 30 October 1934. Five sketches included in *The Radioptimists*.

55A. New production of *School for Crooners*. 8 November 1939. Included in *Mid-Week Matinée*.

55B. New production of *Millionaires*. 28 March 1941. Included in *Everything Stops for Tea*.

56. *Murder in the Midlands*. 13 November 1934. A forty-five minute play. Producer: Martyn C. Webster.

Cast: Hugh Morton, Cecily Gay, John Lang, Godfrey Baseley, Denis Folwell and William Hughes.

Plot summary: A honeymoon couple interrupt their car journey because of thick fog, and when they go to a nearby mansion to seek directions they find it unlocked and discover a corpse in the hallway.

This is significant, as it was the first Durbridge play that was clearly crime fiction. See also his 1945 radio play *Over My Dead Body* (**148**).

57. *Physical Jerks*. 23 November 1934. A sketch included in *The Radioptimists*.
57A. New production. 23 July 1935. Included in *The Radio Follies*.
57B. New production. 2 June 1936. Included in *Mr. Mike Presents*.
57C. New production. 18 September 1937. Included in *Five O'Clock Follies*, presented as *The Children's Hour*. Producer: Martyn C. Webster.
57D. New production. 1 November 1939. Included in *Mid-Week Matinée*.
57E. New production. 23 July 1941. Included in *The Radioptimists*.

58. *World on Wheels*. 27 November 1934. A forty-five minute musical comedy, with music by Michael North and lyrics by Michael North and Peter Gregory. Producer: Martyn C. Webster.

Cast: Godfrey Baseley, Alma Vane, Hugh Morton, John Bentley, Helmar Fernback, Arthur Freeman, Stainton Price, Denis Folwell and Mabel France, with the Revue Orchestra conducted by Jack Wilson.

Plot summary: When the survival of an automobile factory is threatened by a competitor, a lowly inventor steps in and gets the ear of the boss and the heart of the boss's daughter.

59. *In the Country Tonight*, *The Invitation*, *Just Jones* and *Ladies Night*. 14 December 1934. Four sketches included in *The Radio Follies*.

The Radio Follies was a forty-five minute concert party series, created by Michael North and Richard Spencer in the Midland Region, including among its artistes some who had appeared earlier in *The Radioptimists*.

60. *Cuts*, *First Term* and *Service and Civility*. 17 January 1935. Three sketches included in *The Radio Follies*.

60A. New production of *Service and Civility*. 4 October 1939. Included in *Mid-Week Matinée*.

61. *Scandal*. 18 February 1935. A sketch included in *The Radio Follies*.

62. *Dolmans*. 23 February 1935. A one-hour play. Producer: Martyn C. Webster.

Cast: John Lang, Hugh Morton, Denis Folwell, Godfrey Baseley, Janet Joye, Vincent Curran, Mabel France, Cecily Gay, Stuart Vinden, Emily English, John Morley, Valerie Whitehouse, Helmar Fernback, Vera Ashe, Alfred Butler, William Hughes and Constance Needham.

Plot summary: This sequel to *Promotion* (**53**), again set in the Dolmans department store, shows conflict between the young men anxious to run it efficiently and the old managerial staff who meet their onslaught with plots and intrigue.

62A. New production, as *Dolridges: a sequel to the radio play Promotion*. 15 February 1938. Producer: Olive Shapley.

Cast: Frederick Allen, Donald Avison, Alison Bayley, Felix Deebank, Mary Eastwood, D.W. King, Joan Littlewood,

Hugh Morton, David Ormerod, Norman Partridge, Wilfred Pickles, Lucia Rogers, Edith Toms and Mae Bamber.

This was broadcast only in the BBC Northern Region, and it is not clear why the name of the store was changed from Dolmans to Dolridges. Maybe it had been Dolridges also in the Northern Region production of *Promotion* (**53B**), which was only eight months earlier.

63. *Coming Events*, *Midland Parliament* and *Don't Listen To This!* 1 April 1935. Three sketches included in the Midlands revue *How Very Regional*.

64. *Mary Ann*. 29 April 1935. A sketch included in the concert party programme *The Air-Do-Wells*. Producers: Max Kester and Bryan Michie.

64A. New production. 30 November 1935. Included in *Jack Payne's Radio Party*, performed by Janet Joye.

64B. New production. 8 January 1937. Included in the revue *Just Fancy That!* Producer: William MacLurg.

65. *The Shamrock Hat: a Play about Highwaymen in Ulster*. 9 May 1935. A forty-minute play included in *The Children's Hour*, only on BBC Belfast.

66. *Crash* and *Gay Interlude*. 12 June 1935. A one-hour double bill of plays. Producer: Martyn C. Webster.

Cast of *Crash*: Stuart Vinden, Elspeth Marsh, John Morley, Godfrey Baseley, Denis Folwell, Wortley Allen and John Bentley.

Cast of *Gay Interlude*: Vera Ashe and Gerald Martin.

Plot summaries: *Crash* shows a young couple, much in love and both keen aviators, reacting tragically to a financial disaster; whereas the contrasting *Gay Interlude* is a light comedy about the return of a husband from a voyage abroad, and a marital disagreement about whether to spend a quiet evening at home or to go dancing.

Durbridge wrote both plays, although *Crash* was credited to the pseudonymous "Frank Cromwell". The actor "Gerald Martin" was actually Martyn C. Webster. Durbridge later adapted *Crash* to become his 1938 radio play *Information Received* (**111**), with exactly the same characters, broadcast under his own name.

66A. New production of *Crash*. 19 September 1935. Again credited to "Frank Cromwell", and included in a one-hour bill of three plays, together with *The Nutcracker Suite* by J. Leslie Dodd and *Showing Up Shakespeare* by Godfrey M. Hayes and F. Keston Clarke. Producer: Martyn C. Webster.
Cast: Stuart Vinden, Valerie Larg, John Morley, Godfrey Baseley, Denis Folwell, Wortley Allen and John Bentley.

67. *Celebrity Cruise*. 18 July 1935. A one-hour musical comedy, with music by Michael North and lyrics by Charles Hatton. Producer: Martyn C. Webster.
Cast: Helmar Fernback, Marjorie Westbury, John Bentley, Hugh Morton, Godfrey Baseley, Denis Folwell, Dorothy Summers, Alfred Butler, Kathleen Tabberer and Vincent Curran, with Those Three, and the Revue Orchestra conducted by Reginald Burston.

Plot summary: To boost a cruise, a publicist persuades an actress to impersonate the widow of a South American millionaire. She is joined by the author of a best-seller of which he is heartily ashamed, and a film star who is mysteriously poisoned.

Marjorie Westbury, a popular soprano soloist as well as an actress, had already appeared in various Durbridge programmes. This was her first leading role in a Durbridge play, and there were many more to come before she began her long reign as Steve Temple in *Send for Paul Temple Again* in 1945. Hugh Morton, who appeared in numerous Durbridge plays and musical comedies, was to become the first Paul Temple in 1938.

68. *Eighth Cage*. 8 August 1935. A sketch by Durbridge and Max Kester included in *The Air-Do-Wells*, based on Durbridge's unbroadcast sketch *Murder at Malady Manor*.

69. *The Princess Who Couldn't Sleep*. 13 August 1935. A play included in *The Children's Hour*.

70. *The Weather-Cock that Wanted to Crow*. 26 August 1935. A short story, told by Valerie Larg, included in *The Children's Hour*.

71. *Advertising Albert, Nita and Hugh* and *A Soft Hat*. 4 November 1935. Three sketches included in *The Radio Follies*.
71A. New production of *A Soft Hat*. 18 September 1937. Included in *Five O'Clock Follies*, presented as *The Children's Hour*. Producer: Martyn C. Webster.

72. *Love is in the Air Again*. 7 November 1935. For this one-hour "musical mélange" Durbridge wrote the compère script for Martyn C. Webster, who was also the producer.

73. *November Cocktail*. 12 November 1935. This thirty-minute revue included five (unidentified) Durbridge sketches.

74. *Top o' the Tree*. 21 November 1935. A one-hour musical comedy, with music by George Gordon. Producer: Martyn C. Webster.
Cast: Stuart Vinden, Marjorie Westbury, Cecily Gay, Mabel France, Helmar Fernback, Nita Valerie, Denis Folwell and Lee Fox, with the Revue Orchestra conducted by Reginald Burston.
Plot summary: Composer Stephen Nesbet has been proposing marriage to musical comedy actress Anita Sloane for ten years, and he adopts drastic measures to win her consent on the first night of a big show in which she is starring.

75. *Mariella*. 3 December 1935. A one-hour musical comedy, with music and lyrics by Wilfrid Southworth. Producer: Martyn C. Webster.
Cast: Cora Goffin, Mabel France, Charles Brown, Barbara Helliwell, Aubrey Standing, Hugh Morton, Eddie Robinson and Clive Selborne, with the BBC Midland Revue Chorus and the BBC Midland Orchestra conducted by Reginald Burston.
Plot summary: Mariella was adopted as a child by a band of gypsies who had occupied an island in the Mediterranean for generations, and she is asked to intercede when the new owner wants to evict them.
75A. New production, abridged to forty-five minutes. 21 October 1937. Producer: Martyn C. Webster.
Cast: Cora Goffin, Godfrey Baseley, Vera Ashe, Mabel France, Denis Folwell, Dorothy Summers, John Lang, Hugh Morton and Clive Selborne, with the BBC Midland Revue Chorus and the Revue Orchestra conducted by Reginald Burston.
Cora Goffin was married to the theatre impresario Emile Littler, and in the magazine *The Stage* (7 October 1937)

Littler announced that *Mariella* was to be launched as a touring stage production in 1938, but there is no evidence that this actually occurred.

76. *No Alarm* and *On the Spotted Line*. 13 December 1935. Two sketches included in *December Cocktail*.
76A. New production of *No Alarm*. 1 November 1939. Included in *Mid-Week Matinée*.
76B. New production of *No Alarm*. 23 July 1941. Included in *The Radioptimists*.

77. *It Isn't Done, At the Langleys, Full House, Look Before You Leap* and *At the Dance*. 16 January 1936. Five sketches included in *January Cocktail*.
77A. New production of *Full House*. 18 February 1936. Included in *The February Revue of 1936*.

78. *First Instalment*. 30 January 1936. A sketch included in *The Air-Do-Wells*.

79. *All Wrong, Brighter Homes* and *The Valentine*. 15 February 1936. Three sketches included in *February Cocktail*, plus a new production of the sketch *Did You Guess?* (**54A**).

80. *One Over the Twenty-Eight, or Look Before You Leap*. 29 February 1936. A thirty-minute musical comedy, written jointly with Charles Hatton, with music by Jack Hill and lyrics by Charles Hatton. Producer: Martyn C. Webster.
Cast: Laura Bradshaw, Dorothy Summers, Peggy Bryan, Godfrey Baseley and John Bentley, with Jack Wilson at the piano.

Plot summary: The exploits of two spinsters who run a Leap Year matrimonial agency, and two of their clients.

81. *The First Night* and *The House Next Door*. 19 March 1936. Two sketches included in *March Cocktail*.

82. *April Showers*. 1 April 1936. A forty-five minute programme devised by Durbridge, described as "A Fool's Day Revue". Presented as *The Children's Hour*.

83. *Gentle Bonzo*, *A Murder Has Been Deranged*, *One of the Best*, *Personal Tale*, *The Type*, *Who Would Think?* and *Worth Taking*. 30 April 1936. Seven sketches included in *Mr. Mike Presents*.
83A. New production of *One of the Best*. 2 June 1936. Included in *Mr. Mike Presents*.
83B. New productions of *A Murder Has Been Deranged* and *Worth Taking*. 27 July 1936. Included in *Mr. Mike Presents*.
83C. New production of *Worth Taking*. 8 January 1937. Included in the revue *Just Fancy That!* Producer: William MacLurg.
83D. New production of *Worth Taking*. 3 March 1937. Included in the revue *The Time of March*. Producer: Archie Campbell.
83E. New production of *One of the Best*. 11 October 1939. Included in *Mid-Week Matinée*.
83F. New production of *A Murder Has Been Deranged*. 1 November 1939. Included in *Mid-Week Matinée*.

84. *Tonight at 8.30*. 27 May 1936. A sketch included in *This Month of May*, a one-hour revue produced by Archie Campbell.

85. *Excuses*, *Improbable Happening* and *The Knave*. 2 June 1936. Three sketches included in *Mr. Mike Presents*, plus new productions of the sketches *Physical Jerks* (**57B**) and *One of the Best* (**83A**).

85A. New production of *Excuses*. 19 January 1937. Included in *Variety in Miniature*, compèred and produced by Martyn C. Webster.
Cast: Hilary Williams and John Bentley.

85B. New production of *Excuses*. 25 September 1939. Included in *Everything Stops for Tea*.

85C. New production of *The Knave*. 12 March 1940. Read by Lionel Gamlin in *Crime Magazine*. Producer: William MacLurg.

85D. New production of *The Knave*. 7 May 1940. Included in a twenty-minute programme with the story *Mark Conway Tells a Personal Tale of a Long Time Ago* (**126**).

85E. New production of *The Knave*. 8 September 1941. Read by Godfrey Baseley and Martyn C. Webster in the revue *Words and Music*.

85F. New production of *The Knave*. 5 March 1943. Included in the revue *Divertissement*.

86. *Going Short*. 6 June 1936. A sketch included in the revue *A Star Party*, broadcast only in the Western Region.

87. *The New Pupil*. 11 June 1936. A sketch included in the programme *Tale Twisting*. Producer: Frederick Piffard.

88. *Sauce for the Gander*. 14 July 1936. A one-hour musical comedy, with script by Durbridge, music by Michael North and lyrics by Frank Cromwell (a Durbridge pseudonym). Producer: Martyn C. Webster.
Cast: Cora Goffin, John Lang, John Bentley, Hugh Morton, Mabel France, Hal Bryant, Doris Nichols, Stuart Vinden,

Joan Carter and Peggy Bryan, with the Revue Orchestra and the BBC Midland Revue Chorus conducted by H. Foster Clark.

Plot summary: The daughter of an industrialist refuses to marry the son of her father's business associate, and absconds to the centre of the song-publishing business. Simon Deal, the hero, is an unknown lyric writer for whose work the girl secures recognition.

89. *Lady on a Train*. 27 July 1936. A sketch included in *Mr. Mike Presents*, plus new productions of the sketches *A Murder Has Been Deranged* and *Worth Taking* (**83B**).

89A. New production of *Lady on a Train*. 4 October 1939. Included in *Mid-Week Matinée*.

89B. New production of *Lady on a Train*. 17 September 1940. Included in *Bye Bye Blues*.

90. *The Ace*. 18 August 1936. A sketch included in the revue *The Tune You Heard*, for which Durbridge also wrote some song lyrics. Producer: Martyn C. Webster.

90A. New production. 18 September 1937. Included in *Five O'Clock Follies*, presented as *The Children's Hour*. Producer: Martyn C. Webster.

90B. New production. 16 November 1937. Included in the revue *Baker's Dozen*. Producer: William MacLurg.

90C. New production. 11 October 1939. Included in *Mid-Week Matinée*.

90D. New production. 18 October 1940. Included in *Three Sketches by Francis Durbridge* (**129**).
Cast: Bernadette Hodgson and Stuart Vinden.

90E. New production. 7 April 1941. Included in the variety programme *Divertissement*.
Cast: Marjorie Westbury and Alan Robinson.

90F. New production. 10 April 1943. Included in the variety programme *Divertissement*.

91. *Stars at Home*. 4 September 1936. A sketch, starring Warwick Vaughan and Helen Collier, included in *Variety in Miniature*, compèred and produced by Archie Campbell.

92. *A Man about a Dog*. 27 November 1936. A sketch, starring Godfrey Baseley and Doris Nichols, included in *Variety in Miniature*, compèred and produced by Archie Campbell.

93. *It Happened at Christmas*. 22 December 1936. A short play or sketch described as "an interlude", included with Edward J. Mason's pantomime *As You Like It, or Much Ado About Nothing* in the one-hour show *Radio Cracker!* compèred by Percy Edgar. Producer: Martyn C. Webster.
Cast: Dorothy Summers, Hugh Morton, Denis Folwell, Mabel France, Peggy Bryan, Stuart Vinden, John Lang, Alfred Butler and Vincent Curran, with The Revue Orchestra and the BBC Midland Revue Chorus conducted by Reginald Burston.

94. *Hawaiian Interlude*. 19 January 1937. A sketch included in *Variety in Miniature*, compèred and produced by Martyn C. Webster, plus a new production of the sketch *Excuses* (**85A**).
Cast of *Hawaiian Interlude*: Hilary Williams, Maurice Milbourn and Martini and his Music.
94A. New production of *Hawaiian Interlude*. 18 October 1940. Included in *Three Sketches by Francis Durbridge* (**129**).
Cast: Bernadette Hodgson and Stuart Vinden.

95. *Paul Jones*. 12 February 1937. A sketch included in *Variety in Miniature*, compèred and produced by Martyn C. Webster.
Cast: Hugh Morton and Barbara Helliwell.
Plot summary: An encounter after a Paul Jones dance, an earlier version of which had been included in *Summer Showers: A Bright Interval* (**49**).
95A. New production. 8 November 1939. Included in *Mid-Week Matinée*.
95B. New production under the title *Cabaret*. 7 August 1941. Included in *Lunch Interval*.
95C. New production under the title *Cabaret*. 13 June 1942. Included in the revue *Cabaret*, compèred and produced by Martyn C. Webster.
95D. New production under the title *Cabaret*. 11 February 1943. Included in *Revue for Two*.
Cast: Marjorie Westbury and Dudley Rolph.

96. *Does it Pay to Advertise?* and *The Ultimatum*. 5 March 1937. Two sketches included in a variety programme on the BBC Empire Service. Producer: Frederick Piffard.
96A. New production of *Does it Pay to Advertise?* 6 September 1937. Included in *Follow On: a Revue in Miniature*, compèred and produced by Martyn C. Webster.

97. *Follow On*. 25 June 1937. A thirty-minute "little revue", written by Durbridge with music and lyrics by Jack Hill, with each item following on in sketch or song from the item preceding it. Compèred and produced by Martyn C. Webster.
Cast: Marjery Wyn, Dorothy Summers, Denis Folwell and John Bentley, with the Revue Nonet led by Norris Stanley.

98. *Chicken Hearted*, *Expelled* and *Two Chaps*. 10 July 1937. Three "blackout sketches" broadcast on the BBC Empire Service, each lasting less than one minute.

99. *Murder in the Embassy*. 4 August 1937. A one-hour play, with incidental music by Augustus Franzel and lyrics by Ralph Stanley and Lila Field. Producer: Archie Campbell.
Cast: Jack Melford, Norman Shelley, Ernest Sefton, Garda Hall, Jane Carr, Henry Victor, Fred Duprez, Boris Ranevsky, Paul Vernon, Morgan Davies, Edwin Ellis, Barry Ferguson, Ann Codrington and Ruth Beresford, with a Gypsy Orchestra conducted by Augustus Franzel and the BBC Theatre Orchestra conducted by Mark H. Lubbock.
Plot summary: There is mutual distrust between the governments of Westonia and Falkenstein. General Rostard, the Westonian dictator, fears an invasion by Falkenstein and also knows that a longstanding debt to Falkenstein can only be repaid if he can secure funding to develop the Westonian oilfields. Rostard's loathing of Count Sieler, dictator of Falkenstein, is aggravated by the fact that his nephew Captain Michael Rostard is in love with Count Sieler's daughter Elsa. At a glamorous ball in the Westonian Embassy in London, these conflicts come to a head. General Rostard is visiting London to sign a treaty, to secure Britain as an ally against Falkenstein. At the ball he tells Michael that he will be disinherited if he marries Elsa, and he also threatens his ambassador, Baron Von Klemm, with dismissal because he is too friendly towards Falkenstein. Apart from Elsa, the non-Westonians attending the ball include Sir Charles Fanshaw of the UK Foreign Office and Hiram E. Miller, an American authorised to settle Westonia's debt in return for oil development rights but who might be playing a double

game with Falkenstein as an alternative partner. When General Rostard is shot dead in the Embassy's library, Sir Charles Fanshaw assumes the role of detective and identifies various suspects before finally exposing the murderer and opening the way for friendship between Westonia and Falkenstein.

99A. New production, as *Murder at the Embassy*, in the series *Musical Theatre of the Air*. 11 April 1946. Producer: Archie Campbell. "A melodrama with music based on a scenario by Francis Durbridge," adapted by David Kean with incidental music by Augustus Franzel.

Cast: Griffith Jones, Albert Lieven, Frederick Valk, Bernard Rebel, Friedrich Richter, Irène Prador, Charles Farrell, Gwen Catley, Robert Irwin, Olaf Olsen, Jack Williams, Johnnie Schofield, John Clifford, George de Warfaz, Ann Codrington and Thea Wells, with a Gypsy Orchestra led by Augustus Franzel and the Augmented BBC Revue Orchestra conducted by Frank Cantell.

100. *In Training* and *Cowboys*. 6 September 1937. Two sketches included in *Follow On: a Revue in Miniature*, compèred and produced by Martyn C. Webster, plus a new production of the sketch *Does it Pay to Advertise?* (**96A**).

100A. New production of *In Training*. 1 November 1939. Included in *Mid-Week Matinée*.

100B. New production of *In Training*. 1 September 1941. Included in *Everything Stops for Tea*.

101. *Pot Luck*. 27 October 1937. A sketch included in *Follow On: a Revue in Miniature*.

102. *Midland Parade*. 4 November 1937. A forty-five minute programme in which "variety artists of the

Midlands prove that fact is sometimes stranger than fiction", devised and written by Durbridge. Producer: Martyn C. Webster.

Cast: Cora Goffin, Dorothy Summers, Marjorie Westbury, Denis Folwell, Hugh Morton, Helmar Fernback and Godfrey Baseley, with the BBC Midland Revue Chorus and the Revue Orchestra conducted by Reginald Burston.

Plot summary: Actors relate allegedly true experiences from earlier in their careers, for example (according to the *Nottingham Evening Post* in its programme listings) Cora Goffin once reached a theatre in a very strange conveyance, Hugh Morton faced injury when riding a horse for the first time in a film, and Helmar Fernback survived an attack by a knife-wielding assassin.

103. *The Champ* and *Darts*. 12 November 1937. Two sketches included in *Merry-Go-Round: a Revue of Cockney Humour*. Producer: Archie Campbell.

104. *The Kingdom in the Fog*. 13 November 1937. A one-hour musical fantasy, with music and lyrics by Wilfrid Southworth, broadcast as *The Children's Hour*. Producer: Martyn C. Webster.

Cast: Anthony Godfrey, Mabel France, John Bentley, Fred Forgham, Alfred Butler, Dorothy Summers, Marjorie Westbury and Hugh Morton, with the Revue Orchestra conducted by Reginald Burston.

Plot summary: A farmer and his son discover the Kingdom in the Fog.

105. *The Romantic Element*. 16 November 1937. A sketch included in the revue *Baker's Dozen*, plus a new production of the sketch *The Ace* (**90B**). Producer: William MacLurg.

106. *New Voices*. 1 December 1937. A sketch included in a fifteen-minute programme with the same title. Producer: Martyn C. Webster.
Cast: J.G. Thomason and Freida Fenton.

107. *The Guest*. 11 December 1937. A sketch included in the revue *Bits and Pieces*, only in the Northern Region.
107A. New production. 8 November 1939. Included in *Mid-Week Matinée*.

108. *Midland Parade (2)*. 15 December 1937. A forty-five minute programme in which "variety artists of the Midlands prove that fact is sometimes stranger than fiction", devised and written by Durbridge. Producer: Martyn C. Webster.
Cast: Compèred by Hugh Morton, with Gabriel Lavelle, Michael North, Doris Nichols, Vera Ashe, John Lang and Stuart Vinden, with the Revue Orchestra conducted by Reginald Burston.
Plot summary: As with the previous programme on 4 November 1937 (**102**), the Durbridge sketches illustrate unusual experiences in the careers of the actors, true or false.

109. *The Melody Man*. 17 December 1937. A thirty-minute play, with music and lyrics by Norman Hackforth. Producer: Bryan Michie.
Cast: Leslie Hutchinson, Charles Penrose, Diana Morrison, Betty le Brocke, Anthony Eustrel and Edward Stuart, with the BBC Variety Orchestra conducted by Charles Shadwell.
Plot summary: Durbridge wrote this play specially for the singer-pianist Leslie Hutchinson ("Hutch"). He stars as Paul Sanders, a singer who has achieved success on the radio under the name The Melody Man. Paul has secretly

taken a job as a waiter at The Golden Slipper café, to gain experience for his rags-to-riches role in a forthcoming film called "The Singing Waiter". The café proprietor Sam Trexter has booked The Melody Man for his cabaret, so rejects a proposal by his head waiter Monty Rain that Paul should be given a chance to sing. When The Melody Man fails to turn up for his performance, and Paul appears to be singing in his place, Monty explains to Sam that they are one and the same. This play is enhanced by the great voice of "Hutch", performing five original numbers by Norman Hackforth.

110. *The Appeal*. 3 February 1938. A sketch included in *The Children's Hour* in the Midlands.

111. *Information Received*. 25 February 1938. A twenty-five minute play. Producer: Howard Rose.
Cast: Anthony Hulme, Olga Lindo, Dennis Barry, Edward Harben, Dennis Arundell, Norman Scace and Edward Sinclair.
According to the *Radio Times*, "*Information Received*, a rather creepy little play about a young man who is cured of speculating by a story he is told in a club, was broadcast in the Midlands more than two years ago but in a different form." This refers to the play *Crash*, originally broadcast on 12 June 1935 under the Durbridge pseudonym "Frank Cromwell" (**66**), which has exactly the same character names.

112. *Send for Paul Temple*. 8 April - 27 May 1938. Eight twenty-five minute episodes, broadcast in the BBC Midland Region only, although the repeats the following day were broadcast in the BBC Midland and most other Regions.

Cast: Hugh Morton as Temple, Bernadette Hodgson as Steve and Lester Mudditt as Sir Graham Forbes, with Stuart Vinden, Cecily Gay, Courtney Hope, Duncan Blythe, Vincent Curran, Cedric Johnson, William Hughes, John Morley, Hal Bryant, Denis Folwell, Wortley Allen, Butts Marchant and Mabel France.

Plot summary: In this first Paul Temple case he meets journalist Steve Trent, who has changed her name from Louise Harvey in order to pursue a gang of jewel thieves. The murder of her brother, a Scotland Yard man, unites Temple and Steve in their determination to unmask the Knave of Diamonds. In due course they create crime fiction history by deciding to marry. The episodes were entitled "The Green Finger", "Room Seven", "Murder at Scotland Yard", "Reply to a Murder", "Action at the Inn", "The First Penguin", "The Knave of Diamonds" and "Exit the Knave".

Novelised 1938 (**1**) and again in 1951 as *Beware of Johnny Washington* (**7**); stage play 1943 (**191**); filmed 1946 (**202**).

"The First Penguin", the only surviving episode of the original 1938 UK serial, is included in the CD set marketed as *Paul Temple: The Complete Radio Collection: The Early Years 1938-1950*, BBC, 2016. The Canadian production of 1940 (see below) is available on four CDs, BBC, 2015, and is also included in the CD set marketed as *Paul Temple : The Complete Radio Collection: The Early Years 1938-1950*, BBC, 2016.

The *Derby Daily Telegraph* on 20 May 1938 commented: "Who is The Knave? Another revelation, awaited with almost equal breathlessness, will be the names of the cast, which have so far remained anonymous." Indeed the *Radio Times*, throughout the serial's run, adhered to producer Martyn C. Webster's decision that only the character names would be published without details of the cast. The players were identified on air after the final episode in the form that was to be followed by many of the succeeding Temple serials – a brief voice extract, followed by the actor's name - and those now known are listed above. Part of the second movement of Rimsky-Korsakov's *Scheherazade* suite was used as the signature tune for this and all Paul Temple serials until 1947, when it was replaced with *Coronation Scot* by Vivian Ellis for *Paul Temple and the Sullivan Mystery* and all the serials thereafter.

Send for Paul Temple was broadcast twice-weekly in Australia from 25 April to 24 May 1939, and in Canada (produced by Andrew Allen for the CBC Dominion Network) from 31 May to 19 July 1940. The Canadian cast included Bernard Braden as Temple and Peggy Hassard as Steve, and interestingly both actors were later to work in the UK and appear in Durbridge radio serials – Braden as Johnny Washington in 1949 and Hassard in *Paul Temple and the Gilbert Case* in 1954 and the second production of *Paul Temple and the Madison Mystery* in 1955.

The Dutch radio version, *Spreek met Vlaanderen en het komt in orde* (12 February – 2 April 1939, eight episodes), was translated by J.C. van der Horst and produced by Kommer Kleijn, with Theo Frenkel as Vlaanderen and Lily Bouwmeester as Ina.

112A. New production, abridged to one hour. 13 October 1941.

Cast: Carl Bernard as Temple, Thea Holme as Steve and Cecil Trouncer as Sir Graham Forbes, with Ivan Samson, Grizelda Hervey, Amy Veness, Cyril Gardiner, Ivor Barnard, William Trent, Edgar Norfolk, Antony Holles, Arthur Young, Allan Jeayes and John Bryning.

113. *We Were Strangers*. 3 June 1938. A short play, included in the forty-five minute *Three Tales of the Improbable* together with *The Hill of Yesterday* by Colin Howard and *Barking Dog* by L.C. Walters. Producer: Anthony McDonald.
Cast: Hilary Williams, Hugh Morton and William Hughes.
Plot summary: A romantic encounter in a fashionable London jeweller's shop.
Durbridge originally planned to call this *The Enchanted Moment*, and he adapted it as a one-act stage play in 1948 (**192**).
113A. New production, as a separate twenty-minute play. 9 July 1940. Producer: Lance Sieveking.
Cast: Pauline Vilda, D.A. Clarke-Smith and Philip Wade.
113B. New production, as a separate twenty-minute play. 16 September 1941. Producer: Howard Rose.
Cast: Grizelda Hervey, Carl Bernard and Antony Holles.

114. *Paul Temple and the Front Page Men*. 2 November – 21 December 1938. Eight twenty-five minute episodes.
Cast: Hugh Morton as Temple, Bernadette Hodgson as Steve and Lester Mudditt as Sir Graham Forbes, with Cedric Johnson, Neil Tuson, William Hughes, Leslie Bowmar, Cecily Gay, Godfrey Baseley, Percy Dewey, Stuart Vinden, Denis Folwell, Hal Bryant, Vincent Curran, Valerie Larg, Mary Pollock, William Warren, Fred Forgham, Clive Selborne, John Morley and Courtney Hope.
Plot summary: A smash hit detective novel entitled *The Front Page Men* has been published under the well-cloaked pseudonym of Andrea Fortune, and a series of robberies, kidnappings and murders is linked by the calling-card of The Front Page Men and the appearance of a seemingly innocuous piano tuner. The episodes were

entitled "Murder in the Afternoon", "The Glass Bowl", "Crime in the Midlands", "Paul Temple Receives a Warning", "Mr. Goldie's Mistake", "Murder on the Six-Ten", "Herr von Zelton" and "The Front Page Man".
Novelised 1939 (**2**); stage play 1943 (**191**).
"The Front Page Man", the only surviving episode of the original 1938 UK serial, is included in the CD set marketed as *Paul Temple: The Complete Radio Collection: The Early Years 1938-1950*, BBC, 2016.
The Midland Region of the BBC broadcast a ten-minute "trailer" of the new serial on 31 October 1938 under the title *Paul Temple Returns*. As with *Send for Paul Temple* the names of the cast members were kept secret while the serial was running, except that Hugh Morton was confirmed as Temple. Again the *Radio Times* published only the character names, and the players were identified on air after the final episode. The above list is believed to be complete.
The Dutch radio version, *Paul Vlaanderen en de mannen van de frontpagina* (28 May – 16 July 1939, eight episodes), was translated by J.C. van der Horst and produced by Kommer Kleijn, with Theo Frenkel as Vlaanderen and Lily Bouwmeester as Ina.

115. *Between You and Me and the Mike*. 16 February 1939. This thirty-minute Midlands revue, compèred and produced by Martyn C. Webster, included one (unidentified) Durbridge sketch.

116. *Cinderella Comes to Supper*. 26 March 1939. This thirty-minute Midlands revue included one Durbridge sketch (unidentified, but probably the title sketch).

117. *The Daily Dodge: a Family Affair*. 4 April – 27 June 1939. Seven episodes. Included in *For You, Madam*, a fortnightly "magazine programme for every woman". Written by Durbridge and Archie Campbell. Producer: Archie Campbell.

Cast: Kathleen Harrison as Mrs. Dodge, with Edgar Norfolk, Hilda Bruce Potter, Pamela Nell and Leonard Thorne.

Plot summary: In this series of sketches, the Clayton family employs Mrs. Dodge as their daily help (or "char") and they rely on her homespun cockney philosophy to solve many of their difficulties – a sort of early "soap opera"?

For You, Madam was broadcast fortnightly on the National Home Station from 18 October 1938, but the Durbridge contribution did not begin until 4 April 1939. Each episode of *The Daily Dodge*, within this thirty-minute programme, lasted only six or seven minutes. Kathleen Harrison secured the role on the strength of her performances as cockney characters in films and on the stage. This was her debut in a radio series, although she later achieved success as a heart-of-gold Londoner opposite Jack Warner in the 1940s Huggetts series of films, in *Meet the Huggetts* on the radio from 1953 to 1961, and on television as *Mrs. Thursday* from 1966 to 1967.

118. *Mr. Ramsbottom Regrets*. 27 September 1939. A sketch included in *Mid-Week Matinée*.

119. *Rowland's Syrup*. 2 October 1939. A sketch included in *Revue in Miniature*.

120. *Cocktails for Two*. 4 October 1939. A sketch included in *Mid-Week Matinée*, plus new productions of the sketches *Service and Civility* (**60A**) and *Lady on a Train* (**89A**).

121. *Charles*. 18 October 1939. A sketch included in *Mid-Week Matinée*.
121A. New production. 10 January 1942. Included in *Everything Stops for Tea*.
121B. New production. 11 May 1942. Included in *Everything Stops for Tea*.

122. *The Customer's Always Right* and *Parents*. 19 October 1939. Two sketches included in *Everything Stops for Tea*.
122A. New production of *The Customer's Always Right*. 8 May 1942. Included in *Everything Stops for Tea*.

123. *News of Paul Temple*. 13 November – 18 December 1939. Six twenty-five minute episodes.
Cast: Hugh Morton as Temple, Bernadette Hodgson as Steve and Lester Mudditt as Sir Graham Forbes, with Maurice Denham, Clifford Bean, Dick Francis, Diana Morrison, Norman Shelley, Cyril Nash, Gwen Lewis, Mona Harrison, Leo de Pokorny, Alan Howland, Ben Wright, Bruce Winston, Ewart Scott, Ivan Samson, Mary O'Farrell, Geoffrey Wincott and Audrey Cameron.
Plot summary: Iris Archer agrees to appear in one of Temple's plays, but then disappears until he sees her in a Scottish hotel when she is supposed to be in France. But how is this connected with a letter passed to Temple with a plea to deliver it to a Mr. Richmond, and a network of spies with a shadowy leader called Z4? The episodes were entitled "The Stage is Set", "Concerning Z4",

"Instructions for a Murder", "Appointment with Danger", "In which Mrs. Moffat Receives a Visitor" and "Introducing Z4".
Novelised 1940 (**3**); filmed as *Paul Temple's Triumph* 1950 (**204**).
The first Dutch radio version, *Paul Vlaanderen en het Z-4 mysterie* (14 April – 5 May 1940, first four episodes only), was translated by Willem Vogt and produced by Kommer Kleijn, with Theo Frenkel as Vlaanderen and Lily Bouwmeester as Ina. Wartime circumstances prevented episodes 5 and 6 from being transmitted, but on 23 December 1946 a new 145-minute version was broadcast, translated by Willem Vogt and produced by Kommer Kleijn, with Jan van Ees as Vlaanderen and Eva Janssen as Ina.
123A. New production, abridged to one hour. 5 July 1944.
Cast: Richard Williams as Temple, Lucille Lisle as Steve and Laidman Browne as Sir Graham Forbes, with Lewis Stringer, Grizelda Hervey, Molly Rankin, Basil Jones, Alexander Sarner, Cyril Gardiner, Gladys Young, Preston Lockwood, Frank Cochrane, Duncan McIntyre and Arthur Ridley.

124. *Drama*. 12 February 1940. A sketch included in *Revue in Miniature*.

125. *A Case for Sexton Blake*. 12 March – 16 April 1940. Six episodes, included in the programme *Crime Magazine*, adapted from a story by Edward Holmes. Producer: William MacLurg.
Cast: Arthur Young as Sexton Blake and Clive Baxter as Tinker, with John Robinson, Jane Graham, John Morley, Cyril Nash, Foster Carlin, Ewart Scott, Wilfrid Walter, John Rorke, Vera Lennox, Horace Percival and Ben Wright.

Plot summary: Sexton Blake and his assistant Tinker are summoned to a Northumberland castle, where the younger brother of the Marthioly family has been murdered. They not only pursue the murderer, but also the family ghost known as "The Man in the Iron Mask". The theme music was "The Song of Death" by Eric Spear.

126. *Mark Conway Tells a Personal Tale of a Long Time Ago*. 7 May 1940. A short story in a twenty-minute programme, plus a new production of his story *The Knave* (**85D**).

Durbridge had earlier revealed (*Radio Times*, 22 April 1938) that Mark Conway would have been the name of his radio detective if he had not decided upon Paul Temple.

127. *The New Cocktail*. 14 September 1940. A sketch included in *Lunch Interval*.

128. *Cutting*. 17 September 1940. A sketch included in *Bye Bye Blues*, plus a new production of the sketch *Lady on a Train* (**89B**).

128A. New production of *Cutting*. 8 May 1942. Included in *Everything Stops for Tea*.

129. *Sentimental Journey*. 18 October 1940. Included in *Three Sketches by Francis Durbridge*, a twenty-minute programme that also included new productions of *The Ace* (**90D**) and *Hawaiian Interlude* (**94A**). Producer: Martyn C. Webster.

Cast: Bernadette Hodgson and Stuart Vinden.

130. *And Anthony Sherwood Laughed*. 20 December 1940 - 31 January 1941. Six twenty-minute episodes. Producer: Martyn C. Webster.

Cast: Stuart Vinden as Anthony Sherwood, with Janet Joye, Mabel France, Alan Robinson, Godfrey Baseley, Vincent Curran, Lester Mudditt, Hal Bryant, Marjorie Westbury and William Hughes.

Plot summary: This was not a serial, but six short plays about "gentleman and crook" Anthony Sherwood. The episodes were entitled "Make Way for Anthony Sherwood", "The Man with the Perfect Alibi", "The Prince of Rogues", "The Man Who Changed his Mind", "Once Upon a Time" and "Watch Your Step, Mr. Sherwood".

The German radio version, *Bahn frei für Anthony Sherwood* (23 August 1951), was translated by Friedel Schlemmer but consisted only of the first episode.

131. *Mark Conway Returns to the Microphone to Tell a Strictly Personal Tale of How a Certain Gentleman in Chelsea Lost His Braces*. 15 February 1941. A fifteen-minute story on the Forces Programme.

132. *Moods of the Moderns: a Study in Contrasts*. 22 February 1941. A forty-five minute programme about George Gershwin, Noël Coward, Jerome Kern and Cole Porter.

Cast: Evelyn Dall, Sylvia Welling, Ronnie Hill and the Three Radio Graces, with Donald Edge and Charles Groves at two pianos and the BBC Theatre Orchestra conducted by Reginald Burston.

133. *Stranger, Beware*. 18 April 1941. A forty-minute musical comedy, with music by Basil Hempseed and lyrics by Edward J. Mason. Producer: Martyn C. Webster.

Cast: Jack Melford, Marjorie Westbury, Jacques Brown, Pat Rignold, Sidney Keith, Griselda Hervey, Charles Heslop and Joan Miller, with the Revue Orchestra and Ladies' Chorus conducted by Hyam Greenbaum.

134. *Cocktails with Cupid*. 10 May 1941. A fifteen-minute play. Producer: Martyn C. Webster.
Cast: Marjorie Westbury, Alan Robinson and Michael Lynd, with Jack Wilson and his Versatile Five.
Plot summary: A series of conversation pieces, set in the cocktail bar of a large hotel.
134A. New production. 20 June 1942. Producer: Martyn C. Webster.
Cast: Marjorie Westbury, Jack Morrison and Gerald Martin, with Jack Wilson and his Versatile Five.
"Gerald Martin" was actually Martyn C. Webster. Although this production was listed in the *Radio Times*, correspondence in the BBC Written Archives suggests that it was cancelled and it did not appear in *The Times* radio listings.
134B. New production, expanded to twenty-five minutes. 30 March 1943. Producer: Martyn C. Webster.
Cast: Marjorie Westbury, Sydney Tafler and Lewis Stringer, with Jack Wilson and his Versatile Five.

135. *The Man from Washington*. 23 May – 27 June 1941. Six twenty-minute episodes. Producer: Martyn C. Webster.
Cast: Carl Bernard as Johnny Cordell, with Ronald Simpson, Ivor Barnard, Bryan Powley, Cyril Gardiner, Cecil Trouncer, Phyllis Morris, Arthur Young, Betty Hardy, Pamela Brown, Thea Holme, Grizelda Hervey, Fred O'Donovan, Malcolm Graeme and Antony Holles.

Plot summary: American gang-buster Johnny Cordell helps Scotland Yard to smash a dope-smuggling ring, with one gangster biting the dust in each inter-linked instalment. The episodes were entitled "Cards on the Table", "Mr. Michael Sleaman", "The Best of Friends Must Part", "The Guilty Party", "On the Set" and "Guilty or ...". Durbridge originally planned to call this *S.O.S. America!* and given its final title it should not be confused with his later creation, Johnny Washington (**159**).

136. *Hall Mark: A Dramatic Radio Biography of Henry Hall*. 13 July 1941. A forty-minute portrait of the popular bandleader, written jointly with Charles Hatton, featuring Henry Hall and his Orchestra and members of the BBC Drama Repertory Company. Producer: Martyn C. Webster.

137. *The Girl at the Hibiscus*. 22 August – 26 September 1941. Written under the pseudonym Nicholas Vane, jointly with Val Gielgud. Six fifteen-minute episodes. Producers: Val Gielgud for the first episode, the others by Martyn C. Webster.
Cast: Frances Clare as Amanda Smith and Carl Bernard as Hugo Bismarck, with John Laurie, G.R. Schjelderup, Philip Garston-Jones, Marjorie Westbury, Alec Clunes, Edgar Norfolk, Denis Arundell, Arthur Clay and Brenda Bruce.
Plot summary: These were short complete plays about the adventures of Miss Amanda Smith of London, a dance hostess at the Hibiscus night club. The episodes were entitled "The Waltz", "The Wittiest Man in London", "A Man of Honour", "Mr. and Mrs. Royce-Morgan", "Sarah and Johnny" and "The Man Who Was Misunderstood".
Durbridge originally planned to call this *It Started at the Hibiscus*. Five years later, an item in the *Radio Times* (11

October 1946) previewing *Paul Temple and the Gregory Affair* quotes Durbridge as acknowledging the "Nicholas Vane" pseudonym.

138. *Death Comes to the Hibiscus*. 28 November 1941 – 20 February 1942. Written under the pseudonym Nicholas Vane, jointly with Val Gielgud. Twelve fifteen-minute episodes. Producer: Martyn C. Webster.
Cast: Frances Clare as Amanda Smith, Carl Bernard as Hugo Bismarck and Gordon McLeod as Chief Insp. Silence, with Leo de Pokorny, Denis Arundell, Marjorie Westbury, Ivor Barnard, Mary Pollock, Edgar Norfolk, Philip Garston-Jones, Diana Morrison, Kenneth Garratt, Godfrey Baseley, Penelope Shaw, George Brown and Dudley Rolph.
Plot summary: Unlike its predecessor this was a serial, with a murder at the Hibiscus night club that appears to be connected with the plagiarism of a musical composition. More murders follow, but Amanda Smith has felt sure of the culprit from the outset – much to the amusement of the enigmatic Chief Insp. Silence. The episodes were entitled "In which Mr. Bizarre Entertains", "In which we meet Chief Inspector Silence", "In which we hear from Amanda", "In which Amanda is Surprised", "In which Chief Inspector Silence is Amused", "In which we meet Howard Kain", "In which Amanda Receives a Warning", "In which Mr. Bizarre is in the News", "In which Clive Payford is Bewildered", "In which Hugo is Astonished", "In which Silence Investigates" and "In which Amanda Explains".
The theme music was "Frenesi" by Alberto Dominguez.

139. *The House on the Corner*. 24 December 1941. A forty-five minute musical play. Producer: Martyn C. Webster.

Cast: Godfrey Baseley, Mary Jones, William Hughes, Lester Mudditt, Philip Garston-Jones and Marjorie Westbury, with Jack Wilson at the piano and the BBC Midland Light Orchestra conducted by Richard Crean.

140. *Mr. Hartington Died Tomorrow*. 9 February – 6 April 1942. Written under the pseudonym Lewis Middleton Harvey. Eight thirty-minute episodes. Producer: Val Gielgud.

Cast: James McKechnie, Laidman Browne, Philip Cunningham, Phyllis Calvert, Alexander Sarner, Harry Hutchinson, Grizelda Hervey, Tucker McGuire, Malcolm Graeme, Olga Edwards, Ernest Sefton, Roy Emerton, Joan Miller, Jack Livesey, Allan Jeayes, Dino Galvani, John Laurie, Heron Carvic, Muriel Pratt, Lucille Lisle, Finlay Currie, Viki Dobson, Macdonald Parke, Andrea Malandrinos, Ivan Samson, Connie Burnett, Bryan Herbert and G.R. Schjelderup.

Plot summary: Oliver Hartington, the Czar of Hollywood, is found dead at the Blue Stetson club. His poisoning raises the question "Who is Peter London?" The episodes were entitled "Mr. Hartington's Siesta", ""Who is Peter London?", "Makings of a Film Star", "The Second Death", "The Blue Stetson", "Beverley Hills", "The Remarkable Behaviour of Otto Stultz" and "That's My Story!".

This serial was mentioned six months earlier in a preview of forthcoming dramas (*Radio Times*, 15 August 1941), when it was described as "a serial play by a new author, dealing with life (and murder!) in Hollywood's English colony." Evidently the true identity of "Lewis Middleton Harvey" was being concealed at that time – but see the note under *Farewell, Leicester Square!* (**144**).

140A. New production, abridged to one hour. 30 October 1942. Again credited to "Lewis Middleton Harvey". Producer: Val Gielgud.

Cast: James McKechnie, Laidman Browne, Philip Cunningham, Alexander Sarner, Harry Hutchinson, Grizelda Hervey, Malcolm Graeme, Ernest Sefton, Rita Vale, Max Adrian, Preston Lockwood, Naomi Campbell, Penelope Davidson, Richard Williams, Tony Quinn and Harry Ross.

140B. New production. 31 January – 21 March 1950. Again credited to "Lewis Middleton Harvey". Eight thirty-minute episodes. Script editor: Martyn C. Webster. Producer: David H. Godfrey.

Cast: Douglass Montgomery, Richard Williams, Peter Coke, Grizelda Hervey, Rita Vale, Leo de Pokorny, Hamilton Dyce, Catherine Campbell, Tommy Duggan, Jon Farrell, Ian Sadler, Bryan Powley, John McLaren, Charles Leno, Elizabeth Maude, Janet Morrison, Roger Snowdon, Duncan McIntyre, Richard Hurndall, Anthony Jacobs, Alastair Duncan, Stanley Groome, Ivan Samson, Macdonald Parke, Denise Bryer, Marjorie Westbury, Jean Macdonald, Betty Baskcomb, Warren Stanhope, Preston Lockwood, Peter Claughton, John Drexler, Frank Coburn, John Richmond, Eric Lugg, Gordon Tanner and Eddy Reed.

Peter Coke played the mysterious Peter London in this production, with Marjorie Westbury in a supporting role, and four years later they were to get together for the first time as Paul and Steve Temple in *Paul Temple and the Gilbert Case* (**165**).

141. *These Foolish Things*. 18 August 1942. A thirty-minute "programme in reminiscent mood". Producer: Martyn C. Webster.

Cast: Brenda Bruce, Philip Garston-Jones, Marjorie Westbury and Antony Holles.

142. *Paul Temple Intervenes*. 30 October – 18 December 1942. Eight twenty-minute episodes.
Cast: Carl Bernard as Temple, Bernadette Hodgson as Steve and Lester Mudditt as Sir Graham Forbes, with Sydney Tafler, Edgar Norfolk, Godfrey Baseley, Ronald Simpson, Mabel France, David Compton, Philip Garston-Jones, Marjorie Westbury, Hal Bryant, Alan Howland, Vincent Curran, Bessie Love, Geoffrey Wincott, Chris Gittins and John Maddison.
Plot summary: A series of eight murders, with in each case a card bearing the inscription "The Marquis", brings Temple into the hunt for a ruthless master criminal. Suspicion falls on an eminent Egyptologist, but there are other suspects and further murders before the Marquis is identified. The episodes were entitled "The Marquis", "Concerning Sir Felix Reybourn", "Kellaway Manor", "A Warning from the Marquis", "Paul Temple Keeps an Appointment", "Above Suspicion", "The October Hotel" and "Introducing…the Marquis!".
Novelised 1944 (**4**); filmed as *Paul Temple Returns* 1952 (**205**).
Two Audiocassettes / Two CDs of the 1942 broadcast serial, BBC Audio, 2005. Also included in the CD set marketed as *Paul Temple: The Complete Radio Collection: The Early Years 1938-1950*, BBC, 2016.
Marjorie Westbury, who played Dolly Fraser in this production, later became the definitive Steve Temple from 1945 in *Send for Paul Temple Again* (**151**). Durbridge dominated the evening airwaves on 30 October 1942 – with the first episode of *Paul Temple Intervenes* at 6.40 on the Forces Programme and the one-hour version of *Mr.*

Hartington Died Tomorrow (under his Harvey pseudonym) at 9.40 on the Home Service.

The Dutch radio version, *Paul Vlaanderen contra de Markies* (6 April – 25 May 1947, eight episodes), was translated by J.C. van der Horst and produced by Kommer Kleijn, with Jan van Ees as Vlaanderen and Eva Janssen as Ina.

143. *The Essential Heart*. 6 February 1943. Written under the pseudonym Nicholas Vane. A short romantic comedy, in a double bill of thirty minutes with *Goodbye for Now* by Godfrey Heseltine. Producer: Val Gielgud.
Cast: Robert Rendel, Grizelda Hervey and Richard Williams.
Plot summary: The wife of a playwright leaves him for another man but then returns to him, in a play with a Priestley-like time theme.
143A. New production. 22 March 1952. Again credited to "Nicholas Vane", as a separate twenty-minute play on the Midland Home Service. Producer: Trafford Whitelock.
Cast: Peter Wilde, Monica Grey and Ronald Baddiley.

144. *Farewell, Leicester Square!* 8 February – 29 March 1943. Written under the pseudonym Lewis Middleton Harvey, with music by Kenneth Pakeman. Eight twenty-minute episodes. Producer: Martyn C. Webster.
Cast: Ronald Simpson, Olga Edwardes, Carl Bernard, Ernest Sefton, Marjorie Westbury, Belle Chrystall, Shelagh Fraser, Philip Cunningham, Frederick Lloyd, Sydney Tafler, Richard Williams, Arthur Young, Jenny Laird, Robert Rendel, Neville Mapp, Philip Garston-Jones, Preston Lockwood, Allan Jeayes, Grizelda Hervey, Rita Vale, Jack Livesey, Brenda Bruce and Edgar Norfolk.

Plot summary: An aged actor, sitting on a bench in Leicester Square, reminisces about his life in the theatre. Described as "a new musical serial ... a story of London's Theatreland, today and yesterday," it opens with an attempt to persuade an impresario to produce a musical show, and revolves around a group of characters in the theatre world. The episodes were entitled "Introducing the Principals", "Not Enough Comedy", "Danny's Divan", "The Female of the Species", "The Audition", "Chelsea Interlude", "Quentin Barrett – Talent Scout" and "Finale".

The *Radio Times*, previewing this production in its issue of 29 January 1943, described it as "a new serial play of eight instalments, by Francis Durbridge of *Paul Temple* fame." While factually correct this revelation was a slip that the BBC was quick to rectify, and "Lewis Middleton Harvey" was credited in subsequent issues of the *Radio Times* for each serial episode with no mention of Durbridge.

145. *Introducing Gail Carlton*. 10 December 1943 – 21 January 1944. Written under the pseudonym Nicholas Vane. Six fifteen-minute episodes. Producer: Martyn C. Webster.

Cast: Rita Vale as Gail Carlton, with Macdonald Parke, Edgar Norfolk, June Willock, Richard Williams, Robert Rendel, Tommy Duggan, Marjorie Westbury, Bernard Rebel, Alexander Sarner, Carl Bernard, Betty Hardy, Sydney Tafler, Laidman Browne, Gladys Spencer, Ralph Michael, Joan Carol, Preston Lockwood, Ian Sadler, Lucille Lisle, Lester Mudditt, Basil Jones and William Trent.

Plot summary: The adventures of a newspaper woman during the then-current war, in six separate stories entitled "The Bad Lot", "The Carlsruhe Incident", "Change of Heart", "Lucky Dan", "Hotel Toledo" and "The Forsythe Affair".

The theme music was "Revenge with Music" by André Kostelanetz. Durbridge originally planned to call this *Miss Carlton Regrets*, then *Miss Carlton Remembers*. His first idea was to make the central character a romantic lady crook along Raffles lines, but the BBC at the time was not inclined to glamourise criminals. In the 1948 first edition of the book *Send for Paul Temple Again!* a list of "Radio Plays by Francis Durbridge" includes the title *Gail Carlton Remembers*, which is clearly an incorrect reference to *Introducing Gail Carlton* – but at least it is further confirmation that "Nicholas Vane" was Durbridge.

146. *Michael Starr Investigates*. 14 February – 7 August 1944. Twenty-six episodes, a series of brief "weekly detective problems" included in *Monday Night at Eight*. Producer: Harry S. Pepper.
Cast: Henry Oscar as Michael Starr.

147. *The Memoirs of André d'Arnell*. 9 October – 27 November 1944 and 18 December 1944. Nine episodes, a series of brief "weekly detective problems" included in *Monday Night at Eight*. Producer: Harry S. Pepper.
Cast: Kenneth Kent as André d'Arnell, with Linden Travers.

148. *Over My Dead Body*. 11 April 1945. A forty-minute play in the one-hour *Wednesday Matinée*, together with *When You Come Home* by Muriel Levy. Producer: Martyn C. Webster.
Cast: Richard Williams, Belle Chrystall, Alexander Sarner, Cyril Gardiner, Basil Jones, Preston Lockwood and Gladys Spencer. This was the cast published in the *Radio Times*, but a cast list in the BBC Written Archives suggests that Belle Chrystall was replaced by Phyllis Watt.

Plot summary: Actors John and Sheila Nelson have appeared as detective Mark Conway and his wife Myra for longer than they care to remember, and they aspire to more serious roles and more realistic plots. Driving through Essex, they run into thick fog and seek directions at a large house – in which they discover a murdered man, and learn that fact can be as strange as fiction.

There is a tongue-in-cheek element here, as Mark Conway was Durbridge's original idea for his radio detective's name that became Paul Temple, and Conway featured in some earlier Durbridge broadcasts (**126**, **131**). Durbridge originally planned to call this *No Time for Murder*, written for Jessie Matthews and Sonnie Hale and intended to be broadcast on 14 January 1941, but it was postponed indefinitely owing to their theatrical commitments and was never re-scheduled with Matthews and Hale. Given the similarity of plot it was clearly a re-write of Durbridge's 1934 radio play *Murder in the Midlands* (**56**), with the character names changed and one additional character, although evidentially Insp. Dawson appears in both plays.

148A. New production. 7 August 1946. Included in the one-hour *Mystery Playhouse*, together with *The Baron's Room* by Norman Edwards. Producer: Martyn C. Webster. Cast: John Bentley, Phyllis Byford, Finlay Currie, Lee Fox, Bill Gates, Lester Mudditt and Betty Hardy. This was the cast published in the *Radio Times*, but a cast list in the BBC Written Archives suggests that Finlay Currie was replaced by Geoffrey Wincott and Lee Fox by Malcolm Graeme.

The Dutch radio version, *Paul en Ina Vlaanderen incognito* (14 September 1959), was translated by Johan Bennik (pseudonym of Jan van Ees) and produced by Dick van Putten. It replaced the principal characters John and

Sheila Nelson with Paul and Ina Vlaanderen (Jan van Ees and Eva Janssen), and even added Sir Graham Forbes (Louis de Bree).

The German radio version, *Nur über meine Leiche*, was broadcast in 1963. It was translated by Marianne de Barde and produced by Hans Quest, with Jürgen Goslar and Marianne Mosa as the Nelsons. Another German production in 1964 used the same title and the de Barde translation, produced by Wilm Ten Haaf with Peter René Körner and Ricarda Krauf-Benndorf as the Nelsons.

149. *Mr. Lucas*. 3 July 1945. A forty-five minute play. Producer: Howard Rose.

Cast: James Harcourt as Mr. Lucas, with Harold Scott, Sebastian Cabot, Freda Falconer, George Owen, Frank Pettingell, Roger Snowdon, Grizelda Hervey, Gordon McLeod, Stanley Groome, Heron Carvic, Lucille Lisle, Ernest Sefton, Glen Farmer, Frank Partington, Dermot Cathie and Ann Codrington.

Plot summary: A valuable necklace, stolen in Copenhagen, is believed to be in the hands of a courier on a train from London to Carlisle. Among the many passengers is toy trader Mr. Lucas, who might not be all he seems, but when the train crashes the search for the courier and the necklace is thrown into even greater confusion.

Durbridge originally planned to call this *The Mask of Kien Te*. No plot information was given in the *Radio Times* when this play was originally broadcast, and the plot summary above has been obtained from the archives of the Dutch broadcaster BRT. Their version was aired on 26 June 1988, entitled *Mister Lucas*, translated by Luc Van den Broecke and produced by Michel De Sutter, with Anton Cogen in the title role.

150. *Passport to Danger!* 1 August – 5 September 1945. Six thirty-minute episodes. Producer: Vernon Harris.

Cast: Carl Bernard as Tim Valentine and Linden Travers as Linda West, with Philip Leaver, Carleton Hobbs, Norman Shelley, Ian Sadler, Joan Young, Jacques Brown, Finlay Currie, Stephen Jack, Andrea Malandrinos, Dorothy Carless, Wilfred Babbage, Basil Jones, Edna Kaye, Olwen Brooks, Gladys Young, George Owen and Michele De Lys, with music by Hal Evans played by The Dance Orchestra conducted by Stanley Black.

Plot summary: The brother of actress Linda West has vanished overseas on a secret mission, and the only news she receives from him is that he has made an important discovery. After a long wait she decides to follow his trail, accompanied by journalist Tim Valentine, and they are faced with plots and assassinations. The episodes were entitled "In which a Young Lady says 'Yes'", "In which we meet Don Quisando", "In which there is Music in the Air", "In which we visit the El Bassari", "In which there are Cards on the Table" and "In which a Young Lady says 'Yes' again".

Durbridge originally planned to call this *And This Is Stephen Lewis*. No plot information was given in the *Radio Times* when the serial was originally broadcast, and the plot summary above has been obtained from the archives of the Dutch broadcaster AVRO. Their version was aired in six episodes from 8 October 1985, entitled *Een reis vol gevaren*, translated by J.C. van der Horst and produced by Hero Muller, with Manfred de Graaf as Tim Valentine and Barbara Hoffmann as Linda West.

151. *Send for Paul Temple Again*. 13 September – 1 November 1945. Eight thirty-minute episodes.

Cast: Barry Morse as Temple, Marjorie Westbury as Steve and Lester Mudditt as Sir Graham Forbes, with Ralph Truman, Grizelda Hervey, Alexander Sarner, Basil Jones, Laidman Browne, John Blythe, Frank Tickle, William Trent, Cyril Gardiner, Harry Hutchinson, George Owen, Alan Howland, Eric Lugg, Bryan Powley, John Stone, Keith Shepherd, Hilda Davies, Charles Maunsell, Freda Falconer, Dermot Cathie and Preston Lockwood.

Plot summary: A body on a train, the name "Rex" scrawled on the compartment window, and a card with the name "Mrs. Trevelyan" are all linked with further murders and the same names. The case takes Temple to a psychiatrist's consulting room, a dockland rendezvous and a hotel in Canterbury. The episodes were entitled "Paul Temple Takes Over", "Rex Strikes Again", "Concerning Dr. Kohima", "In which Mr. Carl Lathom is Perturbed", "The Girl in Brown", "Who is Rex?", "Temple Makes a Decision" and "Rex".

Novelised as *Send for Paul Temple Again!* 1948 (**5**); filmed as *Calling Paul Temple* 1948 (**203**).

Durbridge originally planned to call this *Paging Paul Temple*. It was Marjorie Westbury's first of twenty-three appearances as Steve.

The Dutch radio version, *Haal Paul Vlaanderen er weer bij!* (17 February – 7 April 1946, eight episodes), was translated by J.C. van der Horst and produced by Kommer Kleijn, with Jan van Ees as Vlaanderen and Eva Janssen as Ina.

151A. New production, as *Paul Temple and the Alex Affair*. 26 February – 21 March 1968 (two episodes per week). Eight thirty-minute episodes.

Cast: Peter Coke as Temple, Marjorie Westbury as Steve and James Thomason as Sir Graham Forbes, with Simon Lack, Barbara Mitchell, Rolf Lefebvre, Basil Jones, Haydn

Jones, Denys Hawthorne, Frank Henderson, Alan Dudley, Ian Thompson, Denis McCarthy, Betty Hardy, Duncan McIntyre, David Brierley, Ann Murray, Ronald Herdman, Antony Viccars, LeRoy Lingwood, Nigel Clayton and Rosalind Shanks.

Two Audiocassettes / Four CDs of the 1968 *Paul Temple and the Alex Affair* broadcast serial, BBC Audio, 2003. Also included in the CD set marketed as *Paul Temple : The Complete Radio Collection: The Sixties 1960-1968*, BBC, 2017.

In this new production of *Send for Paul Temple Again*, the plot closely follows the original but the villain's name is changed from Rex to Alex. The eight episode titles were changed to "Mrs. Trevelyan", "Dr. Kohima", "Mr. Carl Lathom", "Mr. 'Spider' Williams", "Mr. Wilfred Davis", "Mr. Leo Brent", "The Girl in Brown" and "Introducing Alex".

The German radio version, *Paul Temple und der Fall Alex* (16 February – 5 April 1968, eight episodes), was translated by Marianne de Barde and produced by Otto Düben, with Paul Klinger as Temple and Margot Leonhardt as Steve. It is interesting that this began slightly earlier than the UK production.

The Dutch radio version, *Paul Vlaanderen en het Alex mysterie* (7 January – 25 February 1969, eight episodes), was translated by Alfred Pleiter and produced by Dick van Putten, with Johan Schmitz as Vlaanderen and Wieke Mulier as Ina.

152. *A Case for Paul Temple*. 7 February – 28 March 1946. Eight thirty-minute episodes.

Cast: Howard Marion-Crawford as Temple, Marjorie Westbury as Steve and Lester Mudditt as Sir Graham Forbes, with Cyril Gardiner, Olaf Olsen, Gilbert Davis, Rita

Vale, Laidman Browne, Duncan McIntyre, Frank Partington, Lucille Lisle, Tommy Duggan, Alexander Sarner, Dorothy Smith, Vivienne Chatterton, Beryl Calder, Charles Leno, Leslie Perrins, Denis Webb and Frank Atkinson.

Plot summary: Following the deaths of ten young drug addicts, Temple pursues the murderous boss of a drug-dealing ring who is known only as "Valentine". The evidence points to Sir Gilbert Dryden, but Temple keeps an open mind when faced with several others who might not be what they seem. The episodes were entitled "In which Paul Temple hears about Valentine", "In which Steve meets Captain O'Hara", "In which Sir Gilbert Explains", "In which Sir Graham is Surprised", "In which Mr. Layland Tells the Truth", "In which Valentine Strikes", "In which the Net Tightens" and "In which Paul Temple meets Valentine".

The Dutch radio version, *Paul Vlaanderen grijpt in* (6 October – 24 November 1946, eight episodes), was translated by J.C. van der Horst and produced by Kommer Kleijn, with Jan van Ees as Vlaanderen and Eva Janssen as Ina.

The German radio version, *Ein Fall für Paul Temple* (10 February – 7 April 1951, eight episodes), was translated by Marianne de Barde and produced by Eduard Hermann, with René Deltgen as Temple and Elisabeth Scherer as Steve.

The Italian radio version, *Paul Temple, il romanziere poliziotto* (28 January – 18 March 1953, eight episodes), was produced by Umberto Benedetto, with Fernando Farese as Temple and Franca Mazzoni as Betty (not Steve!).

152A. New production. 24 August – 12 October 2011. Eight thirty-minute episodes. Producer: Patrick Rayner.

Cast: Crawford Logan as Temple, Gerda Stevenson as Steve and Gareth Thomas as Sir Graham Forbes, with Greg Powrie, Nick Underwood, Richard Greenwood, Melody Grove, Simon Tait, Jimmy Chisholm, Lucy Paterson, Robin Laing, Eliza Langland, Michael Mackenzie and John Paul Hurley.

Four CDs of the 2011 broadcast serial, AudioGO, 2011. Also included in the CD set marketed as *Paul Temple: The Complete Radio Collection: Paul Temple Returns 2006-2013*, BBC, 2017.

153. *The Caspary Affair*. 11 July 1946. A one-hour play in the series *Musical Theatre of the Air*, with music by Jack Strachey and lyrics by Eric Maschwitz and Alan Stranks. Producer: Vernon Harris.

Cast: Coral Browne, Barry Morse, Hugh Miller, Charles Goldner, Phillip Leaver, Cecile Chevreau, William Trent, Ian Sadler, Eve Becke and John Bentley, with John Blore and his Orchestra and Sidney Crooke at the piano.

Plot summary: A musical comedy actress leaves the stage after her marriage, and later forms a disastrous friendship with a famous pianist.

The Caspary Affair gave rise to a long and interesting chain of events. On 21 November 1960 a Durbridge play called *Preludio al delitto*, translated by Paola Ferroni and produced by Umberto Benedetto, was broadcast in Italy. The cast consisted of Lucio Rama as Sir John Mallion, Nella Bonora as Fay Mallion, Renata Negri as Judy, Alina Moradei as Marian Garson, Antonio Guidi as Alan, Corrado Gaipa as Bill Yorke, Adolfo Geri as Julian Kane and Wanda Pasquini as Charlotte. Its plot indicates that it was based on *The Caspary Affair*, although the character names were changed. Most significant, however, is the fact that the character names in *Preludio al delitto* undoubtedly show that it then enjoyed an even longer life by becoming Durbridge's stage plays *Zaradin 4* in Germany and *Sweet Revenge* in the UK (see **200**).

154. *Paul Temple and the Gregory Affair*. 17 October – 19 December 1946. Ten thirty-minute episodes.
Cast: Kim Peacock as Temple, Marjorie Westbury as Steve, Lester Muddit as Sir Graham Forbes, Frank Partington as Charlie (but Billy Thatcher played Charlie in episodes 9 and 10) and Arthur Ridley as Chief Insp. Vosper, with Olaf Olsen, Geoffrey Wincott, Alexander Sarner, Duncan McIntyre, Rita Vale, Ernest Sefton, Olive Gregg, Charles Leno, Charles Maunsell, Basil Jones, Eddy Reed, Williams Lloyd, Preston Lockwood, David Kossoff, Lee Fox, George Owen, Lionel Stevens, Anne Cullen, Thea Wells, Belle Chrystall, Allan McClelland, Frank Atkinson, Tommy Duggan and Vanessa Thornton.
Plot summary: Sir Graham Forbes seeks Temple's assistance in investigating the murder of a young woman, found in the sea off the Yorkshire coast. Temple is reluctant to become involved until he finds the body of another young woman in his garage, and linking the two murders is the message "With the compliments of Mr. Gregory". The episodes were entitled "With the Compliments of Mr. Gregory", "Introducing Sir Donald Murdo", "The Madrid", "Mr. Davos has an Alibi", "Virginia van Cleeve", "Concerning Mr. Zola", "A Woman's Intuition", "News of Mr. Gregory", "Millgate Steps" and "Presenting Mr. Gregory".
Novelised as *Design for Murder* 1951 (**8**).
The Temples' manservant Charlie and Chief Insp. Vosper both made their first appearance as regular characters.
The Dutch radio version, *Paul Vlaanderen en het Gregory mysterie* (23 November 1947 – 25 January 1948, ten

episodes), was translated by J.C. van der Horst and produced by Kommer Kleijn, with Jan van Ees as Vlaanderen and Eva Janssen as Ina.

The German radio version, *Paul Temple und die Affäre Gregory* (7 November 1949 – 9 January 1950, ten episodes), was translated by Marianne de Barde and produced by Eduard Hermann and Fritz Schröder-Jahn, with René Deltgen as Temple and Anna Maria Ohst as Steve.

The Danish radio version, *Gregory-mysteriet* (3 September – 5 November 1954, ten episodes), was translated by Else Faber and produced by Sam Besekow, with Bendt Rothe as Temple and Inga Schultz as Steve. This was closely followed by a Danish novel with the same title (published by Thorkild Beck in 1954 and reprinted by Editio in 1998), translated and adapted by Else Faber and presumably based on her radio script, as Durbridge had already in 1951 novelised his serial as *Design for Murder* (**8**) with all the character names changed.

The Italian radio version, *Paul Temple e il caso Gregory* (14 March – 16 May 1960, ten episodes), was translated by Ippolito Pizzetti and produced by Giacomo Colli, with Gualtiero Rizzi as Temple and Angiolina Quinterno as Steve.

154A. New production. 3 July – 11 September 2013. Ten thirty-minute episodes. Producer: Patrick Rayner.

Cast: Crawford Logan as Temple, Gerda Stevenson as Steve, Gareth Thomas as Sir Graham Forbes, Greg Powrie as Charlie and Michael Mackenzie as Chief Insp. Vosper, with Simon Donaldson, Meg Fraser, Richard Greenwood, Nick Underwood, Francesca Dymond, Robin Laing and Eliza Langland.

Five CDs of the 2013 broadcast serial, AudioGo, 2013. Also included in the CD set marketed as *Paul Temple: The*

Complete Radio Collection: Paul Temple Returns 2006-2013, BBC, 2017.

155. *Paul Temple and Steve.* 30 March – 18 May 1947. Eight thirty-minute episodes.
Cast: Kim Peacock as Temple, Marjorie Westbury as Steve, Lester Mudditt as Sir Graham Forbes and Kenneth Morgan as Charlie, with Richard Williams, Martin Lewis, Olaf Olsen, Elizabeth Maude, Andrew Crawford, Tommy Duggan, Vivienne Chatterton, Alexander Sarner, Alan Pearce, Clement Scott, Lionel Stevens, Frank Atkinson, Preston Lockwood, Neville Mapp, Harry Hutchinson and Cyril Gardiner.
Plot summary: International criminal Dr. Belasco is Scotland Yard's top target, and the Temples go incognito to meet Belasco's right-hand man Ross Morgan on the Harwich boat train. But Morgan dies when the train crashes, and Temple is faced with the murder of a private detective, cigarette lighters with a distinctive acorn motif, and more murders before Belasco is unmasked. The episodes were entitled "The Notorious Dr. Belasco", "27a Berkeley House Place", "Presenting Ed Bellamy", "Mrs. Forester is Surprised", "David Nelson Explains", "Steve's Intuition", "The Suspects" and "The Final Curtain".
The Dutch radio version, *Paul Vlaanderen en Ina* (3 October – 21 November 1948, eight episodes), was translated by J.C. van der Horst and produced by Kommer Kleijn, with Jan van Ees as Vlaanderen and Eva Janssen as Ina.

155A. New production. 11 June – 30 July 2010. Eight thirty-minute episodes. Producer: Patrick Rayner.
Cast: Crawford Logan as Temple, Gerda Stevenson as Steve, Gareth Thomas as Sir Graham Forbes and Greg Powrie as Charlie, with Jimmy Chisholm, Robin Laing, Nick

Underwood, Candida Benson, Eliza Langland, Richard Greenwood, Michael Mackenzie, Emma Currie, John Paul Hurley and Lucy Paterson.
Four CDs of the 2010 broadcast serial, BBC Audio, 2010. Also included in the CD set marketed as *Paul Temple: The Complete Radio Collection: Paul Temple Returns 2006-2013*, BBC, 2017.

156. *Mr. and Mrs. Paul Temple*. 21 November 1947. A forty-five minute play.
Cast: Kim Peacock as Temple, Marjorie Westbury as Steve and Lester Mudditt as Sir Graham Forbes, with Tommy Duggan, Olaf Olsen, Alexander Sarner, Diana King, Bryan Powley, Frank Atkinson, Vivienne Chatterton, Lionel Stevens, George Owen, Arthur Ridley and Basil Jones.
Plot summary: Having missed a train from Italy to Switzerland, the Temples take the next one with ex-FBI agent Harry McRoy and several suspicious characters. After McRoy tells Temple that the valise he is carrying must be delivered to Sir Graham Forbes, the train crashes and McRoy is killed. Forbes arrives on the scene, but Chief Insp. Vosper is missing and is later found murdered. Vosper went on to appear in several later serials, so today's Temple fans will realise that there is something odd going on here. As this play is unlikely to be broadcast again, it can be revealed that it was all Steve's dream and the final twist was that the train they missed was the one that crashed. The *Derby Daily Telegraph* on 24 November 1947 commented: "Steve's dream sequence was up to Francis Durbridge's usual standard, yet the absence of anticipation of wondering what was going to happen in the next episode decreased the drama."
The broadcast on 21 November 1947 was in the Midland Region only, and the Midland edition of the *Radio Times*

described it as "a new adventure specially written for the BBC Midland Region Jubilee Week by Francis Durbridge," so websites that allege it to be an abridgement of the serial *Paul Temple and Steve* are mistaken. It was repeated nationally on the BBC Light Programme on 23 November 1947, which many websites wrongly record as the first broadcast. No plot details are given in the *Radio Times*, but Charles Norton in his book *Serial Thrillers: The Adventure Serial on British Radio* (Kaleidoscope, 2012) states: "While on holiday, Paul and Steve become lost in a dense fog and stumble across a strange and mysterious mansion." This is incorrect, as my plot summary above is derived from the original script in the BBC Written Archives, whereas Norton's plot summary is reminiscent of both the 1934 radio play *Murder in the Midlands* (**56**) and the 1945 radio play *Over My Dead Body* (**148**), neither of which featured the Temples.

The Dutch radio version, *De heer en mevrouw Paul Vlaanderen* (26 April 1948), was translated by J.C. van der Horst and produced by Kommer Kleijn, with Jan van Ees as Vlaanderen and Eva Janssen as Ina.

157. *Paul Temple and the Sullivan Mystery*. 1 December 1947 – 19 January 1948. Eight thirty-minute episodes.

Cast: Kim Peacock as Temple, Marjorie Westbury as Steve, Lester Mudditt as Sir Graham Forbes and Kenneth Morgan as Charlie, with Tommy Duggan, Olaf Olsen, Laidman Browne, Cyril Gardiner, Vivienne Chatterton, Margaret Inglis, Stanley Groome, Sidney James, Ian Sadler, Tucker McGuire, Leo de Pokorny, Leslie Perrins, Richard Williams, Fritz Krenn, Frank Partington, Basil Jones, Beryl Calder, Joan Clement Scott, Charles Leno, Andrew Churchman, Alec Ross, Arthur Ridley, Betty Baskcomb, Paul Martin, Peter Claughton, Eddy Reed,

Norman Webb, Harry Hutchinson, George Owen, Peter Creswell, Frank Atkinson and David Kossoff.

Plot summary: The Temples, about to travel to Egypt, agree to return a pair of spectacles to Richard Sullivan - but this leads to murder and intrigue, as they find Sullivan elusive and several people have an unhealthy interest in the spectacles. The episodes were entitled "Having a Wonderful Time", "Interlude at Augusta", "Introducing Colonel Marquand", "Cairo", "The House of Bahri", "A Message from Sir Graham", "Mr. Darwin Entertains" and "Still Having a Wonderful Time".

Novelised as *East of Algiers* 1959 under the pseudonym "Paul Temple" (**14**).

Coronation Scot by Vivian Ellis was used as the Paul Temple signature tune for the first time.

The Dutch radio version, *Paul Vlaanderen en het Sullivan mysterie* (6 November – 22 December 1949, eight episodes), was translated by J.C. van der Horst and produced by Kommer Kleijn, with Jan van Ees as Vlaanderen and Eva Janssen as Ina.

157A. New production. 7 August – 2 October 2006. Eight thirty-minute episodes. Producer: Patrick Rayner.

Cast: Crawford Logan as Temple, Gerda Stevenson as Steve, Gareth Thomas as Sir Graham Forbes and Greg Powrie as Charlie, with Richard Greenwood, Michael Mackenzie, Angus MacInnes, Eliza Langland, Nick Underwood, Wendy Seager, Lucy Paterson and John Paul Hurley.

Four Audiocassettes / Four CDs of the 2006 broadcast serial, BBC Audio, 2006. Also included in the CD set marketed as *Paul Temple: The Complete Radio Collection: Paul Temple Returns 2006-2013*, BBC, 2017.

158. *Paul Temple and the Curzon Case*. 7 December 1948 – 25 January 1949. Eight thirty-minute episodes.

Cast: Kim Peacock as Temple, Marjorie Westbury as Steve, Lester Mudditt as Sir Graham Forbes, Billy Thatcher as Charlie and Arthur Ridley as Chief Insp. Vosper, with Grizelda Hervey, Duncan McIntyre, Philip Cunningham, Kenneth Morgan, Hugh Manning, Cyril Gardiner, Tommy Duggan, Leslie Perrins, Olaf Olsen, Peter Mullins, Keith Lloyd, Denise Bryer and Alan Reid.

Plot summary: A plane crash on Dulworth Bay and the disappearance of two schoolboys are linked when Temple pursues the shadowy Curzon, whose name is inscribed on a cricket bat owned by one of the boys. The episodes were entitled "The Baxter Brothers", "Welcome to Dulworth Bay", "Tom Doyle", "Miss Maxwell Keeps an Appointment", "Presenting Carl Walters", "A Message for Charlie", "The Deciding Factor" and "Conclusion".

Novelised as *The Curzon Case* 1972 (**31**).

The Dutch radio version, *Paul Vlaanderen en het Curzon mysterie* (1 October – 19 November 1950, eight episodes), was translated by J.C. van der Horst and produced by Kommer Kleijn, with Jan van Ees as Vlaanderen and Eva Janssen as Ina.

The German radio version, *Paul Temple und der Fall Curzon* (14 November 1951 – 27 February 1952, eight episodes), was translated by Marianne de Barde and produced by Eduard Hermann, with René Deltgen as Temple and Elisabeth Scherer as Steve.

159. *Johnny Washington Esquire*. 12 August – 30 September 1949. Eight thirty-minute episodes. Producer: Martyn C. Webster.

Cast: Bernard Braden as Johnny Washington, with Ivan Samson, David Kossoff, Ina M. Allan, Rita Vale, Michael

Nightingale, Ian Sadler, Madeline Durrant, Marjorie Mars, Frank Atkinson, Raf de la Torre, Alastair Duncan, Catherine Campbell, Laidman Browne, Georgie Henschel, Courtney Hope, Charles Leno, Preston Lockwood, Howieson Culff, Marjorie Westbury, Charles Maunsell, Stanley Groome, Antony Holles, Arthur Ridley, Denise Bryer, Denys Blakelock, Lesley Wareing, Avice Landone, Malcolm Hayes, Duncan McIntyre, Andrew Faulds, Andrew Churchman, Bill Staughton, Gladys Spencer, Charles Lefeaux, Ronald Sidney, Harry Hutchinson, Margaret Vines, Hugh Manning, Lee Fox, Joan Clement Scott, Brian Campbell, Jonathan Meddings, Alan Reid, Martin Lewis, Frederick Peisley and Bryan Powley.

Plot summary: This was not a serial, but eight plays described as "the adventures of a gentleman of leisure", with a young American in London scoring barely legal coups at the expense of social parasites and criminals in Robin Hood style. The episodes were entitled "The Perfect Alibi", "There Was a Young Lady", "A Change of Heart", "The Suspect", "Colonel Wilmington", "Turning the Tables", "The Outsider" and "A False Impression".

Durbridge's 1951 novel *Beware of Johnny Washington* (**7**), although featuring the same central character, is a separate story with an interesting history of its own.

160. *Paul Temple and the Madison Mystery*. 12 October – 30 November 1949. Eight thirty-minute episodes.

Cast: Kim Peacock as Temple, Marjorie Westbury as Steve, Lester Muddit as Sir Graham Forbes, Desmond Carrington as Charlie and Arthur Ridley as Chief Insp. Vosper, with John McLaren, Ivan Samson, Grizelda Hervey, Catherine Campbell, Andrew Faulds, Wendy Gibb, Donald Gray, Olaf Olsen, John Dodsworth, Macdonald Parke, Raf de la Torre, Ian Sadler, Stanley Groome, Hugh

Manning, David Enders, Ellis Chesney, Alan J. Aldridge, Malcolm Farquhar, Gladys Spencer, Geoffrey Bond, Denis Lehrer, Joan Hart and Frank Coburn.

Plot summary: Returning from America by ocean liner, the Temples meet wealthy Sam Portland whose UK agent Hubert Greene has received messages about Portland's past from a private detective called Madison. But Portland dies on board, and Temple is left to unravel a case involving international counterfeiters and the clue of a coin on a watch-chain. The episodes were entitled "A Penny for Your Thoughts", "The Manilla", "Eileen", "Hubert Greene Entertains", "Steve Takes Over", "Just a Red Herring", "The Four Suspects" and "Introducing Madison".

Novelised as *Paul Temple and the Madison Case* 1988 (**39**).

The Dutch radio version, *Paul Vlaanderen en het Madison mysterie* (14 January – 4 March 1951, eight episodes), was translated by J.C. van der Horst and produced by Kommer Kleijn, with Jan van Ees as Vlaanderen and Eva Janssen as Ina.

The German radio version, *Paul Temple und der Fall Madison* (13 January – 2 March 1956, eight episodes), was translated by Helmut Schrey and Dagmar Schorr-Nick and produced by Eduard Hermann, with René Deltgen as Temple and Ursula Langrock as Steve.

160A. New production. 20 June – 8 August 1955. Eight thirty-minute episodes.

Cast: Peter Coke as Temple, Marjorie Westbury as Steve, Lester Mudditt as Sir Graham Forbes, James Beattie as Charlie and T. St. John Barry as Chief Insp. Vosper, with Stan Thomason, Richard Williams, Grizelda Hervey, Marjorie Mars, Michael Turner, Peggy Hassard, Simon Lack, John Carson, Derek Hart, John Gabriel, Richard

Waring, Ian Sadler, Brian Haines, Geoffrey Matthews, Manning Wilson, Hugh David, Peter Claughton, Mairhi Russell, Rolf Lefebvre, Belle Chrystall and Edward Jewesbury.

160B. New production. 16 May – 4 July 2008. Eight thirty-minute episodes. Producer: Patrick Rayner.

Cast: Crawford Logan as Temple, Gerda Stevenson as Steve, Gareth Thomas as Sir Graham Forbes, Greg Powrie as Charlie and Michael Mackenzie as Chief Insp. Vosper, with Robin Laing, Richard Greenwood, Eliza Langland, Emma Currie, Nick Underwood, Lucy Paterson, Angus MacInnes and Jimmy Chisholm.

Four CDs of the 2008 broadcast serial, BBC Audio, 2008. Also included in the CD set marketed as *Paul Temple: The Complete Radio Collection: Paul Temple Returns 2006-2013*, BBC, 2017.

161. *The Night of the Twenty-Seventh*. 27 December 1949. A one-hour play, written by Edward J. Mason. Producer: Martyn C. Webster.

Cast: Kim Peacock as Temple, Marjorie Westbury as Steve, Robert Beatty as Philip Odell, Duncan Carse as Dick Barton, Brian Reece as P.C. 49, Valentine Dyall as The Man in Black, Douglas Burbidge as Dr. Dale and Ellis Powell as Mrs. Dale, with Leon Quartermane, Max Adrian and Malcolm Hayes.

Plot summary: Eight famous radio characters attend a dinner party at the home of a recently deceased man – but is Silas Ephraim really dead, or alive and deranged? A loudspeaker announcement, reminiscent of Agatha Christie's *And Then There Were None*, suggests the latter. Although not written by Durbridge, it is likely that this spoof involved the various characters' original creators somewhere along the way.

162. *Paul Temple and the Vandyke Affair*. 30 October – 18 December 1950. Eight thirty-minute episodes.

Cast: Kim Peacock as Temple, Marjorie Westbury as Steve, Lester Mudditt as Sir Graham Forbes and Michael Harding as Charlie, with Donald Gray, Richard Hurndall, Roger Delgado, Grizelda Hervey, Peter Coke, Tommy Duggan, Joan Hart, Olaf Olsen, Susan Buret, Raf de la Torre, Charles Richardson, Robert Alban, James E. Thompson, David Peel, Pat Jamblin, Alun Owen, Betty Baskcomb, Gladys Spencer, Janet Morrison and Lewis Ward.

Plot summary: A baby and her baby-sitter have disappeared, and the only clue is a note reading "A Mr. Vandyke telephoned. He left no message." In seeking to identify Vandyke, Temple must unravel the significance of a doll, the murder of a man impersonating a police officer, the safe return of the baby, and several other murders. The episodes were entitled "The Sitter-In", "The Marlow Incident", "Introducing Mr. Droste", "Boulevard Seminaire", "Roger Shelly Makes a Suggestion", "Suspect Number One", "Steve Entertains" and "Presenting Mr. Vandyke".

The 1950 broadcast serial is included in the CD set marketed as *Paul Temple: The Complete Radio Collection: The Early Years 1938-1950*, BBC, 2016.

Peter Coke, who played Terry Palmer in this production, became the definitive Paul Temple in 1954.

The Dutch radio version, *Paul Vlaanderen en het Vandyke mysterie* (30 September – 18 November 1951, eight episodes), was translated by J.C. van der Horst and produced by Kommer Kleijn, with Jan van Ees as Vlaanderen and Eva Janssen as Ina.

The German radio version, *Paul Temple und der Fall Vandyke* (12 September – 30 October 1953, eight episodes), was translated by Marianne de Barde and produced by Eduard Hermann, with René Deltgen as Temple and Annemarie Cordes as Steve.

The Danish radio version, *Vandyke-mysteriet* (23 June – 11 August 1961, eight episodes), was translated by Else Faber and produced by Sam Besekow, with Frits Helmuth as Temple and Ghita Nørby as Steve.

162A. New production. 1 January – 19 February 1959. Eight thirty-minute episodes.

Cast: Peter Coke as Temple, Marjorie Westbury as Steve, Richard Williams as Sir Graham Forbes and James Beattie as Charlie, with Frederick Treves, Richard Hurndall, Simon Lack, Grizelda Hervey, Peter Wilde, John Scott, June Tobin, Rolf Lefebvre, Betty Hardy, Armine Sandford, Catherine Salkeld, Haydn Jones, David Spenser, John Bryning, Jon Farrell, Betty Baskcomb, Beatrice Ormonde, David March, John Graham and James Thomason.

Two Audiocassettes / Five CDs of the 1959 broadcast serial, BBC Audio, 2004 – the fifth CD is *The Radio Detectives – Send for Paul Temple* by Prof Jeffrey Richards, originally broadcast on 20 May 1998. Also included in the CD set marketed as *Paul Temple: The Complete Radio Collection: The Fifties 1954-1959*, BBC, 2016.

This was Richard Williams' first appearance as Sir Graham, although he had played various parts in previous Temple serials and had once played Temple himself (**123A**).

163. *Paul Temple and the Jonathan Mystery*. 10 May – 28 June 1951. Eight thirty-minute episodes.

Cast: Kim Peacock as Temple, Marjorie Westbury as Steve, Lester Mudditt as Sir Graham Forbes and Frank Partington as Charlie, with George Margo, Grizelda Hervey, Duncan McIntyre, Rita Vale, Martin Lewis, Olaf Olsen, Belle Chrystall, Stanley Groome, David Peel, Frank Atkinson,

Courtney Hope, Michael Holt, Charles Lefeaux, Lewis Ward, Leslie Parker, Ronald Sidney, Spencer Hale, Dorothy Smith, Hamilton Dyce, Gabrielle Blunt, Arthur Bush, Frank Coburn, Malcolm Hayes, Alan Reid, Roger Delgado, Harry Hutchinson and Bryan Powley.

Plot summary: The Temples meet the Fergusons when travelling home from New York, but are later told that the Fergusons' son Richard has been murdered at his university. The only leads are a postcard signed "Jonathan" and Richard's missing signet ring. The episodes were entitled "The Fergusons", "That Good Old Intuition", "The Ring", "The Encounter", "Concerning Richard Ferguson", "A Surprise for Mavis Russell", "An Invitation for Mr. Elliot" and "Jonathan".

Novelised as *Dead to the World* 1967 (**24**).

The Dutch radio version, *Paul Vlaanderen en het Jonathan mysterie* (25 January – 29 March 1953, eight episodes), was translated by J.C. van der Horst and produced by Kommer Kleijn, with Jan van Ees as Vlaanderen and Eva Janssen as Ina.

The German radio version, *Paul Temple und der Fall Jonathan* (17 September – 5 November 1954, eight episodes), was translated by Elfriede Engelmann and produced by Eduard Hermann, with René Deltgen as Temple and Annemarie Cordes as Steve.

The Italian radio version, *Chi è Jonathan?* (12 – 23 April 1971, ten episodes), was translated by Franca Cancogni and produced by Umberto Benedetto, with Mario Feliciani as Temple and Lucia Catullo as Steve.

163A. New production. 14 October – 2 December 1963. Eight thirty-minute episodes.

Cast: Peter Coke as Temple, Marjorie Westbury as Steve, James Thomason as Sir Graham Forbes and James Beattie as Charlie, with John Glen, Grizelda Hervey, Simon Lack,

Isabel Rennie, William Fox, Anthony Hall, Valerie Kirkbright, Rolf Lefebvre, Gabriel Woolf, Frederick Treves, John Baddeley, Eva Stuart, Lee Fox, David Spenser, Vivienne Chatterton, Jo Manning Wilson, Frank Partington, Peter Bartlett, Glyn Dearman, Alan Haines and Lewis Stringer.

Two Audiocassettes / Four CDs of the 1963 broadcast serial, BBC Audio, 2004. Also included in the CD set marketed as *Paul Temple: The Complete Radio Collection: The Sixties 1960-1968*, BBC, 2017.

This was James Beattie's last appearance as Charlie.

164. *Paul Temple and Steve Again*. 8 April 1953. A one-hour play in the series *Curtain Up*.

Cast: Kim Peacock as Temple, Marjorie Westbury as Steve, Lester Mudditt as Sir Graham Forbes and James Beattie as Charlie, with Ivan Samson, Rolf Lefebvre, Anthony Jacobs, Mary Williams, Norman Claridge, Garard Green, Cyril Shaps, Susan Richmond, Daphne Maddox, Lisa Sibley, Lee Fox, John Cazabon, Stanley Groome, Douglas Hayes, Arthur Lawrence, Susan Neil, Aubrey Richards and Margaret Ward.

Plot summary: Temple re-opens a cold case when he is urged by a discharged convict to visit Fowey to meet Harry King, a grocer and local councillor – but what has the man who died in a Knightsbridge hotel to do with Harry King, what has the bottle of medicine to do with Dr. Schumann, and how is all of this connected with the Duke of Westfield's jewellery?

The Dutch radio version, *Paul Vlaanderen en het mysterie van de Westfield juwelen* (11 January 1954), was translated by Johan Bennik (pseudonym of Jan van Ees) and produced by Kommer Kleijn, with Jan van Ees as Vlaanderen and Eva Janssen as Ina.

165. *Paul Temple and the Gilbert Case.* 29 March – 17 May 1954. Eight thirty-minute episodes.

Cast: Peter Coke as Temple, Marjorie Westbury as Steve, Lester Mudditt as Sir Graham Forbes and James Beattie as Charlie, with Duncan McIntyre, Charles Leno, Grizelda Hervey, Richard Williams, Olaf Olsen, Peggy Hassard, Alec Ross, Cyril Shaps, David Peel, Anne Cullen, Robert Rietty, Elizabeth London, Geoffrey Bond and Arthur Lawrence.

Plot summary: Wilfrid Stirling asks Temple to investigate the murder of his daughter, for which her boyfriend Howard Gilbert has already been convicted and sentenced to hang. As Temple races against time there are more murders, but why has a shoe been taken from each victim? The episodes were entitled "The Unlucky One", "The Third Shoe", "Peter Galino", "La Martella", "That Good Old Intuition", "A Warning from Miss Wayne", "The Note" and "The Guilty Party". The title of the final episode was changed from "The Guilty Party" to "Mr. Hamilton" for the new production of 1959/60 (**165A**).

Novelised as *Another Woman's Shoes* 1965 (**22**).

Two Audiocassettes of the 1954 broadcast serial, BBC Audio, 2001. Three CDs of the 1954 broadcast serial, BBC Audio, 2003. Also included in the CD set marketed as *Paul Temple: The Complete Radio Collection: The Fifties 1954-1959*, BBC, 2016.

This was Peter Coke's first appearance as Temple.

The Dutch radio version, *Paul Vlaanderen en het Gilbert mysterie* (3 October – 21 November 1954, eight episodes), was translated by Johan Bennik (pseudonym of Jan van Ees) and produced by Kommer Kleijn, with Jan van Ees as Vlaanderen and Eva Janssen as Ina.

The German radio version, *Paul Temple und der Fall Gilbert* (4 January – 22 February 1957, eight episodes), was translated by Elfriede Engelmann and produced by Eduard Hermann, with René Deltgen as Temple and Annemarie Cordes as Steve.

The Danish radio version, *Gilbert-mysteriet* (5 July – 23 August 1957, eight episodes), was translated by Niels Locher and produced by Søren Melson, with Gunnar Lauring as Temple and Else Højgaard as Steve.

165A. New production. 22 November 1959 – 10 January 1960. Eight thirty-minute episodes.

Cast: Peter Coke as Temple, Marjorie Westbury as Steve, Richard Williams as Sir Graham Forbes and James Beattie as Charlie, with Duncan McIntyre, Douglas Storm, Eva Stuart, Simon Lack, John Hollis, June Tobin, George Hagan, David Spenser, Peter Wilde, John Bennett, Kathleen Helme, Joan Matheson, Ronald Baddiley and James Thomason.

The 1959/60 broadcast serial is included in the CD set marketed as *Paul Temple: The Complete Radio Collection: The Sixties 1960-1968*, BBC, 2017.

Richard Williams died on 6 January 1960, four days before the last episode of this serial was broadcast. He had appeared as Paul Temple in the one-hour abridgement of *News of Paul Temple* in 1944, played various roles in many of the Temple serials, and finally succeeded Lester Mudditt in the role of Sir Graham Forbes for just one year, appearing in 1959 in a revival of *Paul Temple and the Vandyke Affair*, the new serial *Paul Temple and the Conrad Case*, and this revival of *Paul Temple and the Gilbert Case*.

166. *Paul Temple and the Lawrence Affair*. 11 April – 30 May 1956. Eight thirty-minute episodes.

Cast: Peter Coke as Temple, Marjorie Westbury as Steve, Lester Mudditt as Sir Graham Forbes, James Beattie as

Charlie and Arthur Ridley as Chief Insp. Vosper, with Simon Lack, Brewster Mason, Brian Haines, Belle Chrystall, John Gabriel, Marjorie Mars, Dorothy Holmes-Gore, Richard Williams, Cecile Chevreau, Allan McClelland, Leonard Trolley, Manning Wilson, Geoffrey Hodson, Denis Goacher, Hamilton Dyce, Gordon Davies, Molly Rankin, Gretta Gouriet, Annette Kelly, George Merritt, Jeffrey Segal, James Thomason and Michael Turner.

Plot summary: On a boat trip from the fishing village of Downburgh, the Temples are shot at and later the boatman dies in a cliff-top fall. Back in London, the daughter of the head of MI5 has disappeared and it soon transpires that there is a connection. The episodes were entitled "The Little Things", "Salty West", "The Handbag", "Return to Downburgh", "A Present for Steve", "News from Sir Graham", "Another Suspect" and "Return to London".

Two Audiocassetes / Four CDs of the 1956 broadcast serial, BBC Audio, 2003. Also included in the CD set marketed as *Paul Temple: The Complete Radio Collection: The Fifties 1954-1959*, BBC, 2016.

The Dutch radio version, *Paul Vlaanderen en het Lawrence mysterie* (30 September - 18 November 1956, eight episodes), was translated by Johan Bennik (pseudonym of Jan van Ees) and produced by Kommer Kleijn, with Jan van Ees as Vlaanderen and Eva Janssen as Ina.

The German radio version, *Paul Temple und der Fall Lawrence* (12 September – 31 October 1958, eight episodes), was translated by Dagmar Schnorr-Nick and produced by Eduard Hermann, with René Deltgen as Temple and Annemarie Cordes as Steve.

The Italian radio version, *Paul Temple e l'uomo di Zermatt* (17 July – 4 September 1961, eight episodes), was translated by Pietro Robespi and produced by Umberto Benedetto, with Adolfo Geri as Temple and Renata Negri as Steve.

167. *Paul Temple and the Spencer Affair*. 13 November 1957 – 1 January 1958. Eight thirty-minute episodes.
Cast: Peter Coke as Temple, Marjorie Westbury as Steve, Lester Mudditt as Sir Graham Forbes, James Beattie as Charlie and Hugh Manning as Chief Insp. Vosper, with Brewster Mason, Thomas Heathcote, Isabel Dean, Frank Partington, Simon Lack, June Tobin, Lockwood West, John Graham, James Thomason, Hamilton Dyce, Denis Goacher, Frank Windsor, Haydn Jones, Beryl Calder, Malcolm Hayes, Will Leighton, Trevor Martin, Molly Rankin, David Spenser and Norman Tattersall.
Plot summary: Drama student Mary Dreisler is murdered, and her father asks Temple to investigate. The only clue is a package containing a gramophone record called "My Heart and Harry", with a message from the mysterious Spencer. The episodes were entitled "My Heart and Harry", "Concerning Judy Milton", "Introducing Pete Roberts", "That Old Intuition", "A Surprise for Pete Roberts", "Home Again", "Dinner at The Stardust" and "A Party of Four".
Two Audiocassettes of the 1957/58 broadcast serial, BBC Audio, 2000. Four CDs of the 1957/58 broadcast serial, BBC Audio, 2004. Also included in the CD set marketed as *Paul Temple: The Complete Radio Collection: The Fifties 1954-1959*, BBC, 2016.
Durbridge originally planned to call this *Paul Temple and the Ambrose Affair*, until he was alerted by the BBC to the fact that Philip Levene's serial *Ambrose in London* was

about to be broadcast. *Paul Temple and the Spencer Affair* was Lester Mudditt's last appearance as Sir Graham Forbes, a role he had played from the outset in 1938. The serial was specially repeated 29 October – 17 December 1992, to celebrate Durbridge's 80th birthday. A notable date for Durbridge was 13 November 1957, as that evening saw the premières of two of his serials - *Paul Temple and the Spencer Affair* on the BBC Light Programme at 8.00, followed immediately by *A Time of Day* on BBC television at 8.30.

The Dutch radio version, *Paul Vlaanderen en het Spencer mysterie* (19 January - 9 March 1958, eight episodes), was translated by Johan Bennik (pseudonym of Jan van Ees) and produced by Kommer Kleijn, with Jan van Ees as Vlaanderen and Eva Janssen as Ina.

The German radio version, *Paul Temple und der Fall Spencer* (2 October – 20 November 1959, eight episodes), was translated by Marianne de Barde and produced by Eduard Hermann, with René Deltgen as Temple and Annemarie Cordes as Steve.

The Italian radio version, *Cabaret* (21 March – 1 April 1977, ten episodes), was translated by Franca Cancogni and produced by Umberto Benedetto, with Luigi Vannucchi as Temple and Lia Zoppelli as Steve.

168. *Paul Temple and the Conrad Case.* 2 March – 20 April 1959. Eight thirty-minute episodes.
Cast: Peter Coke as Temple, Marjorie Westbury as Steve, Richard Williams as Sir Graham Forbes, James Beattie as Charlie and Hugh Manning as Chief Insp. Vosper, with Jeffrey Segal, James Thomason, Rolf Lefebvre, Virginia Winter, June Tobin, Hilda Schroder, Dorothy Holmes-Gore, John Bryning, Joan Matheson, Dorothy Smith, George Hagan, John Bennett, Peter Wilde, John Hollis,

Jane Jordan Rogers, Ronald Baddiley, John Boddington, John Cazabon, Sheila Grant, Beatrice Ormonde, John Graham, Judy Bailey, Frank Partington, Peggy Gow, Jonathan Scott and Frederick Treves.

Plot summary: Temple is asked to investigate the disappearance of Betty Conrad from her finishing school in Bavaria, and he has to clutch at the clue of an unusual cocktail stick. The episodes were entitled "The Man from Munich", "Concerning Elliot France", "Hotel Reumer", "A Visit to Innsbruck", "A Dry Martini", "Concerning Captain Smith", "Coffee for Miss Conrad" and "Person Unknown".

Two Audiocassettes of the 1959 broadcast serial, BBC Audio, 1989. Four CDs of the 1959 broadcast serial, BBC Audio, 2004 – the final track of CD4 is an interview with Durbridge by Jack de Manio. Also included in the CD set marketed as *Paul Temple: The Complete Radio Collection: The Fifties 1954-1959*, BBC, 2016.

The set of audiocassettes issued by the BBC in 1989 is incorrectly listed as a published book in various bibliographies (including Allen J. Hubin's *Crime Fiction IV: A Comprehensive Bibliography 1749-2000*), but this title was never novelised.

The Dutch radio version, *Paul Vlaanderen en het Conrad mysterie* (27 September – 15 November 1959, eight episodes), was translated by Johan Bennik (pseudonym of Jan van Ees) and produced by Dick van Putten, with Jan van Ees as Vlaanderen and Eva Janssen as Ina.

The first German radio version, *Paul Temple und der Fall Conrad* (26 November 1959 – 21 January 1960, eight episodes), was translated by Marianne de Barde and John Lackland and produced by Willy Purucker, with Karl John as Temple and Rosemarie Fendel as Steve. A slightly later German radio version, *Paul Temple und der Fall Conrad* (13 January – 3 March 1961, eight episodes), was translated by Marianne de Barde and produced by Eduard Hermann, with René Deltgen as Temple and Annemarie Cordes as Steve.

The Italian radio version, *La ragazza scomparsa* (17 – 28 February 1975, ten episodes), was translated by Franca Cancogni and produced by Umberto Benedetto, with Alberto Lupo as Temple and Lucia Catullo as Steve.

169. *Paul Temple and the Margo Mystery*. 1 January – 19 February 1961. Eight thirty-minute episodes.

Cast: Peter Coke as Temple, Marjorie Westbury as Steve, James Thomason as Sir Graham Forbes and James Beattie as Charlie, with Simon Lack, Tommy Duggan, Julian Somers, June Tobin, Jon Rollason, Mary Wimbush, Hugh Manning, Joan Matheson, Duncan McIntyre, Tom Watson, Dorit Welles, Janet Morrison, George Merritt, Douglas Storm, Malcolm Hayes, Beatrice Kane, Nigel Anthony, Peter Wilde, William Eedle, Haydn Jones, Armine Sandford, Sara Nash, Peter Watts, Kathleen Helme, Peter Pratt, Frank Partington, Kenneth Dight and Eva Stuart.

Plot summary: Flying home from America, Temple is asked by Mike Langdon to persuade his employer's daughter Julia Kelburn to give up her boyfriend, pop singer Tony Wyman. Arriving to meet Temple at the airport, Steve is drugged and kidnapped – but released unharmed, she unaccountably finds herself in possession of a coat bearing the label "Margo". The episodes were entitled "The Coat", "Concerning Ted Angus", "A Change of Mind", "Bill Fletcher's Story", "Breakwater House", "Mainly about Wyman", "A Time to Worry" and "The Visitor".

Novelised 1986 (**38**).

Two Audiocassettes / Four CDs of the 1961 broadcast serial, BBC Audio, 2004. Also included in the CD set marketed as *Paul Temple: The Complete Radio Collection: The Sixties 1960-1968*, BBC, 2017.

Durbridge originally planned to call this *Paul Temple and the Stewart Case*. James Thomason made his first appearance as Sir Graham Forbes, a role he also played in the 1963 revival of *Paul Temple and the Jonathan Mystery* and the 1968 *Paul Temple and the Alex Affair*.

The German radio version, *Paul Temple und der Fall Margo* (23 February – 13 April 1962, eight episodes), was translated by Marianne de Barde and John Lackland and produced by Eduard Hermann, with René Deltgen as Temple and Annemarie Cordes as Steve.

The Dutch radio version, *Paul Vlaanderen en het Margo mysterie* (30 September – 18 November 1962, eight episodes), was translated by Johan Bennik (pseudonym of Jan van Ees) and produced by Dick van Putten, with Jan van Ees as Vlaanderen and Eva Janssen as Ina.

The Italian radio version, *Margò* (19 – 30 June 1967, ten episodes), was translated by Franca Cancogni and produced by Guglielmo Morandi, with Aroldo Tieri as Temple and Lia Zoppelli as Steve.

170. *What Do You Think?* 12 September 1962. A play in the series *Thirty Minute Theatre*. Producer: Martyn C. Webster.

Cast: Rolf Lefebvre, Peggy Butt, Lewis Stringer, Frank Partington, Sheila Grant, John Pullen, Jonathan Scott, William Eedle and Lee Fox.

Plot summary: Successful crime writer Felix Layton is inclined to confuse fact with fiction, which rather perplexes the police, but is this a case of "crying wolf"?

Three German radio productions of this play, translated by Marianne de Barde and John Lackland, were entitled *Zu viele Geständnisse* (produced by S.O. Wagner), *Kaum zu glauben* (produced by Heinz-Günter Stamm) and *Der Fall Greenfield* (produced by Oskar Nitschke). They were aired several months earlier than the UK production, as was the broadcast in Switzerland of *Kaum zu glauben* produced by Amido Hoffmann. A Dutch radio translation by Guy Bernaert was produced by Herman Niels on 30 October 1977, called *Wat denk jij?*

171. *Paul Temple and the Geneva Mystery*. 11 April – 16 May 1965. Six thirty-minute episodes.
Cast: Peter Coke as Temple, Marjorie Westbury as Steve and John Baddeley as Charlie, with Patrick Barr, Isabel Dean, Nigel Graham, Simon Lack, Polly Murch, Wilfrid Carter, Isabel Rennie, Frederick Treves, Anthony Hall, Pat Connell, Alan Haines, Peter Bartlett, Hamlyn Benson, Bruce Beeby, Malcolm Terris, James Thomason, Barbara Barnett, Fraser Kerr, Rex Graham, Gordon Faith, Bryan Colvin, Gordon Gardner, Garard Green, Madi Hedd, Noel Howlett, LeRoy Lingwood, Michael McClain, Peter Marinker, Antony Viccars and Martin Muncaster.
Plot summary: Maurice Lonsdale asks Temple to investigate the apparent death of his brother-in-law Carl Milbourne, who might still be alive. The mystery appears to have its roots in Switzerland – but what is the significance of the phrase "too young to die"? The episodes were entitled "Too Young to Die", "Concerning Mrs. Milbourne", "A Note for Danny", "A Change of Mind", "A Surprise for Mrs. Milbourne" and "See You in London".
Novelised as *The Geneva Mystery* 1971 (**30**).
Two Audiocassettes of the 1965 broadcast serial, BBC Audio, 2002. Three CDs of the 1965 broadcast serial, BBC Audio, 2004. Also included in the CD set marketed as *Paul*

Temple: The Complete Radio Collection: The Sixties 1960-1968, BBC, 2017.

The Dutch radio version, *Paul Vlaanderen en het Milbourne mysterie* (2 January – 6 February 1966, six episodes), was translated by Johan Bennik (pseudonym of Jan van Ees) and produced by Dick van Putten, with Jan van Ees as Vlaanderen and Eva Janssen as Ina.

The first German radio version, *Paul Temple und der Fall Genf* (25 February – 1 April 1966, six episodes), was translated by Marianne de Barde and produced by Otto Düben, with René Deltgen as Temple and Irmgard Först as Steve. Another German radio version, *Paul Temple und der Fall in Genf* (later in 1966, four episodes), was translated by Marianne de Barde and produced by Wilm ten Haaf, with Siegfried Dornbusch as Temple and Ricarda Benndorf as Steve.

172. *La Boutique*. 2 October – 16 October 1967 (two episodes per week). Five thirty-minute episodes. Producer: Martyn C. Webster.

Cast: Simon Lack as Robert, Isabel Dean as Eve and William Fox as Lewis, with Barbara Mitchell, Haydn Jones, Beatrice Kane, Carol Marsh, Margaret Robertson, Noël Hood, Ronald Herdman, Alan Dudley, Dorit Welles, Jon Rollason, Antony Viccars, Frank Henderson, Duncan McIntyre, Humphrey Morton, Tommy Duggan, Yvonne Andre, Madi Hedd and Beth Boyd.

Plot summary: La Boutique is the chic London dress shop owned by Eve, the ex-wife of internationally acclaimed song-writer Lewis Bristol. Lewis comes from Los Angeles to London with important information for his brother, Supt. Robert Bristol of Scotland Yard, but soon Durbridge-like things begin to happen.

Among the European productions of *La Boutique* were the 1967 German translation by Marianne de Barde, produced by Dieter Munck, with Karl Michael Vogler as Robert, Ursula Dirichs as Eve and Wolfgang Weiser as Lewis; the 1968 Swiss production, translated and produced by Hans Hausmann, with René Deltgen as Robert, Maria Magdalena Thiesing as Eve and Maximilian Wolters as Lewis; and the 1968 Italian production, translated by Amleto Micozzi and produced by Umberto Benedetto, with the character names changed.

Paul Temple and the Alex Affair. 26 February – 21 March 1968. Often described as the last Paul Temple radio serial, this was actually a revised version of Durbridge's 1945 serial *Send for Paul Temple Again* (see **151A**).

WORKS FOR TELEVISION

The Brass Candlestick and *Stupid like a Fox* are two Durbridge television serials frequently mentioned, but he never used either of these titles on UK television. The first is easily dismissed, as confirmed in my Foreward and the note under the film *The Vicious Circle* (**211**). *Stupid like a Fox* was listed in Durbridge's *Who's Who* entry as a television serial of 1971 and again in his obituary in *The Times*, and I incorrectly speculated in my earlier book *Francis Durbridge: A Centenary Appreciation* that this was possibly the working title of his 1971 television serial *The Passenger*. Further research has since revealed that it was certainly a working title, but that of the 1971 German television serial *Das Messer*. This was originally to be called *Dumm wie ein Fuchs* (which translates as *Stupid like a Fox*), and it was a greatly amended and much later version of his third Tim Frazer television serial *The Mellin Forest Mystery* (**181C**).

It is also worth noting that in 1954, following Durbridge's success with his first three television serials, it was reported that he had written a one-off play for television. Indeed the *Yorkshire Post* (8 September 1954), previewing the autumn BBC television season, mentioned that "Plays include a specially commissioned thriller by Francis Durbridge". Durbridge's own financial records, on 24 June 1954, referred to the receipt of a half fee in advance for a "single 90-minute television play", but there is no evidence that a one-off Durbridge play was ever produced or transmitted. Abundantly clear, therefore, is the fact that the only television works by Durbridge remain his serials as detailed below.

The following list gives the inclusive dates of the original transmissions, but repeats are not listed. In each case the fullest available details of cast members are given, and it will be seen that various names appear and re-appear from the roll of great twentieth-century British television actors. In particular it is worth noting that several actors were each cast more than once in leading parts, and they were presumably considered the epitome of the stalwart yet tortured Durbridge protagonist and perhaps even given the seal of approval by the writer himself – namely Patrick Barr in *The Teckman Biography* (**175**) and *Portrait of Alison* (**176**); Stephen Murray in *My Friend Charles* (**177**), *A Time of Day* (**179**) and *The Scarf* (**180**); Tony Britton in *The Other Man* (**178**) and *Melissa* (**183**); Gerald Harper in *A Man Called Harry Brent* (**184**) and *A Game of Murder* (**185**); and Peter Barkworth in the new production of *Melissa* (**183A**) and *The Passenger* (**188**). Incidentally Gerald Harper later appeared as the leading man in two of Durbridge's stage plays in London's West End – *Suddenly at Home* (**193**) and *House Guest* (**196**). But among the regular supporting actors in Durbridge's television serials it is impossible to resist mentioning the wonderful Brian Wilde (1927-2008), who before his long comedy runs on television as Prison Officer Barrowclough in *Porridge* and Foggy Dewhurst in *Last of the Summer Wine* played deadly serious and contrasting roles in *Portrait of Alison* (**176**), *The World of Tim Frazer* (**181A**), *Melissa* (**183**) and *A Man Called Harry Brent* (**184**).

For many years there were very few DVDs of Durbridge television productions, but by 2016 all of his serials from 1963 to 1980 had become available. In addition there are DVDs of some episodes of the 1969/71 Paul Temple series starring Francis Matthews and the 1997 Alan Bleasdale revival of *Melissa*. These are all listed below under the respective productions.

Several European countries produced their own versions of Durbridge television serials, many of which are identified here with brief information. They varied considerably in the number and duration of episodes, ranging from two long episodes to nineteen episodes of barely ten minutes, but arguably the most effective were those that retained the trademark Durbridge format with their original cliff-hangers. The German versions in particular remained faithful to Durbridge's plots and scripts in most cases, as did the French versions (albeit using French character names and settings). Some of the Italian versions, however, strayed far from Durbridge's plotlines and even his dénouements.

173. *The Broken Horseshoe*. 15 March - 19 April 1952. Six thirty-minute episodes. Producer/Director: Martyn C. Webster.
Cast: John Robinson, John Byron, Andrew Crawford, Elizabeth Maude, Robert Adair, Barbara Lott, Daphne Maddox, Tristan Rawson, Michael Yannis, Marc Sheldon, Alec Ross, Russell Hunter, John Witty, Fred Griffiths, Delphi Lawrence, John Baker, Frank Atkinson, Noel Howlett, Peter Fox, Max Barrett, Arthur Ridley, Violet Loxley, Jacqueline Lacey and Alun Owen.
Plot summary: Surgeon Mark Fenton is drawn into a murder case when a man is the victim of a hit-and-run, and this appears to be connected with a woman who is involved in an international racehorse-doping ring. The episodes were entitled "Mr. Constance", "Mr. Felix Gallegos", "Miss Jackie Leroy", "Mr. Ernest Carrel", "Mr. Mark Fenton" and "Operation Horseshoe".

Filmed 1953 (**206**).

The theme music was "Atlantis" by Edward Stanley de Groot as "Edward Stanelli". Durbridge originally planned to call this *The Mark Fenton Story*. It was the first thriller serial on British television, transmitted live from Alexandra Palace.

174. *Operation Diplomat*. 25 October - 29 November 1952. Six thirty-minute episodes. Producer/Director: Martyn C. Webster.

Cast: Hector Ross, Pamela Galloway, Reginald Hearne, Hugh Kelly, David Peel, Ivan Sampson, Elizabeth Maude, Raymond Huntley, Arthur Ridley, Nancy Manningham, Lillian Christine, Duncan McIntyre, Cecil Winter, James Beattie, Brian Badcoe, Mary Horn, Christopher Rhodes, Alun Owen, Peter Coke, Raf de la Torre, Venetia Barrett, Kathleen Canty, Arthur Mason, Frank Singuineau, Nickola Sterne, Ann Totten, Dorit Welles, Fanny Carby, Roger Delgado, Charles Leno and Stanley Groome.

Plot summary: Surgeon Mark Fenton is involved in another murder case, although this time played by Hector Ross rather than John Robinson. He is abducted and forced to operate on a man whom he recognises as a missing diplomat, but when he comes under suspicion he feels compelled to pursue the person behind the plot. The episodes were entitled "Sir Oliver Peters", "Two Dozen Carnations", "Under Suspicion", "Gida", "A Change of Plan" and "The Other Man".

Filmed 1953 (**207**).

The theme music was "Atlantis" by Edward Stanley de Groot as "Edward Stanelli". Peter Coke, who played Edward Schroder in this serial, was to appear for the first time in 1954 as Paul Temple on BBC radio.

175. *The Teckman Biography*. 26 December 1953 - 30 January 1954. Six thirty-minute episodes. Producer / Director: Alvin Rakoff.
Cast: Patrick Barr, Pamela Alan, John Witty, Peter Coke, Ivan Samson, Anthony Nicholls, Paul Whitsun-Jones, James Raglan, Margaret Boyd, Maureen Pryor, Michael Bates, John Laurie, Harry Brunning, Harry Towb, James Beattie, June Petersen, Vera McKechnie, Ann Murray, Frank Pendlebury, Peter Bathurst, Leslie Kyle, Eddie Sutch, Stuart Nichol and Clare James.
Plot summary: Philip Chance, a writer researching the biography of a supposedly dead test pilot, finds a colleague of the pilot murdered. His own life is threatened when he suspects that the pilot is still alive and in hiding. The episodes were entitled "The Proposition", "Charmaine", "47 Harrison Court", "A Cable from Kesner", "The Man" and "Third Person Singular".
Filmed as *The Teckman Mystery* 1954 (**208**).
The theme music was "The Shadow Waltz" by Clive Richardson and Sam Heppner as "Paul Dubois". Peter Coke, who played Maurice Miller in this serial, became Paul Temple on BBC radio three months later.

176. *Portrait of Alison*. 16 February – 23 March 1955. Six thirty-minute episodes. Producer/Director: Alan Bromly.
Cast: Patrick Barr, Lockwood West, Anthony Nicholls, Brian Wilde, Arnold Bell, Peter Dyneley, William Lucas, Helen Shingler, William Kendall, Elaine Wodson, Elaine Dundy, Edward Dain, Patrick Jordan, Anne Ridler, Gretchen Franklin and Grace Webb.
Plot summary: Tim Forester is commissioned to paint a portrait from a photograph of Alison Ford, who was apparently killed with his brother in a car crash in Italy.

Then a model wearing Alison's dress is found murdered in his studio, and Alison herself reappears.
Filmed 1955 (**209**). Novelised 1962 (**19**).
The theme music was "Deep Night" by Charles Henderson.

177. *My Friend Charles*. 10 March – 14 April 1956. Six thirty-minute episodes. Producer/Director: Alan Bromly.
Cast: Stephen Murray, John Arnatt, Anne Ridler, Bryan Coleman, Gillian Raine, Francis Matthews, Rupert Davies, Geoffrey Chater, Ena Moon, Marvin Kane, Marianne Brauns, Victor Brooks, June Ellis, Anton Diffring, Bryan Kendrick and Peter Wayn.
Plot summary: Harley Street doctor Howard Latimer meets an actress from the airport as a favour for his friend Charles Kaufmann, but soon afterwards she is murdered. It seems that Kaufmann is being impersonated and Latimer is being framed, but in seeking to clear himself he becomes increasingly ensnared in a complex web.
Filmed as *The Vicious Circle* 1957 (**211**). Novelised 1963 (**20**).
The theme music was "The Blue Parrot" by Merrano.

178. *The Other Man*. 20 October – 24 November 1956. Six thirty-minute episodes. Producer/Director: Alan Bromly.
Cast: Tony Britton, Duncan Lamont, Patricia Driscoll, Victor Brooks, Jack Lambert, Brenda Dean, Peter Copley, Philip Guard, Brenda Cowling, Ronald Baddiley, David Tilley, John Kidd, Vanda Godsell, Ian Whittaker, Marla Landi, John Arnatt, William Patenall and Peter Morny.
Plot summary: What was schoolmaster David Henderson doing on the houseboat before the body of Paul Rocello was found? Det. Insp. Ford knows Henderson well, as his

son is one of Henderson's pupils, but he has to investigate the schoolmaster's suspicious behaviour as the evidence mounts up and another murder occurs.
Novelised 1958 (**13**).
The theme music was "Soft Lights" by Monia Liter.
The German television version was *Der Andere* (5 – 16 October 1959, six episodes), translated by Marianne de Barde and directed by Joachim Hoene.
The Italian television version was *Lungo il fiume e sull'acqua* (13 – 27 January 1973, five episodes), translated by Franca Cancogni, adapted by Biagio Proietti and directed by Alberto Negrin.

179. *A Time of Day*. 13 November - 18 December 1957. Six thirty-minute episodes. Producer/Director: Alan Bromly.
Cast: Stephen Murray, Dorothy Alison, Raymond Huntley, John Sharplin, Marianne Walla, Annabel Maule, Gerald Cross, Ernest Hare, Angela Ramsden, Hazel Hughes, Robert Hunter, Richard Bebb, Anne Ridler, Frank Pemberton, Maurice Durant, Hedger Wallace, Iris Baker, Anna Barry, Edwin Brown, Lane Meddick, Peter Halliday, Freddie Watts, Edward Dentith and Frank Pettitt.
Plot summary: Research scientist Clive Freeman and his wife Lucy are on the brink of a divorce when their daughter is kidnapped, but they need to work together to fathom the cryptic words in her exercise book. This leads them to a duplicitous photographer, and Clive's involvement in the death of a mysterious Mr. Nelson.
Novelised 1959 (**16**).
The theme music was "Piano concerto no.2, 1st movement" by Boris Blacher.

The German television version was *Es ist soweit* (21 October – 7 November 1960, six episodes), translated by Marianne de Barde and directed by Hans Quest.

The Italian television version was *Paura per Janet* (2 – 18 December 1963, six episodes), translated by Franca Cancogni and directed by Daniele D'Anza.

The Polish television version was *W bialy dzień* (11 – 25 November 1971, three episodes), translated by Kazimierz Piotrowski and directed by Jan Bratkowski.

180. *The Scarf*. 9 February – 16 March 1959. Six thirty-minute episodes. Producer/Director: Alan Bromly.

Cast: Stephen Murray, Donald Pleasence, Bryan Coleman, Peter Halliday, Lockwood West, Diana King, Leo Britt, Patrick Troughton, Edward Higgins, Vilma Ann Leslie, Anthony Valentine, Anne Ridler, Alan Edmiston, Reginald Barratt, Frank Pemberton, Neal Arden, June Ellis, Frank Sieman, Margery Fleeson, Lane Meddick, Norrie Carr, Fred Ferris, Jennifer Jayne, Arnold Bell, Edward Dentith, Diana French, Frank Pettitt and Stephen Scott.

Plot summary: Fay Collins is found strangled in a farm tractor trailer, and suspicion falls on publisher Clifton Morris. As the evidence against Morris accumulates, Det. Insp. Yates does not favour the obvious solution and has several other suspects.

Novelised 1960 (**17**).

The theme music was "The Girl from Corsica" by Trevor Duncan.

The German television version was *Das Halstuch* (3 – 17 January 1962, six episodes), translated by Marianne de Barde and directed by Hans Quest.

The Swedish television version was *Halsduken* (20 November - 9 December 1962, eight episodes), translated by Börje Lindell and Ulla Barthels and directed by Hans Lagerkvist.

The Finnish television version was *Huivi* (4 -15 December 1962, six episodes), translated by Seija Vihma and directed by Juhani Kumpulainen.

The Italian television version was *La Sciarpa* (11 – 27 March 1963, six episodes), translated by Franca Cancogni and directed by Guglielmo Morandi.

The French television version was *L'écharpe* (17 – 24 September 1966, two episodes), translated by Abder Isker and Yves Jamiaque and directed by Abder Isker.

The Polish television version was *Szal* (12 March – 9 April 1970, three episodes), translated by Kazimierz Piotrowski and directed by Jan Bratkowski.

Durbridge later updated and revised *The Scarf*, changing the character names and occupations, to become *Breakaway – The Local Affair* (**190B**) in 1980.

181. *The World of Tim Frazer*. 15 November 1960 – 14 March 1961. Eighteen thirty-minute episodes, three separate stories of six episodes each. The theme music was "The Willow Waltz" by Cyril Watters. At the time, this was the longest serial ever transmitted by BBC Television. It qualified as a continuous serial by using the audience-holding technique of a cliff-hanger ending to each episode, with the changeover in stories taking place during episodes seven and thirteen. It was well promoted by the BBC, with the front cover of the *Radio Times* of 10 November 1960 (a first for Durbridge) devoted to a photograph of Jack Hedley as Tim Frazer.

There is evidence in Durbridge's financial records that early in 1960 he was working on a serial to be called *Deadline for Harry*, and it can be speculated that this referred to the elusive Harry Denston who is mentioned below in the first serial of *The World of Tim Frazer*. Soon after, when this was to be developed into three separate stories, Durbridge first planned to call the overall series *The World of David Marquand*. The final change from David Marquand to Tim Frazer cemented the latter's place in Durbridge history.

181A. The first story, *The World of Tim Frazer*, was transmitted 15 November - 20 December 1960. Written jointly with Clive Exton. Producer/Director: Alan Bromly.

Cast: Jack Hedley as Tim Frazer and Ralph Michael as Charles Ross, with Heather Chasen, Gerald Cross, Fred Ferris, Brian Wilde, Barbara Couper, Redmond Phillips, Donald Morley, Alan Rolfe, Ann Way, John Dearth, Peter Hammond, Janina Faye, Steve Plytas, Karal Gardner, Vi Stevens, Arthur R. Webb, Frank Sieman, Anthony Wingate, Frank Pettitt, Maurice Durant, Neil Hunter, Donald Pelmear, Dennis Edwards, Christopher Rhodes and Jack Rodney.

Plot summary: When engineer Tim Frazer pursues his ex-partner Harry Denston, who has left him with a bankrupt business, the trail takes him to the fishing village of Henton and leads to his recruitment as an undercover agent. To solve a case of murder and espionage, he must unravel the significance of a model sailing ship.

Novelised 1962 (**18**).

The German television version was *Tim Frazer* (14 – 25 January 1963, six episodes), translated by Marianne de Barde and directed by Hans Quest.

The Italian television version was *Traffico d'armi nel golfo* (12 – 26 November 1977, three episodes), translated by Franca Cancogni, adapted by Aurelio Chiesa and directed by Leonardo Cortese.

181B. The second story, *The Salinger Affair*, was transmitted 27 December 1960 – 31 January 1961.

Written jointly with Barry Thomas and Charles Hatton. Producer/Director: Terence Dudley.

Cast: Jack Hedley as Tim Frazer and Ralph Michael as Charles Ross, with Patricia Haines, Francis Matthews, Michael Aldridge, Patricia Marmont, Anthony Bate, Kenneth J. Warren, Hamish Roughead, Donald Stewart, Bridget Armstrong, Veronica Wells, Victor Brooks, Cameron Hall, John Gill, Gertan Klauber, Robert Henderson, George Street, Brian Vaughan, Richard Rudd, Lee Richardson, Alan Rolfe and Anthony Jennett.

Plot summary: Special agent Leo Salinger is run down by a car in Amsterdam, and Frazer's task is to tail the woman who was at the wheel. He returns to a murder in London, and further complications involving a bulb catalogue and a metronome.

Novelised as *Tim Frazer Again* 1964 (**21**).

The German television version was *Tim Frazer – Der Fall Salinger* (10 – 20 January 1964, six episodes), translated by Marianne de Barde and directed by Hans Quest.

The French television version was *La mort d'un touriste* (3 October – 7 November 1975, six episodes), translated and directed by Abder Isker.

181C. The third story, *The Mellin Forest Mystery*, was transmitted 7 February – 14 March 1961. Written jointly with Barry Thomas and Charles Hatton. Producer/ Director: Richmond Harding.

Cast: Jack Hedley as Tim Frazer and Ralph Michael as Charles Ross, with Hazel Hughes, Jack Watling, Laurence Hardy, Walter Horsbrugh, Prysor Williams, David Langton, Ellen McIntosh, David Lander, John Glyn-Jones, Helen Lindsay, Patrick McAlinney, Douglas Blackwell, Alan Stuart, Colin Douglas, Murray Evans, John Stevenson Lang, Martin Boddey, Edward Palmer, Clifford Cox, Howell Evans, Meurig Wyn-Jones, Ballard Berkeley, Edward

Brooks, Thomas Gallagher, Robert Croudace, John Pike and Balbina.

Plot summary: Frazer's assignment is to investigate the murder of a British agent near a guest house in Wales, and the link between this death and the disappearance of a German scientist.

Novelised as *Tim Frazer Gets the Message* 1978 (**35**).

The German television version was *Das Messer* (30 November – 4 December 1971, three episodes), translated by Marianne de Barde and directed by Rolf von Sydow. Durbridge was himself involved in the creation of this production ten years after his original UK serial, so perhaps it is not surprising that it became almost a new story. The changes included the re-naming of characters (Tim Frazer became Jim Ellis and Charles Ross became George Baker), with many amendments to the plot and even the revelation of a different guilty party.

This German production also provides us with the solution to the mystery of why Durbridge listed in his *Who's Who* entry a 1971 television serial entitled *Stupid like a Fox*, as on 1 September 1970 the newspaper *Hamburger Abendblatt* reported that Rolf von Sydow was to direct a new Durbridge serial called *Dumm wie ein Fuchs* (which translates as *Stupid like a Fox*) for transmission in autumn 1971. There were other German magazine articles that gave similar coverage, and this date and mention of Rolf von Sydow shows that the serial in question was *Das Messer* and that *Dumm wie ein Fuchs* was the original working title. It is therefore now understandable, given Durbridge's close collaboration in the development of *Das Messer*, that he counted it among his television serials in *Who's Who* (albeit quoting the English translation of the original German working title, *Stupid like a Fox*).

182. *The Desperate People*. 24 February – 31 March 1963. Six thirty-minute episodes. Producer/Director: Alan Bromly.

Cast: Denis Quilley, Hugh Cross, Renny Lister, Garard Green, June Ellis, Nigel Hawthorne, Stanley Meadows, Barry Jackson, Shirley Cain, Gerard Heinz, Artro Morris, David William, Hilary Crane, John Flint, Frances Collier, Edward Brooks, Clifford Earl, Colin Pinney, Philip Guard, Rosemary Rogers, Steve Kirby, Stanley Walsh, Valerie Stanton, Stuart Hutchison, Peter Thornton, Tony Poole, Diana Oxford, Peter Ducrow, Hugh Lund, Yvonne Antrobus, Leonie Forbes, Pam Reece, Janet Davies, Kenneth Keeling, William Kendrick, Desmond Cullum-Jones, Michael Hunt, Frank Dunne, Brian Proudfoot and Thelma Holt.

Plot summary: Philip Martin, home from Germany on army leave, apparently commits suicide in a hotel – leaving his photographer brother Larry and Det. Insp. Hyde to unravel many inconsistencies among Philip's military friends.

Novelised 1966 (**23**).

DVD of the 1963 production, included in the DVD set marketed as *Francis Durbridge Presents Volume 1*, BBC/Madman, 2016.

The theme music was "Dalilia", aka "The Desperadoes", by Roger Roger. This serial gave Durbridge his second *Radio Times* cover, a full-page photograph of Denis Quilley as Larry Martin, on 21 February 1963.

The German television version was *Die Schlüssel* (18 – 22 January 1965, three episodes), translated by Marianne de Barde and adapted and directed by Paul May.

The Polish television version was *Desperaci* (26 September – 10 October 1974, three episodes), translated by Kazimierz Piotrowski and directed by Anna Minkiewicz.

183. *Melissa*. 26 April – 31 May 1964. Six thirty-minute episodes. Producer/Director: Alan Bromly.

Cast: Tony Britton, Brian Wilde, Helen Christie, Kerry Jordan, Brian McDermott, Norman Scace, Elizabeth Weaver, Richard Wilding, Ian Norris, Martin Norton, Reg Pritchard, Sydney Dobson, Mark Powell, Carole Mowlam, Michael Collins, Elizabeth Craven, Petra Davies, John Bryans, Richard Aylen, Denis Cleary, Patricia Marmont, Stanley Walsh, Arthur R. Webb, Edward Brooks, Clifford Parrish, Lennard Pearce, Anthony Sagar, Ann Wrigg and Marjorie Somerville.

Plot summary: Who murdered Melissa, the wife of writer Guy Foster? Things look bad for Guy, as he is beset by people who pretend to be somebody else and strangers who falsely claim to know him.

Novelised as *My Wife Melissa* 1967 (**25**).

DVD of the 1964 production, included in the DVD set marketed as *Francis Durbridge Presents Volume 1*, BBC/Madman, 2016.

The theme music was "Searching for Frankie" by Trevor Duncan. *Melissa* set the pace for BBC2 television serials when the new channel opened in the London area in April 1964, and it was repeated later that year as more regions began to receive BBC2.

The German television version was *Melissa* (10 – 14 January 1966, three episodes), translated by Marianne de Barde and adapted and directed by Paul May.

The Italian television version was *Melissa* (23 November – 28 December 1966, six episodes), translated by Franca Cancogni and directed by Daniele D'Anza.

The French television version was *Mélissa* (29 June – 6 July 1968, two episodes), translated and directed by Abder Isker.

The Polish television version was *Melissa* (3 – 17 December 1970, two episodes), translated by Kazimierz Piotrowski and directed by Jan Bratkowski.

Apparently there was also a Swedish television production of *Melissa* in 1966, and according to IMDb there was a Finnish version with the same title beginning on 13 June 1966 – but further details have proved impossible to trace.

183A. New production, in colour. 4 – 18 December 1974. Three fifty-minute episodes. Script Editor: Simon Masters. Producer: Morris Barry. Director: Peter Moffatt.

Cast: Peter Barkworth, Philip Voss, Joan Benham, Ronald Fraser, Ray Lonnen, Lyndon Brook, Elizabeth Bell, Moira Redmond, Desmond Jordan, Leonard Gregory, Robert King, Richard Borthwick, John Horsley, Ursula Hirst, Godfrey Jackman, Pat Gorman, Zuleika Robson, Godfrey James, Marcia Ashton, Roy Spencer, Alan Charles Thomas, James Appleby, Reg Cranfield and Sheelah Wilcocks.

DVD of the 1974 production, BBC/Acorn Media, 2007 - includes filmographies of the main cast and a Francis Durbridge biography.

The theme music was "Snowdrops and Raindrops" by Steve Gray. This three-episode remake of *Melissa* was the first Durbridge serial to be shown on US television, but not until 1982, when some newspaper critics regarded it as *passé*.

183B. New production (Channel Four). 12 – 20 May 1997. Five one-hour episodes (12 May, 13 May, 14 May, 19 May, 20 May). Written by Alan Bleasdale. Script Supervisor: Sheila Wilson. Producer: Keith Thompson. Director: Bill Anderson.

Cast: Tim Dutton, Jennifer Ehle, Julie Walters, Adrian Dunbar, Bill Paterson, Diana Weston, Gary Cady, Christopher Ryan, Andrew Schofield, Michael Angelis,

Gary Bleasdale, Hugh Quarshie, Neil Conrich, Trevor Thomas, Tom Marty, David Ross, Laura Davenport, Kevin Rooney, Yuri Stepanov, Paul Hargreaves, Michael Fleming, Ian Sanders, Beaux Bryant, Keith Clifford, Joy Harrison, John Ringham, Julie Livesey, Clarence Smith, Harry Audley, Faith Edwards, Philip O'Brien, Nigel Pegram, Neville Phillips, Alice Brighton, Joan Hooley, Terence Harvey, Paul Henry, Tunde Oba, Alibe Parsons, Gordon Sterne, Jona Jones, Cliff Kelly, Lucy Blair, Andrew Johns, Steven Brough, Morgan Deare, Laura Brattan, James Aidan, Paul Jerricho, Henry Woolley, Matthew Zajak, Mary Conlon, Josie Netherwood, Richard Bebb, Ben Miles, Mark Straker, James Ryland, Giles Watling, Tom Keller, Jill West, Paul Blake, Richard Morant, Richard Trice, Sam Rumbelow, Sharon Hinds, Chuck Julian, Chris Adamson, Jamie Foreman, Morgan Jones, Eddie Webber, Cameron Stewart and Jonah Russell.

Two DVDs of the 1997 Bleasdale production, Channel 4, 2006 - the second DVD includes an interview with Alan Bleasdale.

The original music was by Richard Harvey and Stephen Baker. Alan Bleasdale was a longtime admirer of Durbridge, and this was his tribute. Updated to the 1990s and longer than the previous versions, its first half was a prequel to the Durbridge plot – although Nancy Banks-Smith commented in *The Guardian* (21 May 1997) that "you could always see the join." This version also deviated extensively from the original Durbridge story line, which is not surprising in view of Bleasdale's credentials as the author of such gritty social dramas as *Boys from the Blackstuff* and *The Monocled Mutineer*.

184. *A Man Called Harry Brent*. 22 March – 26 April 1965. Six thirty-minute episodes. Producer/Director: Alan Bromly.

Cast: Edward Brayshaw as Harry Brent, with Gerald Harper, Jennifer Daniel, Bernard Brown, Peter Ducrow, Brian Wilde, Christopher Wray, John Horsley, Judy Parfitt, Alan Hockey, Leon Shepperdson, Michael Warren, Gerald Young, Marion Mathie, Raymond Huntley, Audine Leith, Winifred Dennis, John Falconer, Michael Harding, Penny Lambirth, Joseph Cuby, James Locker, Brian Cant, Harry Davis, Stewart Guidotti, Hugh Halliday, Anna Wing, Denis Cleary, Frank Barrie, Ray Marioni, David J. Grahame, Richard Wilding, Desmond Cullum-Jones, Fred Ferris, Diana Chapman, Norman Atkyns, Graham Ashley, Stanley Walsh, Edward Webster and John Scott Martin.

Plot summary: Carol Vyner meets travel agent Harry Brent, and although she knows little about him she breaks off her engagement to Det. Insp. Alan Milton. When Carol's employer is murdered, not only does it appear to Milton that Carol and Brent are implicated but there is a key puzzle to be resolved – who exactly is Harry Brent? The episodes were entitled "The Flowers", "Jacqueline", "The Pen", "The Problem", "Tolly Changes His Mind" and "The Third Person".

Novelised 1970 (**29**).

DVD of the 1965 production, included in the DVD set marketed as *Francis Durbridge Presents Volume 1*, BBC/Madman, 2016.

The theme music was "Hysteria" by Trevor Duncan.

The German television version was *Ein Mann namens Harry Brent* (15 – 19 January 1968, three episodes), translated by Marianne de Barde and directed by Peter Beauvais.

The Italian television version was *Un certo Harry Brent* (1 – 17 November 1970, six episodes), translated by Franca Cancogni, adapted by Biagio Proietti and directed by Leonardo Cortese.

The Polish television version was *Harry Brent* (1 – 15 June 1972, three episodes), translated by Kazimierz Piotrowski and directed by Andrzej Zakrzewski.

The French television version was *Un certain Richard Dorian* (23 November – 11 December 1973, sixteen episodes), translated and directed by Abder Isker.

According to IMDb there was a Finnish television version entitled *Mies nimeltä Harry Brent*, but further details have proved impossible to trace and this might have been simply the UK production dubbed into Finnish.

185. *A Game of Murder*. 26 February – 2 April 1966. Six thirty-minute episodes. Producer/Director: Alan Bromly.

Cast: Gerald Harper, David Burke, June Barry, Conrad Phillips, John Harvey, Christopher Wray, Peter Copley, Dorothy White, Diana King, John Carlin, Dorothy Frere, Kenneth Hendel, Lesley Carole, Murray Hayne, Patricia Shakesby, Anthony Sagar, Bernard G. High, Donald Oliver, Elizabeth Hopkinson, Alan Lynton, Derek Martin, Bernard Stone, Richard Jacques, Donald Hoath, Christopher Gilmore, Kenneth Waller, Brian Cant and Reg Whitehead.

Plot summary: A retired athlete is found dead on a golf course, and his son (Det. Insp. Jack Kerry) refuses to accept that it was an accident. When Kerry investigates the secrets of his father's private life, he is intrigued by the mystery of a dog's collar.

Novelised 1975 (**33**).

Three DVDs of the 1966 production, BBC/Danann, 2014. Also included in the DVD set marketed as *Francis Durbridge Presents Volume 1*, BBC/Madman, 2016.

The theme music was one of Sidney Torch's "Off-Beat Moods".

The Italian television version was *Giocando a golf una mattina* (28 September – 16 October 1969, six episodes), translated by Franca Cancogni and directed by Daniele D'Anza.

The French television version was *La Mort d'un champion* (4 – 5 February 1972, two episodes), translated and directed by Abder Isker.

The Polish television version was *Brutalna gra* (30 September – 14 October 1976, three episodes), translated by Kazimierz Piotrowski and directed by Anna Minkiewicz.

The German television version was *Die Kette* (18 – 20 December 1977, two episodes), translated by Marianne de Barde and Hubert von Bechtolsheim and directed by Rolf von Sydow.

186. *Bat Out of Hell*. 26 November – 24 December 1966. Five thirty-minute episodes. Producer/Director: Alan Bromly.

Cast: Sylvia Syms, John Thaw, Dudley Foster, Stanley Meadows, June Bland, June Ellis, Emrys Jones, Clive Graham, Ann Windsor, David Quilter, Patsy Smart, Paddy Glynn, Noel Johnson, Bernard Martin, Norman Scace and Patrick Ellis.

Plot summary: The apparent murder of estate agent Geoffrey Stewart by his wife Diana and her lover Mark Paxton is not all it seems, as the body disappears and Diana then receives a telephone call from the deceased. Mark and Diana find they have to deal with blackmail and further murders, with Det. Insp. Clay in close pursuit.

Novelised 1972 (**32**).

DVD of the 1966 production, BBC/Danann/Luxin, 2016. Also included in the DVD set marketed as *Francis Durbridge Presents Volume 2*, BBC/Madman, 2016.

The theme music was "Riot Squad" by Paul Gerard and Dennis Farnon.

The German television version was *Wie ein Blitz* (9 – 12 April 1970, three episodes), translated by Marianne de Barde and directed by Rolf von Sydow.

The French television version was *À corps perdu* (22 – 29 September 1970, two episodes), translated and directed by Abder Isker.

The Italian television version was *Come un uragano* (28 November – 12 December 1971, five episodes), translated by Franca Cancogni, adapted by Biagio Proietti and directed by Silverio Blasi.

The Polish television version was *Jak błyskawika* (19 October – 2 November 1972, three episodes), translated by Kazimierz Piotrowski and directed by Jan Bratkowski.

According to IMDb there was a Finnish television version from 17 August 1967 as *Salama kirkkaalta taivaalta*, but further details have proved impossible to trace and this might have been simply the UK production dubbed into Finnish.

187. *Paul Temple*. 23 November 1969 – 1 September 1971. Fifty-two fifty-minute episodes. Various writers provided original screenplays, but Durbridge was prominently credited as the creator. The BBC and Taurus Film GMBH of Munich jointly produced these modern Temple exploits, aimed at an international audience. Many of them used locations outside the UK, and the cast list was a cornucopia of familiar British television faces. The venture ended surprisingly, as there had been some twenty-five million viewers in Germany every week and it had proved popular from Russia to Australia.

Francis Matthews starred as Paul Temple, with Ros Drinkwater as Steve. Other regular characters were the "domestics" Kate and Eric (June Ellis and Blake Butler), who disappeared soon after the second series began, with rough diamond Sammy Carson (George Sewell) and his sidekick Paddy (Derek Martin) appearing from the second series.

The screenwriters of the fifty-two episodes, leaving aside the possibility that some of them might have been pseudonyms for one another, from the most to the least number of scripts were - John Tully (6), Jeremy Burnham (4), David Roberts (4), David Ellis (3), Lindsay Galloway (3), Bill Strutton (3), Cyril Abraham (2), David Chantler (2), Michael Chapman (2), John Lucarotti (2), Wolf Rilla (2) and David Simon (2), with single scripts from Patrick Alexander, Michael J. Bird, Eddie Boyd, Marc Brandel, Victor Canning, Paul Erickson, Moris Farhi, John Gould, Donald James, Peter Miller, Derry Quinn, John Roddick, Derrick Sherwin, Dennis Spooner, David Whitaker, John Wiles and Michael Winder. Given that this list included many of the top writers of television thrillers, it is strange that the *Paul Temple* series was poorly received by critics in the UK and is not held in high esteem today by Durbridge fans, although this reaction can perhaps be explained in just four words – it was not Durbridge.

The theme music was by Ron Grainer, with incidental music by Dudley Simpson.

A set of DVDs was marketed as *Francis Durbridge's The Paul Temple Collection*, BBC/Acorn Media, 2009. This contains the episodes *Games People Play* (**187B.3**); *Corrida* (**187C.4**); *The Specialists* (**187C.7**); *Has Anybody Here Seen Kelly?* (**187C.8**); *Motel* (**187C.10**); *Cue Murder!*

(**187C.11**); *Death of Fasching* (**187C.12**); *Catch Your Death* (**187C.13**); *Ricochet* (**187D.3**); *With Friends Like You, Who Needs Enemies?* (**187D.4**); and *The Quick and the Dead* (**187D.6**). The first disc includes the extra features "Being Paul Temple: An Interview with Francis Matthews"; "The Women of Paul Temple"; "Fashion Statements"; "Francis Durbridge Biography"; and "Selected Cast Filmographies". This boxed set bears the comment that "The Paul Temple Collection represents the surviving colour episodes," although a further two DVDs were later marketed as the box set *Francis Durbridge's The Paul Temple Black & White Collection*, BBC/Acorn Media, 2012. This contains the final five episodes – *The Guilty Must Die* (**187D.9**); *Game, Set and Match* (**187D.10**); *Long Ride to Red Gap* (**187D.11**); *Winner Take All* (**187D.12**); and *Critics, Yes! But This is Ridiculous!* (**187D.13**). The first disc includes the extra features "Francis Durbridge Biography" and "Selected Cast Filmographies". These episodes were originally shown in black and white in Commonwealth countries, as most sets were at the time unable to receive colour, and it is unlikely though not impossible that others will now be rescued.

187A. The first series of thirteen fifty-minute episodes (23 November 1969 – 15 February 1970) was produced by Alan Bromly, with Barry Thomas as script editor, and consisted of:

187A.1. *Who Dies Next?* 23 November 1969. Writer: Peter Miller. Director: Douglas Camfield. Cast: Matthews, Drinkwater, Ellis, Butler, Bernard Archard, David Butler, Bobbie Oswald, Olaf Pooley, Roy Evans, Hubert Rees, Ian Fairbairn, Bernard G. High, Ahmed Khalil and Tom McCall.

Plot summary: The Temples discover that their flat has been burgled, and books have been taken from shelves as if the intruder has been searching for something.

187A.2. *Message from a Dead Man*. 30 November 1969. Writer: John Roddick. Director: Paul Ciappessoni. Cast: Matthews, Drinkwater, Raymond Huntley, Madge Ryan, Derek Benfield, Rosalie Westwater, Robert Howay, Paula Tate, Shay Gorman, Lindsay Campbell and John Rolfe.

Plot summary: Temple is sceptical about a visitor's story that he overheard a murder being planned on the telephone, but then a corpse turns up.

187A.3. *There Must Be a Mr. X*. 7 December 1969. Writer: David Ellis. Director: Eric Hills. Cast: Matthews, Drinkwater, Ellis, Butler, Maggie London, Geoffrey Palmer, Brian McDermott, Walter Gotell, Dudley Jones, William Dexter and Arnold Peters.

Plot summary: Steve is misled by Temple when he tells her he has spent the night with a friend, whereas he escorted a night club hostess back to her flat.

187A.4. *Missing Penny*. 14 December 1969. Writer: Cyril Abraham. Director: Tina Wakerell. Cast: Matthews, Drinkwater, Butler, Martin Jarvis, Lans Traverse, Christine Finn, John Humphry, Dan Meaden, John Warner, Gwen Cherrell, Enid Lindsey and Edward Kelsey.

Plot summary: At his weekend retreat, Temple follows up the strange story of a woman who has disappeared without trace.

187A.5. *The Man Who Wasn't There*. 21 December 1969. Writer: John Tully. Director: Douglas Camfield. Cast: Matthews, Drinkwater, Ellis, Lillias Walker, Catherine Lacey, Renny Lister, Alethea Charlton, Clifford Earl, Peter Miles, Peter Forbes-Robertson and Michael Bird.

Plot summary: An acquaintance of the Temples has been reported killed in an air crash, so how did the dead man manage to call at their home afterwards?

187A.6. *Which One of Us is Me?* 28 December 1969. Writer: David Chantler. Director: Paul Ciappessoni. Cast: Matthews, Drinkwater, Ellis, Butler, William Squire, John Lee, Glyn Houston, Barbara Shelley, Nita Lorraine, Veronica Strong, Milton Johns and Prentis Hancock.

Plot summary: Temple is told by Howard Haythorn that someone is threatening his marriage and reputation and even his sanity, and that the culprit is Howard Haythorn himself.

187A.7. *Inside Information.* 4 January 1970. Writer: David Ellis. Director: Tina Wakerell. Cast: Matthews, Drinkwater, Ellis, Butler, Tracy Reed, Leonard Maguire, Edward Evans, Kevin Lindsay, Patricia Maynard and Michael Gwynn.

Plot summary: It seems that Steve wants a divorce, when she hires a private detective to prove Temple's infidelity.

187A.8. *The Masked Lady*. 11 January 1970. Writer: John Tully. Director: Rex Tucker. Cast: Matthews, Drinkwater, Ellis, Butler, Clive Morton, Beatrix Lehmann, Basil Dignam, George Howe, Tristram Jellinek, Tony Thawnton, Wendy Lingham and Wilfrid Downing.

Plot summary: An actress disappears from a film set, and Temple finds that this mirrors the original disappearance of the actress's Masked Lady character.

187A.9. *Swan Song for Colonel Harp*. 18 January 1970. Writer: David Chantler. Director: Tina Wakerell. Cast: Matthews, Drinkwater, Ellis, Butler, Patrick Troughton, William Lucas, Ilona Rodgers, James Cossins, Hilary Mason, Norah Gordon, Michael McClain, David Engers and Michael Mulcaster.

Plot summary: Colonel Harp is terrified by a stranger and flees to a cottage in the country, but then Temple's man

Eric is asked by the same stranger to take a trunk to Harp's cottage.

187A.10. *Mr. Wallace Predicts*. 25 January 1970. Writer: John Tully. Director: Eric Hills. Cast: Matthews, Drinkwater, Ellis, Peter Copley, Dennis Bowen, Kathleen Byron, Emrys Leyshon, Sheila Brownrigg, Geraldine Moffatt, Angela Ellis and Richard Pescud.

Plot summary: When Mr. Wallace uses extra-sensory perception to foretell accidents, he is always too late.

187A.11. *Letters from Robert*. 1 February 1970. Writer: John Tully. Director: Prudence Fitzgerald. Cast: Matthews, Drinkwater, Ellis, Butler, Rachel Kempson, Timothy Bateson, Angela Pleasence, Michael Johnson, John Collin, Stella Moray, Sarah Craze and David Monico.

Plot summary: A woman whose lover disappeared twenty years earlier appears to be receiving letters from him.

187A.12. *The Man from the Sea*. 8 February 1970. Writer: Cyril Abraham. Director: Philip Dudley. Cast: Matthews, Ellis, Butler, Donald Morley, Sheila Fearn, Arthur Pentelow, Reginald Barratt, Reg Lye, Jill Allen, Eric McCaine, Gertan Klauber, David Quilter, Marcelle Samett, Pitt Wilkinson and Jack Le White.

Plot summary: Temple investigates when a body is washed ashore and a lighthouse keeper behaves suspiciously.

187A.13. *The Victim*. 15 February 1970. Writer: David Whitaker. Director: Douglas Camfield. Cast: Matthews, Drinkwater, Ellis, Butler, Ray McAnally, Ellen McIntosh, Angharad Rees, Warwick Sims, Rosemary Rogers, Carol Haddon, Terence Brook, Les Clark, Michael Miller, Stan Sanders, Richie Stewart, Gordon Stothard and Terry Walsh.

Plot summary: A wealthy industrialist thinks that a competitor is plotting against him, but Temple is not so sure.

187B. The second series of thirteen fifty-minute episodes (5 April – 26 July 1970, split by a month's break for the Football World Cup) was produced by Peter Bryant and Derrick Sherwin, with firstly Trevor Ray and later Martin Hall as script editor, and consisted of:

187B.1. *Right Villain*. 5 April 1970. Writer: Derrick Sherwin. Director: Ken Hannam. Cast: Matthews, Drinkwater, Ellis, Sewell, Martin, Caroline Blakiston, John Gill, Richard Hampton, Tom Oliver, Patsy Smart, Elizabeth Digby-Smith and Jay Neil.

Plot summary: Temple is offered a new car by Sammy Carson, a reformed criminal who badly needs his help.

187B.2. *Kill or Cure*. 12 April 1970. Writer: Bill Strutton. Director: Christopher Barry. Cast: Matthews, Drinkwater, Butler, Wolfgang Preiss, Christiane Krüger, Jerome Willis, Angus Mackay, Peter Porteous, Alan Bennion, Eric Hillyard, Virginia Lester, John Dawson, John Rapley and Edward Topps.

Plot summary: Temple investigates the disappearance of the niece of a pharmaceutical manufacturer, ignoring advice to stay out of it.

187B.3. *Games People Play*. 19 April 1970. Writer: John Gould. Director: Philip Dudley. Cast: Matthews, Drinkwater, George Baker, Angela Browne, Moray Watson, Michael Gothard, Tony Vogel, Penny Spencer and Joe Zammit Cordina.

Plot summary: In Malta, the Temples meet an arrogant actor and his hangers-on who devise dangerous games to relieve their boredom with thrills.

187B.4. *The Artnappers*. 26 April 1970. Writer: Bill Strutton. Director: Ken Hannam. Cast: Matthews, Drinkwater, Sewell, Martin, Terence Alexander, Hugh Cross, Jenny Till, Christopher Benjamin, Edwina Carroll, Kenneth Edwards, Esmond Webb, Ray Ford, Del Baker, John Caesar and Reginald Peters.

Plot summary: Temple links a series of art thefts with an insurance company.

187B.5. *The Black Room*. 3 May 1970. Writer: Moris Farhi. Director: Christopher Barry. Cast: Matthews, Drinkwater, Julian Glover, Michael Deacon, Helen Downing, Patrick Newell, Edward Burnham, Rudolph Walker, Joan Haythorne, Geoffrey Lumsden, Simon Merrick, Stan Hollingsworth, David Simeon and Brian Vaughan.

Plot summary: Temple finds that a victim's violent memories can be manipulated by mind games.

187B.6. *Antique Death (1)*. 10 May 1970. Writer: Michael Chapman. Director: John Matthews. Cast: Matthews, Drinkwater, Ellis, John Franklyn Robbins, Noel Willman, Peter Carsten, Eric Pohlmann, Marie Versini, Russell Napier, Peter Hutchins, Christopher Owen, Paul Nemeer and Noel Schomaker.

Plot summary: Temple's newly-acquired copy of an Etruscan figurine of Apollo is stolen, and he pursues it in Amsterdam.

187B.7. *Antique Death (2)*. 17 May 1970. Writer: Michael Chapman. Director: John Matthews. Cast: Matthews, Drinkwater, Jean Anderson, Noel Willman, Peter Carsten, Yvonne Antrobus, Jan Conrad, Cyril Shaps, Wolf Frees, Andreas Malandrinos and Cynthia Bizeray.

Plot summary: In Bruges, Temple discovers that his stolen figurine is linked with a gang trading in fake art works.

187B.8. *Double Vision*. 24 May 1970. Writer: Jeremy Burnham. Director: Ken Hannam. Cast: Matthews,

Drinkwater, Martin, Andrew Faulds, Janet Key, Dennis Waterman, John Grieve, David Healy, Jack Le White and John Scholes.

Plot summary: On a trip to Edinburgh for a crime writers' convention, Temple finds that a request to read a budding author's novel is more dangerous than expected.

187B.9. *Steal a Little Happiness*. 28 June 1970. Writer: Bill Strutton. Director: Philip Dudley. Cast: Matthews, Drinkwater, Micaela Esdra, Jack Woolgar, John Abineri, Yvonne Bonnamy, Alex Scott, George Selway, Christopher Robbie, Frank Mann, Giuseppe Gerola, Raffaele Pezzoli, Doris Apostoloff, Gaby Vargas and Walter Villani.

Plot summary: A girl hitch-hiker and an old man both require the assistance of the Temples when they are visiting Italy.

187B.10. *The Suitcase*. 5 July 1970. Writer: John Tully. Director: John Matthews. Cast: Matthews, Drinkwater, Martin, Jack Watling, Alan MacNaughtan, Tenniel Evans, Scott Forbes, Daphne Anderson, Mysie Monte, John Kelland, Jason Kemp, Lloyd Lamble, Jenny Lee, Richard Gregory, John Rolfe and Walter Horsbrugh.

Plot summary: An exploding suitcase in a country house in Surrey leaves Temple uncertain whether this is espionage or a purely domestic matter.

187B.11. *Murder in Munich (1)*. 12 July 1970. Writer: David Roberts. Director: Michael Ferguson. Cast: Matthews, Drinkwater, Dieter Borsche, Maria Perschy, Jack Hedley, Corin Redgrave, Stanley Meadows, Wolf Petersen, Janos Kurucz, Siegfried Brandl, Yvette Rees, Ernst Walder, Paul Hansard, Joanna Ross, Derrick Slater, Me Me Lai and Gordon Sterne.

Plot summary: On a visit to Munich, Temple is mistaken for a contract killer and expected to do his job.

187B.12. *Murder in Munich (2)*. 19 July 1970. Writer: David Roberts. Director: Michael Ferguson. Cast: Matthews, Drinkwater, Dieter Borsche, Maria Perschy, Jack Hedley, Corin Redgrave, Wolf Petersen, Janos Kurucz, Siegfried Brandl, Yvette Rees, Ernst Walder, Wolfgang Völz, Steve Peters and John Herrington.
Plot summary: Still enmeshed in the Munich case, Temple has to extricate himself when framed for murder.
187B.13. *Re-Take*. 26 July 1970. Writer: Paul Erickson. Director: Douglas Camfield. Cast: Matthews, Drinkwater, Sewell, Martin, Kate O'Mara, Daniel Moynihan, Betty Alberge, Shirley Cooklin, Anthony Dutton, Freddie Earlle, Susanna East, George Giles, Roy Macready, Eve Ross, Michael Segal, Mark Sinclair, Vicki Woolf and Ralph Arliss.
Plot summary: Temple links a child's disappearance in London with an earlier series of crimes in Rome.

187C. The third series of thirteen fifty-minute episodes (10 January - 11 April 1971) was produced by Peter Bryant and/or Derrick Sherwin as noted, with Martin Hall as script editor, and consisted of:
187C.1. *House of the Dead*. 10 January 1971. Writer: David Roberts. Producer: Derrick Sherwin. Director: George Spenton-Foster. Cast: Matthews, Drinkwater, Moira Redmond, Gerald Flood, Petra Davies, Sean Caffrey, Richard Caldicot, Jane Sherwin and Sylvia Coleridge.
Plot summary: Temple investigates a past case of murder when he is invited to an abandoned house.
187C.2. *Sea Burial*. 17 January 1971. Writer: David Roberts. Producers: Peter Bryant and Derrick Sherwin. Director: Ronald Wilson. Cast: Matthews, Drinkwater, Fulton Mackay, Gunnar Hellström, Godfrey James, Lauritz Faulk, Monica Nordquist, Lawrence Trimble, Jan Karlsson and Bibbi Landelius.

Plot summary: Temple is drawn into investigating an ingenious crime in Sweden.

187C.3. *Night Train*. 24 January 1971. Writer: Michael J. Bird. Producer: Derrick Sherwin. Director: Douglas Camfield. Cast: Matthews, Drinkwater, Robert Urquhart, Gerald Sim, Geoffrey Chater, Barry Jackson, Linda Liles, George Moon, Peter Halliday, George Waring, John Acheson, John Muirhead, Harold Reece, Denis Plenty, Ian Elliott and Jack Le White.

Plot summary: When Temple takes the night train, he wonders why a familiar face is working as the sleeping-car attendant.

187C.4. *Corrida*. 7 February 1971. Writer: Lindsay Galloway. Producer: Derrick Sherwin. Director: Ken Hannam. Cast: Matthews, Drinkwater, Edward De Souza, Frederick Jaeger, Hugh Sullivan, Georges Lambert, Jeremy Higgins, Peter Miles, Paul Armstrong, Colette Martin, Michael Forrest, Michael Mellinger and Jean Driant.

Plot summary: The Temples witness a shooting in an otherwise deserted bullring, and seek the connection between this and the deaths of two children in an explosion.

187C.5. *Death for Divers' Reasons*. 14 February 1971. Writer: John Lucarotti. Producer: Derrick Sherwin. Director: Ken Hannam. Cast: Matthews, Drinkwater, Richard Hurndall, Stephanie Bidmead, Geoffrey Russell, Marcus Hammond, Kit Taylor, Patrick Durkin and George Tovey.

Plot summary: The Temples go yachting, but it proves not to be the relaxing break they were hoping for.

187C.6. *A Greek Tragedy*. 21 February 1971. Writer: Lindsay Galloway. Producer: Peter Bryant. Director: George Spenton-Foster. Cast: Matthews, Drinkwater, Valerie Gearon, Francis De Wolff, John Bennett, Wolfe

Morris, Colin Jeavons, Denis Carey, John Barrett, John Barrard, John Cazabon and Meadows White.

Plot summary: Temple has to look back to events almost thirty years earlier, when faced with a tragedy in a Greek village and the refusal of the locals to co-operate.

187C.7. *The Specialists*. 28 February 1971. Writer: Michael Winder. Producer: Peter Bryant. Director: Eric Price. Cast: Matthews, Drinkwater, Sewell, Emrys Jones, Wendy Gifford, Elisabeth Murray, Hans Meyer, Garfield Morgan, John Line, Hugh Morton, Alister Williamson and Laurie Webb.

Plot summary: Temple believes that a contract has been agreed to kill a businessman friend, and finds that no-one can be trusted.

187C.8. *Has Anybody Here Seen Kelly?* 7 March 1971. Writer: Dennis Spooner. Producer: Derrick Sherwin. Director: Eric Price. Cast: Matthews, Drinkwater, Peter Barkworth, Richard Vernon, Glyn Owen, David Sumner, Virginia Wetherell, Griffith Jones, Alan Curtis, Terence Brook, Nicolette Roeg, Colin Rix and Frank Littlewood.

Plot summary: In a port on the French Riviera, the Temples learn that an artist friend has disappeared under suspicion of murder - but why are two public school gentlemen so interested?

187C.9. *Requiem for a Don*. 14 March 1971. Writer: Jeremy Burnham. Producer: Derrick Sherwin. Director: Christopher Barry. Cast: Matthews, Drinkwater, Lana Morris, Cyril Luckham, Derek Francis, Alison Fiske, Bernard Kay, Oscar Quitak, Aubrey Richards, George Cormack, Richard Burrell, Patrick Godfrey, Freddy Foote, Sarah Gibson, David Lyell, Steve Emerson and Eric Kent.

Plot summary: Temple investigates the death of a university professor.

187C.10. *Motel.* 21 March 1971. Writer: David Simon. Producer: Derrick Sherwin. Director: Simon Langton. Cast: Matthews, Drinkwater, Robert MacLeod, Gay Hamilton, Tony Steedman, Patricia Haines, Reginald Marsh, James Donnelly, John Bindon, Dan Meaden, John Moore and Angus Lennie.

Plot summary: The Temples check into an isolated Scottish motel in a snowstorm and find it is the rendezvous for a criminal gang, which leads to murder.

187C.11. *Cue Murder!* 28 March 1971. Writer: David Simon. Producer: Derrick Sherwin. Director: George Spenton-Foster. Cast: Matthews, Drinkwater, Donald Houston, Katharine Blake, Philip Madoc, Madge Ryan, Alison Leggatt, Michael Lees, Sonia Dresdel, Joseph Fürst, Elizabeth Begley, Anna Korwin, Tristan Rogers, Jackie Rohan and John Abbott.

Plot summary: The audience in a television studio witnesses Temple exposing a murderer.

187C.12. *Death of Fasching.* 4 April 1971. Writer: Wolf Rilla. Producer: Derrick Sherwin. Director: Viktors Ritelis. Cast: Matthews, Drinkwater, Georg Marischka, George Pravda, Isa Miranda, Catherine Schell, Bruno Dietrich, Kenneth Garner, Michael Gahr, Alexander Allerson, Terence Woodfield and Sarah Grazebrook.

Plot summary: In Munich, the Temples' enjoyment of the Fasching festivities is marred by kidnapping and revolutionaries.

187C.13. *Catch Your Death.* 11 April 1971. Writer: Patrick Alexander. Producer: Derrick Sherwin. Director: Frank Cox. Cast: Matthews, Drinkwater, Sewell, John Carson, Patrick Barr, Allan Cuthbertson, Donald Morley, Brian Lawson, Karin MacCarthy, Roger Rowland, Frederick Peisley, John Garrie, John Atkinson, Jimmy Gardner, Hope

Jackman, Peter Diamond, Paul Nemeer, David Griffin and Graham Berown.
Plot summary: A bungled break-in at a medical research establishment leaves the burglar frozen to death, but a second more successful attempt means that Temple must recover a potentially fatal virus.

187D. The fourth series of thirteen fifty-minute episodes (9 June - 1 September 1971) was produced by Derrick Sherwin unless otherwise noted, with Martin Hall as script editor, and consisted of:

187D.1. *Paper Chase*. 9 June 1971. Writer: Jeremy Burnham. Director: George Spenton-Foster. Cast: Matthews, Drinkwater, Norman Bird, Kenneth Griffith, John Le Mesurier, Tamara Ustinov, Barry Dennen, Ellen Pollock, Jackie Rohan, Ray Edwards, Geoffrey Frederick, John Hamill, Oliver Maguire and Michael Wolf.
Plot summary: Temple investigates an affair involving shadowy political warfare in London.

187D.2. *Death Sentence*. 16 June 1971. Writer: David Ellis. Director: Douglas Camfield. Cast: Matthews, Drinkwater, Sewell, Brian Worth, Marjie Lawrence, Miranda Connell, Nicholas Smith, Natalie Kent, Michael McStay, Sally James, Bruce Myles, Philip Ryan, Derek Ware and Bernard G. High.
Plot summary: Someone is attempting to murder a woman who seemingly has no enemies.

187D.3. *Ricochet*. 23 June 1971. Writer: Marc Brandel. Director: Darrol Blake. Cast: Matthews, Drinkwater, David Bauer, Christopher Chittell, Ilona Grübel, Franco Derosa, Frederick Schiller, Paul Hansard, Leonardo Pieroni, Frans Van Nord and Kenneth Benda.
Plot summary: In a hotel in St. Moritz, the Temples meet a ruthlessly ambitious man who plans to ensure that his son

wins the Cresta Run, and a girl is menaced by an Italian criminal.

187D.4. *With Friends Like You, Who Needs Enemies?* 30 June 1971. Writer: Victor Canning. Director: Michael Ferguson. Cast: Matthews, Drinkwater, Sewell, Victor Maddern, Garfield Morgan, Christine Shaw, Monique Messine, André Charisse, Terry Walsh and Florence Marchandau.

Plot summary: In a French resort, the Temples' friend Sammy Carson is framed for murder.

187D.5. *Party Piece.* 7 July 1971. Writer: Lindsay Galloway. Director: Ken Hannam. Cast: Matthews, Drinkwater, Sewell, Bernard Archard, Jill Dixon, Cyd Hayman, Ray Lonnen, Denis Carey, David Dundas, Chris Cunningham, Brian Glover, John F. Landry and Maxine Casson.

Plot summary: A crime requires Temple's attention when Sammy Carson meets an old jazz-pianist buddy.

187D.6. *The Quick and the Dead.* 14 July 1971. Writer: Derry Quinn. Director: George Spenton-Foster. Cast: Matthews, Drinkwater, Peter Sallis, Tenniel Evans, John Stratton, Terence Edmond, Barbara Lott, Jeremy Brock, Avril Elgar, Graham Haberfield, Brian Smith, Derek Newark, Jay Neil, Jane Pilcher, Michael Mulcaster and Gladys Bacon.

Plot summary: Archaeological excavations in an English village result in murder, with evidence of the revival of pagan rituals.

187D.7. *The Man Who Forged Real Money.* 21 July 1971. Writer: John Lucarotti. Director: Ken Hannam. Cast: Matthews, Drinkwater, Sewell, Barrie Cookson, Gabriel Woolf, Mark Heath, Johnny Sekka, Sheila Scott-Wilkinson, Thomas Baptiste, Christopher Biggins, Bernard Spear,

Milo Sperber, Gloria Stewart, Cyril Varley and John Boswall.

Plot summary: Temple is drawn into a conspiracy in an African embassy in London.

187D.8. *A Family Affair*. 28 July 1971. Writer: Wolf Rilla. Director: David Maloney. Cast: Matthews, Drinkwater, Walter Rilla, Michael Cramer, Roland Astor, Paul Ambrose, Ingrid Kelemen, Ingeborg Schöner, Roy Scammell and Janos Kurucz.

Plot summary: Treachery within a family involves Temple when he takes a trip to Hamburg.

187D.9. *The Guilty Must Die*. 4 August 1971. Writer: John Tully. Director: Douglas Camfield. Cast: Matthews, Drinkwater, Sewell, Sylvia Syms, Patrick Mower, Joe Melia, Michael Sheard, Keith James, David Butler, Godfrey Jackman, Jenny Lee-Wright, Deirdre Costello, Norman Hartley, Jorund Camfield and George Giles.

Plot summary: While Temple is away Steve tries to dissuade a friend from marrying an unscrupulous car salesman, but on his return Temple suspects that it will all end in murder.

187D.10. *Game, Set and Match*. 11 August 1971. Writer: Jeremy Burnham. Director: Darrol Blake. Cast: Matthews, Drinkwater, John Gregg, Del Henney, Veronica Strong, Dilys Watling, Ed Devereaux, Edmund Pegge, Kurt Christian, Robert Oates, Ian Elliott, Colin Thatcher, Peter Cockburn, Anthony Nash, Ken Fletcher and Tony Hammond.

Plot summary: On a visit to London for a tournament, an Australian tennis player needs the Temples' help when pursued by debt collectors.

187D.11. *Long Ride to Red Gap*. 18 August 1971. Writer: John Wiles. Director: George Spenton-Foster. Cast: Matthews, Drinkwater, Sewell, Martin, Kevin Stoney,

Anthony Sagar, Christopher Gray, Will Leighton, Jonathan Deans, Shane Raggett, Ian Ramsey and Paul Burton.

Plot summary: Sammy Carson is ambushed by Red Indians – near Guildford!

187D.12. *Winner Take All*. 25 August 1971. Writer: Donald James. Producer: Peter Bryant. Director: Christopher Barry. Cast: Matthews, Drinkwater, Claire Nielson, Peter Dyneley, Mark Kingston, Edward Cast, Charles Lamb, James Hall, Jon Croft, John Dickinson, Esmond Webb, Timothy Craven, Philip Ryan, Brian Nolan, Lena Ellis and Peter O'Sullevan.

Plot summary: Against a horse-racing background, the Temples find that a struggle for control of a crime syndicate involves far more than horses.

187D.13. *Critics, Yes! But This is Ridiculous!* 1 September 1971. Writer: Eddie Boyd. Director: Michael Ferguson. Cast: Matthews, Drinkwater, William Gaunt, Maurice Roëves, Morag Hood, Andrew Crawford, Prentis Hancock, Simon Lack, Angus Lennie, Joanna Cooper, Elaine Baillie, Philip Dunbar, Marilyn Fridjon, Dean Harris, Robert Robertson, Stanley Stewart, James Gibson and Don McKillop.

Plot summary: Someone has vandalised Temple's novels in a Scottish library, and in seeking the reason he finds that this trifling matter becomes a case of double murder.

188. *The Passenger*. 23 October – 6 November 1971. Three forty-five minute episodes. Producer: Gerard Glaister. Director: Michael Ferguson.

Cast: Peter Barkworth, Joanna Dunham, Melissa Stribling, Michael McStay, Arthur Pentelow, Paul Grist, Christine Shaw, Mona Bruce, David Knight, James Kerry, Derek Bond, Paul Hastings, Roger Booth, Beth Morris, Hugh Murray, Jim Collier, Jane Blackburn, Anthony Gylby

Garner, Sally Avery, Patrick Durkin, Derek Chafer, Ric Felgate, Alan Chuntz, Billy Franks, Denis Cleary and Terry Walsh.

Plot summary: Toymaker David Walker gives a lift to a young woman, but he runs out of petrol and when he returns to the car she has disappeared. She is later found strangled, and Det. Insp. Martin Denson's investigation becomes even more complex when Walker himself appears to have committed suicide.

Novelised 1977 (**34**).

Two DVDs of the 1971 production, BBC/Pidax, 2016, under the German title *Die Spur mit dem Lippenstift* but containing the English and the German (dubbed) versions. Also included in the DVD set marketed as *Francis Durbridge Presents Volume 2*, BBC/Madman, 2016.

The theme music was "Dark Theme" by The Pretty Things. The three episodes were amalgamated and televised as a single programme of two hours on 5 October 1973.

The French television version was *La Passagère* (6 December 1974 – 2 January 1975, nineteen episodes), translated and directed by Abder Isker.

The UK production of *The Passenger* was shown in Germany, dubbed, as *Die Spur mit dem Lippenstift* (6 - 8 September 1983, three episodes).

189. *The Doll*. 25 November – 9 December 1975. Three fifty-five minute episodes. Producer: Bill Sellars. Director: David Askey.

Cast: John Fraser, Anouska Hempel, Geoffrey Whitehead, Derek Fowlds, Cyril Luckham, Roger Milner, William Russell, Sheila Keith, Olive Milbourne, Corinna Marlowe, Sarah Brackett, Paul Williamson, Roger Gartland, John Pennington, Dolly Landon, Rod Beacham, Marjorie Hogan, Jacqueline Stanbury, Ken Kennedy, Eric Mason, John

Livesey, Linal Haft, Alexandra Taylor, George Lowdell, Douglas Jones, Ray Callaghan, Richard Borthwick and Sarah Nash.

Plot summary: Publisher Peter Matty meets the widowed Phyllis du Salle, who tells him that her late husband collected dolls in national costumes and that soon after his death she found one of them in her bathroom. Matty later finds a Tyrolean doll floating in his own bath, then learns that Phyllis's friend Linda Braithwaite has been murdered.

Novelised 1982 (**37**).

Two DVDs of the 1975 production, BBC/Pidax, 2013, under the German title *Die Puppe* but containing the English and the German (dubbed) versions. Also included in the DVD set marketed as *Francis Durbridge Presents Volume 2*, BBC/Madman, 2016.

The theme music was "Counterspy" by Roger Webb.

The Italian television version was *Dimenticare Lisa* (9 – 23 October 1976, three episodes), translated by Franca Cancogni and directed by Salvatore Nocita.

The UK production of *The Doll* was shown in Germany, dubbed, as *Die Puppe* (4 – 5 June 1982, two episodes).

190. *Breakaway*. 11 January – 28 March 1980. Twelve thirty-minute episodes, two separate stories of six episodes each. The theme and incidental music were by Joe Griffiths. The series was promoted by a *Radio Times* cover (5 January 1980) headed "The Radio Times Murder Game", with eight caricatures of the cast depicted on playing-cards as Cluedo-type figures.

190A. The first story, *Breakaway - The Family Affair*, was transmitted 11 January – 15 February 1980. Producer: Ken Riddington. Director: Paul Ciappessoni.

Cast: Martin Jarvis, Glyn Houston, Angela Browne, Derek Farr, John Lee, Paul Shelley, Hilary Ryan, Simon Oates, Norman Hartley, Derek Benfield, Gilly McIver, Patrick Westwood, Jason James, Clifton Jones, Samuel Holland, Lockwood West, Joan Benham, Richard Caldicot, Paul Grinbergs, John Cannon, Reg Turner, Martin Fisk, Mike Lewin, James Muir, Mela White, Rebel Russell, Geoffrey Beevers, Pat Gorman, Jerry Judge, Ray Knight and Brian Peck.

Plot summary: Det. Supt. Sam Harvey decides to resign from the force after writing a successful children's book, but stays on when his parents are murdered. Why had they cancelled a trip to Australia after Sam left them at the airport, and why were their bodies in a van marked Marius of Rye?

Novelised as *Breakaway* 1981 (**36**).

DVD of the 1980 production, included in the DVD set marketed as *Francis Durbridge Presents Volume 2*, BBC/Madman, 2016.

The UK production of *Breakaway - The Family Affair* was shown in Germany, dubbed, as *Auf eigene Faust – Eine Familienangelegenheit* (6 – 18 May 1982, four episodes).

The UK production of *Breakaway - The Family Affair* was shown in Italy, dubbed, as *Addio, Scotland Yard – Affari di famiglia* (3 – 5 June 1985, three episodes).

190B. The second story, *Breakaway – The Local Affair*, was transmitted 22 February – 28 March 1980. Producer: Ken Riddington. Director: Michael E. Briant.

Cast: Martin Jarvis, Ed Bishop, Judy Geeson, David Collings, Edward Peel, Michael Culver, William Marlowe, Robert Morris, Miles Fothergill, Paul Luty, Lynn Dalby, Vivien Merchant, Gillian Rhind, Sandra Bryant, Susan Field, Eric Mason, Margaret John, John Abineri, Suzan Farmer, Jack McKenzie, Elizabeth Rider, Richard Seagar,

Elizabeth Chambers, Clark Stephens, David Griffin and Juliette James.

Plot summary: While serving his notice Det. Supt. Sam Harvey is sent to Market Cross, to be faced with conflicting information about a body in a wood. He finds that this is far from a one-off murder, but is part of a complex web of blackmail.

DVD of the 1980 production, included in the DVD set marketed as *Francis Durbridge Presents Volume 2*, BBC/Madman, 2016.

Although the character names and occupations are changed, this is clearly a new production of his 1959 television serial *The Scarf* (**180**).

The UK production of *Breakaway – The Local Affair* was shown in Germany, dubbed, as *Auf eigene Faust – Kleinstadtaffäre* (20 May – 1 June 1982, four episodes).

The UK production of *Breakaway – The Local Affair* was shown in Italy, dubbed, as *Addio, Scotland Yard – Affari locali* (6 – 11 June 1985, three episodes).

According to IMDb there was a Finnish television version from 24 June 1981 as *Irtautuminen*, but further details have proved impossible to trace and it is not known if this Finnish production covered both of the *Breakaway* serials or only one. It is also likely that it was simply the UK production dubbed into Finnish.

To conclude this section, it is necessary to mention one unresolved European query. On Danish television in May 1980 a two-episode Durbridge serial was transmitted called *Die Abrechnung*, and sadly the UK origin of this remains a mystery. There is no evidence in the Danish television archives to clarify the matter, and its English translated title *The Payoff* is no help, but given its date it might possibly have been a version of *The Passenger*, *The*

Doll or *Breakaway*. It was probably also the case that it was the UK television version, dubbed into Danish.

STAGE PLAYS

There are two oddities in respect of Francis Durbridge stage plays – and the first, *The Grandma Game*, is debunked below. The other, *Murder Diary*, was listed in Durbridge's *Who's Who* entry and dated as 1986 – and as there is no further evidence of a production with this title, see the note under *A Touch of Danger* (**198**).

The Grandma Game is listed on many websites as a Durbridge play that was produced in Brighton in 1980. Indeed a review by G.D. Hammerton was published in *The Stage and Television Today* (26 June 1980) under the heading "BRIGHTON / The Grandma Game", which is where the confusion originated. The body of this review does not re-quote the title of the play, but it mentions Durbridge and then proceeds with comments that clearly relate to his earlier play *Murder with Love* (**195**). A previous issue of *The Stage and Television Today* (5 June 1980), in "Regional Production News", had already announced a new production of *Murder with Love* to be performed at the Derby Playhouse from 11 to 28 June, and Hammerton's review mentions the director of the Derby Playhouse and the Derby actors. There can be no doubt, therefore, that Hammerton's review should have been captioned "DERBY / Murder with Love" and not "BRIGHTON / The Grandma Game". And to complete the picture, a week after Hammerton's review there was another review by Charles Plumley (*The Stage and Television Today*, 3 July 1980), again using the heading "BRIGHTON / The Grandma Game", but this time it related to a play by Edward A. Barton that really was entitled *The Grandma Game* and was then running in Brighton.

It can therefore be positively confirmed that Durbridge never wrote a play called *The Grandma Game*, but delight at resolving this is tempered with frustration at having spent many hours searching the files of four Brighton newspapers for a non-existent Durbridge play! How the heading could have been misprinted in *The Stage and Television Today* remains a mystery, but it has bred errors up to the present day. For example various websites continue to suggest, albeit with little conviction, that a Durbridge play produced in Germany called *Zaradin 4* might have been a translation of the mysterious *The Grandma Game*.

So to finalise the puzzle, given that *The Grandma Game* was never a Durbridge play, what was the origin of the play *Zaradin 4*? There is now no doubt that this was an early German version of the stage play that later became *Sweet Revenge*, and indeed Durbridge's original typescript for *Sweet Revenge* contains his handwritten amendment of the murderous drug's name from Zaradin 4 to Zarabell Four. Furthermore there is incontrovertible evidence that this play had an even earlier and more complicated history, as explained under *Sweet Revenge* (**200**) below.

In the theatre world, when a new play has its première or tryout it might never achieve a London West End opening, but conversely it might become a great success. In some cases it might only reach the West End after its provincial run has convinced the director and/or author that alterations must be made to it. The following listing is the best possible attempt to identify all of Durbridge's provincial premières and pre-London runs, showing only the opening date in each case. London West End runs are given in full, but neither provincial nor West End runs can be taken as evidence of the success or otherwise of Durbridge plays because today they still continue to be performed worldwide.

These plays, with the exception of *Send for Paul Temple* and *We Were Strangers*, have frequently been presented throughout Europe. Nevertheless information here is confined to the German stage productions as these had a particular significance, given the fact that it was in Germany that Francis Durbridge's successful career as a stage dramatist can now be shown to have begun. In addition, details are provided here about various European television versions of his stage plays.

191. *Send for Paul Temple*. First produced at the Alexandra Theatre Birmingham from 25 October to 6 November 1943. Based on his 1938 radio serials *Send for Paul Temple* and *Paul Temple and the Front Page Men* (**112** and **114**).

This Birmingham production was announced at the time in the theatre listings of the *Birmingham Post* as "Send for Paul Temple – A New Adventure of Radio's Most Popular Detective, by Francis Durbridge." According to a review by "T.C.K." in the *Birmingham Post* of 26 October 1943: "There are some strange goings-on this week at the Alexandra Theatre where Paul Temple, the detective who has made a reputation on the radio, is in session. To provide incident for this exciting sitting, it seems that the Newgate Calendar has been combed for material. A couple of kidnappings head the list and lead on to sterner stuff in the form of poisonings, shootings and dope dealing. Bodies fall out of lifts; screams rend the night; an innocent-looking gramophone spits forth bullets; and cyanide finds its way into harmless brandy flasks … Of course, this nefarious exercise is the work of a gang (and) in the final scenes the case resolves itself into a chase after the mysterious leader … Strongly as we have suspected A and B, it turns out to be X after all." The review mentions "Robert Ginns's likeable Paul Temple, Vernon Fortescue and Denis Goacher as the men from Scotland Yard, Angela Wyndham-Lewis as the discreetly intelligent woman journalist indispensable to the modern detective and Andrew Buck as Dr. Brightman, the perverted practitioner indispensable to the modern crime."

The play was also noted in the "Chit Chat" column of *The Stage* (4 November 1943): "A new detective play, called *Send for Paul Temple* by Francis Durbridge, has been doing well at the Alexandra, Birmingham, where it was presented last week … In this there are four assorted murders, committed in view of the audience, and the same number off-stage. Under the direction of George Owen, the Alexandra Repertory Company have made a creditable production. Robert Ginns in the name part displays a pleasing personality, and Angela Wyndham-Lewis makes the most of limited opportunities as the reporter-heroine."

A review in the *Birmingham Gazette* of 26 October 1943 names Angela Wyndham-Lewis's character as Steve Trent (rather than Steve Temple), which would normally identify it as an adaptation of the 1938 radio serial *Send for Paul Temple* in which Temple and Steve first meet. From the play's typescript deposited in the British Library, however, it can clearly be seen that it owes more to the second radio serial, *Paul Temple and the Front Page Men*.

This was certainly Francis Durbridge's first professionally-produced stage play, and there was no evidence of further performances until recently. On 15 November

2015, *Send for Paul Temple* was presented for one night only at Middle Temple Hall in London in support of the charity The Kalisher Trust. It was directed by Joe Harmston with a high profile professional cast including Stanley Tucci as Temple and Sophie Ward as Steve, together with Hugh Dennis, Jason Watkins, Ray Fearon, Mark Farelly, Paul Hertzberg, Daniel Hill, Cassie Raine, Andrew Paul, Keith Myers, Sarah Berger, Martin Fisher, Simon Cole and Iain Christie. This semi-staged production recreated the atmosphere and sound effects of the original radio serials, and appears to have been an adapted and abridged version of the 1943 Birmingham play.

192. *We Were Strangers*. One-act play, dated 1948 in the published collection *One-Act Plays for the Amateur Theatre*, Ed. Max H. Fuller, Harrap, 1949. Originally presented as a radio play on 3 June 1938 (**113**).

193. *Suddenly at Home*. Samuel French, 1973 [November]. Two-act play, first produced at the Theatre Royal Windsor from 8 June 1971 and subsequently at the Fortune Theatre London from 30 September 1971 to 16 June 1973 (over seven hundred performances). Director: Basil Coleman.
The Fortune Theatre cast: Gerald Harper, Jennifer Daniel, Veronica Strong, Penelope Keith, Terence Longdon, Rula Lenska, Frederick Farley and John Horton. On 12 June 1972 a change of cast introduced Patricia Shakesby, Kate O'Mara, Rachel Herbert, Patricia Dermott and Vernon Joyner, leaving only Gerald Harper, Terence Longdon and Frederick Farley from the original cast. On 22 January 1973 Simon Oates succeeded Gerald Harper as the leading man, and the almost complete change of cast

introduced Harriet Philpin, Lesley Goldie, Moira Foot, Annette Andre and Richard Poore, leaving only Terence Longdon and Frederick Farley from the original cast.

Plot summary: Salesman Glenn Howard plans to kill his wealthy wife and implicate her former lover, but everything becomes much more complicated than he intended.

The German stage production was *Plötzlich und unerwartet*, translated by Maria Weiser. Its première in Essen, directed by Heinz Drache, was in the early 1970s during the long London run of *Suddenly at Home* – probably in 1972.

The Italian television version, *A casa una sera* (23 – 24 September 1976, two episodes), was adapted and directed by Mario Landi from a script by Franca Cancogni.

The German television version, *Plötzlich und unerwartet* (20 January 1985), was adapted and directed by Thomas Engel from the translation by Maria Weiser.

194. *The Gentle Hook*. Samuel French, 1975 [October]. Two-act play, first produced at the Yvonne Arnaud Theatre Guildford from 30 September 1974, the King's Theatre Southsea from 7 October 1974, the Theatre Royal Brighton from 14 October 1974 and the Rex Theatre Wilmslow from 21 October 1974, and subsequently at the Piccadilly Theatre London from 21 December 1974 to 26 April 1975. Director: Basil Coleman.

The Piccadilly Theatre cast: Dinah Sheridan, Jack Watling, Raymond Francis, Hazel Bainbridge, Tony Anholt, John Quentin, Charles Stapley and Brian Moorhead.

Plot summary: Successful interior designer Stacey Harrison, who is seeking a divorce from her barrister husband, returns from a trip to Paris and is shortly afterwards attacked by a stranger whom she kills. But is he really a stranger, and how is this mystery and a second killing linked with a plot to forge paintings?

The German stage production was *Dies Bildnis ist zum Morden schön*, translated by Max Faber. Its première in Hamburg on 27 February 1975, directed by Ulrich Erfurth, was during the London run of *The Gentle Hook*.

The first German television version, *Der elegante Dreh* (11 March 1979), was directed in the GDR by Hanns Anselm Perten. It was not adapted or edited for television, but simply took Max Faber's stage script and reproduced it scene-by-scene.

The Italian television version, *Poco a poco* (30 November – 7 December 1980, three episodes), was adapted by Giuseppe D'Agata and directed by Alberto Sironi, from a script by Franca Cancogni. The setting was Milan, and it had little in common with the original play *The Gentle Hook*.

The later German television version, *Dies Bildnis ist zum Morden schön* (23 November 1987), was adapted by Dorothee Dhan and directed by Günter Gräwert from the translation by Max Faber.

195. *Murder with Love*. Samuel French, 1977 [September]. Two-act play, first produced at the Theatre Royal Windsor from 2 March 1976, the Playhouse Harlow from 22 March 1976, the Civic Theatre Corby from 29 March 1976, the Civic Theatre Darlington from 5 April 1976, the Theatre Royal Bath from 12 April 1976, the Grand Theatre Wolverhampton from 19 April 1976, the Adeline Genée Theatre East Grinstead from 26 April 1976, Devonshire Park Theatre Eastbourne from 3 May 1976, the Arts Theatre Cambridge from 10 May 1976, the Alexandra Theatre Birmingham from 17 May 1976, the New Theatre Hull from 24 May 1976, the King's Theatre

Southsea from 31 May 1976, the Ashcroft Theatre Croydon from 7 June 1976, the Belgrade Theatre Coventry from 14 June 1976, the Wyvern Theatre Swindon from 21 June 1976, the Crucible Theatre Sheffield from 28 June 1976, the Theatre Royal Brighton from 5 July 1976, the Theatre Royal Norwich from 26 July 1976, the Grand Theatre Leeds from 2 August 1976, Richmond Theatre from 9 August 1976 and the Rex Theatre Wilmslow from 16 August 1976. Director: Hugh Goldie.

Cast: Peter Byrne, Dermot Walsh, Ann Kennedy, Jenny Till, David Sterne, Peter Myers, Mike Hall, Michael Howe and Patricia Moore.

Plot summary: Barrister David Ryder is framed for the murder of a man who once had an affair with his late wife, but several other suspects emerge when it transpires that the dead man's activities involved much more than womanising. A tantalising twist is provided by a second murder.

This play clearly originated earlier, as is evident from the fact that the French television adaptation *Sang froid* was transmitted on 6 July 1972 whereas the stage play *Murder with Love* was not produced in the UK until 2 March 1976. In fact it has an even longer history, as it was first staged in Germany as early as 1964 with the title *Wettlauf mit der Uhr*, and its première in Mainz was covered in the newspaper *Hamburger Abendblatt* dated 17 November 1964.

There was another early German stage version, called *Ein lückenloses Alibi*. Translated by Marianne de Barde, its script clearly identifies the English title as *Murder with Love*. *Ein lückenloses Alibi* is longer than the Windsor 1976 play, with additional dialogue and two more characters – Hibberd and Fred Ogden - but it excludes the second murder which occurs in the Windsor 1976 play.

As the November 1964 Mainz production of *Wettlauf mit der Uhr* was reported in the press as a première, it is likely that this was the very first production of the play that later became *Murder with Love*. The theatre programme of a Munich 1966 production of *Wettlauf mit der Uhr*, directed by Isebil Sturm, gives the English title as *Murder with Love* and the translator as Marianne de Barde – but the cast list, compared with *Ein lückenloses Alibi*, excludes Mrs. Bedford and Fred Ogden.

Almost certainly the title *Wettlauf mit der Uhr* was used first, and Durbridge or de Barde soon made changes when it became *Ein lückenloses Alibi* (adding Mrs. Bedford and Fred Ogden). *Ein lückenloses Alibi* was produced in Berlin in 1968, directed by Hans Schweikart and starring Albert Lieven. Again the theatre programme quotes the English title as *Murder with Love*. Given the eminence of the director and the cast, and the fact that this was less than four years after the Mainz première of *Wettlauf mit der Uhr*, it is very likely that this Berlin production was the première of the re-written *Ein lückenloses Alibi*.

It is worth noting that the character Jack Keller, who is sometimes included in the cast list of this play both in the UK and abroad, is mentioned in the play but does not actually appear on stage.

To summarise, this play clearly originated in the very early 1960s. It was written by Durbridge, in English of course, and the German scripts and theatre programmes show that he used the title *Murder with Love* from the very beginning. He might originally have written it especially for German translation and performance, but it is more likely that he simply failed (or did not attempt) to secure an English stage production in the 1960s as he was not at the time recognised in the UK as a stage dramatist. On the other hand, in Germany the radio and television adaptations of his serials had given him a huge fan-base which could easily have encouraged German producers to give him this opportunity.

Some years later than the German productions, Durbridge made considerable changes to the play (including adding a second murder and removing the characters Hibberd and Fred Ogden) before *Murder with Love* was eventually "premièred" in Windsor in 1976. The English title *Greatly Missed*, which for some reason is quoted in the opening credits of the German television version *Kein Alibi für eine Leiche* (1986), was never used in the UK.

The French television version, *Sang froid* (6 July 1972), was adapted and directed by Abder Isker. The setting is France and the characters are French, but it follows closely the scenes and cast of *Ein lückenloses Alibi*. There is no second murder, which was not introduced until the Windsor play of 1976.

The Polish television version, *Odwet* (16 May 1985), was adapted and directed by Bogdan Augustyniak from a script by Krzysztof Nowicki. It retains the English characters and closely follows the scenes of the 1976 *Murder with Love*, including the second murder.

The German television version, *Kein Alibi für eine Leiche* (19 October 1986), was adapted by Dorothee Dhan from a script by Max Faber and directed by Wolf Dietrich. It retains the English characters and closely follows the scenes of the 1976 *Murder with Love*, with a few additional location scenes. It includes the second murder, but for dramatic effect this happens in different circumstances. As this television version credits a German script by Max Faber, and as it was Marianne de Barde who translated the earlier stage versions, it appears that Faber might possibly have written a new translation of the final Durbridge stage version (Windsor, 1976) of

Murder with Love, which might also have been produced on the stage in Germany.

196. *House Guest*. Samuel French, 1982 [January]. Two-act play, first produced at the Yvonne Arnaud Theatre Guildford from 10 February 1981, the Richmond Theatre from 2 March 1981 and the Rex Theatre Wilmslow from 6 April 1981, and subsequently at the Savoy Theatre London from 29 April 1981 to 27 March 1982. Director: Val May.

The Savoy Theatre cast: Susan Hampshire, Gerald Harper, Philip Stone, Barry Stokes, Richard Gale, Jane Cussons, Sarah Bullen and Barbara Atkinson. In August 1981 Sylvia Syms succeeded Susan Hampshire as the leading lady, followed by Barbara Murray in February 1982; also in February 1982, Gerald Harper was succeeded by Simon Ward and Philip Stone by Clifford Rose.

Plot summary: Actor Robert Drury and his wife Stella learn that their son has been abducted, but not for ransom. They must simply allow the kidnapper to stay in their house for forty-eight hours.

The German stage production was *Der Gast*, translated by Max Faber.

The German television version, *Der Besuch* (18 March 1984), was directed by Jürgen Roland. It was not adapted or edited for television, but simply took Max Faber's stage version and reproduced it scene-by-scene.

197. *Deadly Nightcap*. Samuel French, 1986 [April]. Two-act play, first produced as *Nightcap* at the Yvonne Arnaud Theatre Guildford from 6 July 1983, the Theatre Royal Plymouth from 8 August 1983, the Theatre Royal Bath from 29 August 1983, the Ashcroft Theatre Croydon from

5 September 1983 and the Theatre Royal Nottingham from 19 September 1983. Director: Val May.

Cast: Nyree Dawn Porter, Jack Hedley, Derek Waring, Barbara Murray, Robin Halstead, Christine Russell, Maitland Chandler, Suzanne Church, John Clegg and Jeremy Hawk.

Subsequently produced as *Deadly Nightcap* at the Westminster Theatre London from 19 June to 8 November 1986. Director: Val May.

Cast: Nyree Dawn Porter, Peter Byrne, Dermot Walsh, Elisabeth Scott, Andrew Cuthbert, Mary Bradley, Maitland Chandler, Julie Teal, Geoffrey Lea and Charles Stapley.

Plot summary: Estate agent Jack Radford plots to kill his wife Sarah, by firstly disposing of her brother and convincing everyone that she is mentally unstable. He then plans to fake her suicide, but it appears that Sarah is far from unstable.

The German stage production was *Mord am Pool*, translated by Max Faber. Its script quotes the original title as *Nightcap*, which indicates that the translation was from Durbridge's first version of the play. The initial UK run of *Nightcap* clearly inspired Durbridge to re-write this play very considerably as *Deadly Nightcap*, for which he even changed the identity of the murderer. Comparing *Mord am Pool* with the published edition of *Deadly Nightcap* shows the German version to have many script differences and it retains the original murderer, which is further evidence that it was a translation of *Nightcap* rather than *Deadly Nightcap*.

There was also a later German stage version called *Mord um Mitternacht*, directed by Wolfgang Wahl and starring Karin Baal, Heike Ulrich and Volker Eckstein. As this was produced in March 1987, it might have been a new translation of the 1986 *Deadly Nightcap* rather than the

1983 *Nightcap*, but could equally have been simply *Mord am Pool* with a new title.

The German television version, *Mord am Pool* (11 May 1986), was directed by Gerhard Klingenberg. This took the German stage version by Max Faber and reproduced it scene-by-scene, with some editing – although strangely Faber was not mentioned in the credits. It closely follows the story and scenes of the stage play *Mord am Pool*, including the original murderer as in the 1983 *Nightcap*.

198. *A Touch of Danger*. Samuel French, 1989 [July]. Two-act play, first produced at the Theatre Royal Windsor from 21 July 1987, the Theatre Royal Nottingham from 21 September 1987, the Key Theatre Peterborough from 19 October 1987, the Chichester Festival from 2 November 1987, the Eden Court Theatre Inverness from 10 November 1987, the Devonshire Park Theatre Eastbourne from 16 November 1987, the Thorndike Theatre Leatherhead from 19 January 1988, the Theatre Royal Brighton from 8 February 1988, the Grand Theatre Wolverhampton from 22 February 1988, the Civic Theatre Darlington from 29 February 1988, the Richmond Theatre from 7 March 1988, the Ashcroft Theatre Croydon from 14 March 1988, the Theatre Royal York from 21 March 1988 and the Horsham Arts Centre from 28 March 1988, and subsequently at the Whitehall Theatre London from 12 September 1988 to 4 March 1989. Director: Mark Piper.

The Whitehall Theatre cast: William Franklyn, Virginia Stride, Pauline Yates, Derren Nesbitt, William Lucas, Charles Rea, Max Mason, Cathy Flanagan and Sarah Beeson.

Plot summary: Following reports of author Max Telligan's death in Munich, he reappears in London and finds that the CID, the CIA and a terrorist organisation are all interested in a calculator he has brought back from Germany and the diary he has been preparing for publication.

The German stage production was *In der Nähe des Todes*, translated by Max Faber, and its première in Munich in September 1988 was directed by Theodor Grädler. This was almost certainly translated from the original 1987 Windsor script of *A Touch of Danger* rather than the 1988 Whitehall Theatre London script, as Durbridge introduced various changes for the latter. Further evidence is provided by the fact that the scripts of *In der Nähe des Todes* and the London 1988 *A Touch of Danger* show considerable differences, with the German version including an extra Act 2 Scene 5 and an additional flashback sequence as well as some different dialogue. Similarly the false report of Telligan's death, which opens the 1988 London version, is not included in *In der Nähe des Todes*.

The German typescript quotes the English title as *A Touch of Murder*, which could be a simple transcription error as this play has always been presented in the UK as *A Touch of Danger*. Strangely the German television version *Tagebuch für einen Mörder* quotes yet another English title, *A Touch of Fear*, but this again is incorrect and has never been used in the UK.

The German television version, *Tagebuch für einen Mörder* (4 July 1988), was adapted by Dorothee Dhan and directed by Franz Josef Gottlieb. It credits Max Faber's German script, but compared with *In der Nähe des Todes* it includes various new features that appeared in the 1988 London production of *A Touch of Danger*, such as the report of Telligan's "death", but excludes the extra scene that appeared in *In der Nähe des Todes*. The television *Tagebuch für einen Mörder* also includes various location scenes, extra dialogue, four additional characters and greater physical action, all of which was presumably intended to produce a television thriller rather than simply transferring a one-set play to the screen. As it was transmitted some two months before the revised UK version of *A Touch of Danger* opened in London, it would appear that Max Faber (or more probably Dorothee Dhan) had access to Durbridge's revised playscript, or indeed that Durbridge was himself involved in *Tagebuch für einen Mörder*.

The latter possibility might explain why a play entitled *Murder Diary* was listed in Durbridge's *Who's Who* entry and dated as 1986, in spite of the fact that no Durbridge stage play with this title has ever existed. It might have been his working title that became *A Touch of Danger*, as this prominently features a diary; but it is more likely to relate to Durbridge's involvement in the German television play *Tagebuch für einen Mörder*, the title of which is convincingly explicit.

199. *The Small Hours*. Samuel French, 1992 [January]. Two-act play, first produced at the Thorndike Theatre Leatherhead from 22 January 1991, the King's Theatre Southsea from 18 February 1991, the Theatre Royal Brighton from 25 February 1991, the Liverpool Playhouse from 11 March 1991, the Forum Billingham from 25 March 1991, the Theatre Royal Bath from 15 April 1991, Devonshire Park Theatre Eastbourne from 29 April 1991, the Theatre Royal Windsor from 6 May 1991, the Ashcroft Theatre Croydon from 3 June 1991 and the Key Theatre Peterborough from 24 June 1991. Director: Sebastian Graham-Jones.

Cast: Patrick Mower, Pamela Salem, Carole Mowlem, Douglas Fielding, Norman Eshley, Richard Walker, Neil West and Sallyann Webster.

Plot summary: Carl Houston, a Sussex hotelier, returns from Australia and finds his life threatened when he seeks the connection between a koala bear, a devious chef and an emerald necklace.

The German stage production was *Tief in der Nacht*, translated by Max Faber. Its première in Munich, directed by Siegfried Lowitz, was on 19 September 1992. In 2000 the Faber translation was broadcast in Germany as a radio play, adapted by Caroline Walburg and produced by Christoph Dietrich.

200. *Sweet Revenge*. Samuel French, 1993 [November]. Two-act play, first produced at the Thorndike Theatre Leatherhead from 12 January 1993, the Yvonne Arnaud Theatre Guildford from 1 February 1993, the Swan Theatre High Wycombe from 15 February 1993, the Gordon Craig Theatre Stevenage from 22 February 1993, Devonshire Park Theatre Eastbourne from 1 March 1993, the Grand Opera House Belfast from 8 March 1993, the Key Theatre Peterborough from 15 March 1993, the Crucible Theatre Sheffield from 22 March 1993, the Connaught Theatre Worthing from 12 April 1993, the Churchill Theatre Bromley from 19 April 1993, the New Theatre Hull from 3 May 1993, the Playhouse Harlow from 10 May 1993 and the Palace Theatre Manchester from 31 May 1993. Director: Val May.

Cast: Richard Todd, Meg Davies, Abigail Thaw, Ben Robertson, Lesley North, Peter Cartwright, David Baron, Hayward Morse, Christopher Birch and Jo McLaren-Clark.

Plot summary: Ross Marquand, a prominent cardiac consultant, is suspected of the murder of his wife's lover –

but several others have strong motives, making this play a genuine whodunit.

Sweet Revenge has a very long history, and is a perfect example of Durbridge's penchant for re-cycling his plots. Although it is usually considered to be an original Durbridge play that premièred in Leatherhead in 1993, it can actually be traced back to the 1940s.

A radio play by Durbridge called *Preludio al delitto*, translated by Paola Ferroni and produced by Umberto Benedetto, was broadcast in Italy on 21 November 1960. This was clearly based on Durbridge's much earlier UK radio play *The Caspary Affair*, broadcast on 11 July 1946, which had different character names but a similar plot (see **153**).

Preludio al delitto was eventually to become the stage play *Sweet Revenge*, with very similar character names, but next in line chronologically was a longer version written for the stage which was translated into German by Max Faber in 1988 as *Zaradin 4*. A production in September 1990 in Munich, directed by Günter Penzoldt, might have been the première – but as it was a touring production by Berliner Tournee-Theater Kühnen, this might equally have been just one of the tour venues. Faber's translation must have been made from Durbridge's first English stage version, which at that time had not been performed in the UK, and which was presumably entitled either *Zaradin 4* or *Sweet Revenge* (no English title is mentioned in the German script credits). The eight characters in *Zaradin 4*, with some slight name changes, correspond exactly with the eight characters in *Preludio al delitto*.

Durbridge then revised this play considerably before it became *Sweet Revenge* and had its 1993 "première" in Leatherhead, as can be seen when comparing the published script of *Sweet Revenge* with Faber's German typescript of *Zaradin 4*. The same cast of characters was retained, again with some slight name changes, but Durbridge added two new principal parts – Dr. Sam Kennedy and Chief Insp. Norman Sanders. This involved substantial re-writing and expansion, transforming the six scenes of *Zaradin 4* into the nine scenes of *Sweet Revenge*. When working on *Sweet Revenge*, Durbridge changed the name of the fatal drug from Zaradin 4 to Zarabell Four and introduced an entirely different murderer. In fact *Sweet Revenge* became virtually a new play using the earlier central idea.

In Germany in 1993, Max Faber translated *Sweet Revenge* under the title *Stich ins Herz*, although it is unclear if this was a new German adaptation or simply a revival of Faber's *Zaradin 4* with a new title. The latter is more likely, given the fact that *Stich ins Herz* had only seven characters whereas *Sweet Revenge* had ten.

201. *Fatal Encounter*. Samuel French, 2002. Two-act play, written in the mid-1990s, but published posthumously with no indication that it had ever been produced professionally.

It reached the professional stage in a 2005 production directed by Bruce James, which toured to towns including Weston-super-Mare, Lowestoft and Chesterfield.

Cast: Benjamin Roddy, Kate Burrell, Jane Shakespeare, Neill Bull, Patrick Bird, Aaron Bixley, Jacqueline Roberts and Quinn Patrick.

Slightly later in 2005, a tour directed by Hugo Myatt for Charles Vance Productions included theatres in Stoke-on-Trent and Wolverhampton.

Cast: Owen Oldroyd, Louise Faulkner, Jan Hirst, Robert Armes, Hugo Myatt, Nick Barclay, Leann Young and Edward Handoll.

A particularly extensive tour in 2009/10 directed by Ian Dickens included theatres in Guildford, Windsor, Stevenage, Buxton, Eastbourne, Basingstoke, Colchester, Worthing, Crewe, Darlington, Tunbridge Wells, Plymouth and Cheltenham.

Cast: Michael Howe, Susan Skipper, Anita Harris, Neil Stacy, Nicholas Ball, Aaron Bixley, Miranda Magee and Michael Kirk.

It can therefore be seen that *Fatal Encounter*, though not produced professionally in Durbridge's lifetime, later became a regular fixture in repertory seasons outside London.

Plot summary: Publisher Howard Mansfield is suspicious of his wife's movements, and in particular her stories that she was attacked by a dog and later mugged. Events take a more sinister turn when he finds that she has shot a man known to them both, allegedly in self-defence, but there is a second attempted murder before the complications of a major blackmail plot are unravelled.

The German stage production was *Begegnung mit Folgen*, translated by Max Faber.

To conclude this section, an important footnote must be added regarding the origin of Francis Durbridge's stage plays, given that a German theatre programme for an early 1970s performance of *Plötzlich und unerwartet* (*Suddenly at Home*) contains an article that refers to *Wettlauf mit der Uhr* and *Ein lückenloses Alibi* (the two German titles for *Murder with Love*). It follows that these plays must have been staged in Germany before *Plötzlich und unerwartet*, and indeed it is now firmly established that this was as early as 1964.

This leads to a very significant conclusion, because apart from the one-off 1943 Birmingham production of *Send for Paul Temple* there were no Durbridge plays staged in the UK before *Suddenly at Home* in 1971 (which has usually been described as his first stage play). However, as *Murder with Love* was written for translation and production in Germany in the early 1960s, it is indisputable that Durbridge's successful theatrical career actually began in Germany. This is also confirmed by the fact that a German newspaper (*Dürener Zeitung*, 17 January 1962) reported that Durbridge was then working on his first stage play – presumably the play that was not produced in the UK at that time, but was first translated into German as *Wettlauf mit der Uhr / Ein Lückenloses Alibi*. Indeed this is further verified by the fact that Durbridge's cash ledger, in an entry dated 16 February 1963, recorded the receipt of £617 for the rights of a play that even at that early stage he called *Murder with Love*.

CINEMA FILMS

As an introduction to this section it is worth mentioning the Birmingham-born actor John Bentley (1916–2009), who was the leading man in three of the four Paul Temple films. The producer Ernest G. Roy cast Bentley in *Calling Paul Temple* (1948), having been impressed by his performance in *The Hills of Donegal* (1947) which had given him his first leading film role. This launched Bentley into a career in many "B-movies" of decent quality including those featuring John Creasey's character The Toff, and later he appeared on television in the series *African Patrol* and the daily "soap opera" *Crossroads*. He had, however, been associated with Durbridge from a much earlier era, when after successfully auditioning as a teenager for BBC Midland Region producer Martyn C. Webster he became a leading player on the regional airwaves. As an actor and singer he was a regular broadcaster in the 1930s and 1940s, and his name appears frequently in the foregoing listing of Durbridge's radio programmes.

There are several oddities in respect of Durbridge's contributions to the cinema. In particular the 1956 British film *Town on Trial*, while it certainly exists, does not have any proven Durbridge connection and is covered in the note below (**210**). Then there is one that might be described as "the film that never was", as revealed by the columnist and Durbridge fan "Collie Knox" in the *Daily Mail* on 8 August 1953: "Francis Durbridge is livid over the announcement that he has written a Temple film for the Nettlefold Studios called *The Notting Hill Case*, based on the Christie murders." Durbridge was quoted as saying: "Nothing would induce me to write a story with such a title or on so unsavoury a case. I am most upset." This was highly sensitive at the time, because J.R.H. Christie's conviction for the murders of several women was then very recent and he was hanged less than a month before the *Daily Mail* item appeared. While a digression, it is worth noting that the passage of time eventually freed writer Clive Exton and director Richard Fleischer to produce the film *Ten Rillington Place* in 1971 with Richard Attenborough as Christie.

The Austrian film *Tim Frazer jagt den geheimnisvollen Mister X* ("Tim Frazer Chasing the Mysterious Mister X"), made by Melba Film Wien in 1964, was also released in Belgium as *Tim Frazer à la poursuite du mystérieux Monsieur X*, in Italy as *Tim Frazer caccia il misterioso Mister X* and in the USA as *Case 33: Antwerp*. It was directed by Ernst Hofbauer, who also wrote the screenplay from a story by Anton van Casteren; and although Durbridge was credited on the film's poster and trailer as the creator of Tim Frazer he received no acknowledgement on the film itself. Indeed Durbridge had no direct involvement in this tale of Tim Frazer pursuing drug smugglers and a knife murderer in Antwerp, which was a blatant attempt to ride on the bandwagon of the two genuine Durbridge television serials produced in Germany as *Tim Frazer* (1963) and *Tim Frazer – Der Fall Salinger* (1964) while emulating the style of the famous German Edgar Wallace thrillers of that time.

It was a similar situation with the 1963 German film *Piccadilly null Uhr zwölf*, which exploited Durbridge's name at a time when he was enormously popular following successful foreign versions of his television serial *The Scarf*. In this case, however, he was fully credited and the film is therefore discussed below (**212**).

Durbridge made two other contributions to cinema history that are not generally known, and they are indeed surprising. Both are proven rather than rumoured or apocryphal, as they are mentioned in his financial records. The first of these, which was amazing rather than simply surprising, is the major part he played in finalising the screenplay of the 1961 film comedy *Raising the Wind* that showed music college students in what can only be described as "Carry On" mode. The film's credited writer and musical director was Bruce Montgomery (who composed many film themes and also wrote detective novels as Edmund Crispin), but it is likely that Durbridge was asked to refine it by producer Peter Rogers and director Gerald Thomas because they had already been impressed with his work on their earlier film *The Vicious Circle* (**211**). Durbridge was never credited for *Raising the Wind*, and one can only speculate that this was at his own insistence because it deviated markedly from the genre with which he was primarily associated and would have done little for his reputation.

A further aspect of Durbridge's unknown film career is in direct contrast. While he might have been reluctant to be revealed as a writer of *Raising the Wind*, he would surely have been proud of the fact that the internationally acclaimed film producer Dino De Laurentiis recognised his skills and commissioned him to write a major movie. In 1962 Durbridge wrote a treatment of over one hundred pages for *Zakary*, an enthralling story of espionage and personal relationships with a Japanese setting spanning the years from 1910 to just after the 1941 attack on Pearl

Harbor. If this film had been made, it might have become a blockbuster capable of enhancing Durbridge's name as far more than a writer of mystery thrillers – but regrettably, as with countless film treatments over the years, it never saw the light of day.

Durbridge films have been shown with sub-titles or dubbed in numerous countries including Russia, so the following mentions of film titles in foreign languages are far from comprehensive.

202. *Send for Paul Temple*. Butchers/Nettlefold, 1946. Based on his 1938 radio serial (**112**). Screenplay: John Argyle and Durbridge. Producer/Director: John Argyle. Original music by Sidney Torch.
Cast: Anthony Hulme as Temple, Joy Shelton as Steve and Jack Raine as Sir Graham Forbes, with Tamara Desni, Beatrice Varley, Hylton Allen, Maire O'Neill, Michael Golden, Richard Shayne, Edward V. Robson, Phil Ray, Leslie Weston, Olive Sloane, H. Victor Weske, Norman Pierce, Melville Crawford and Charles Wade.
Plot summary: See **112**.
DVD, Renown Pictures, 2009. Also included in the DVD set marketed as *The Paul Temple Collection Limited Edition*, Renown Pictures, 2011. Also available as one DVD containing the English and German (dubbed) versions - *Der Grüne Finger*, Pidax, 2015.
See also his 1943 stage play (**191**).
The film *Send for Paul Temple* was released in the USA as *Mystery of the Green Finger* and *The Green Finger*; in Germany as *Der Grüne Finger*; in Austria as *Die Todesfalle*; in France as *L'Auberge des tueurs*; and in Denmark as *Den grønne finger*.

203. *Calling Paul Temple*. Butchers/Nettlefold, 1948. Based on his 1945 radio serial *Send for Paul Temple Again* (**151**). Screenplay: A.R. Rawlinson, Durbridge and Kathleen Butler. Producer: Ernest G. Roy. Director: Maclean Rogers. Original music by Percival Mackey and Steve Race.
Cast: John Bentley as Temple, Dinah Sheridan as Steve and Jack Raine as Sir Graham Forbes, with Margaretta Scott, Abraham Sofaer, Celia Lipton, Alan Wheatley, Hugh Pryse, John McLaren, Michael Golden, Ian MacLean, Shaym Bahadur, Merle Tottenham, Mary Midwinter, Wally Patch, Aubrey Mallalieu, Hugh Miller, Maureen Glynne, Paul Sheridan, George Merritt, Harry Herbert, Gerald Rex, Marion Taylor, Steve Race and Michael Ward.
Plot summary: See **151**.
DVD, Renown Pictures, 2009. Also included in the DVD set marketed as *The Paul Temple Collection Limited Edition*, Renown Pictures, 2011. Also available as one DVD containing the English and German (dubbed) versions – *Wer ist Rex?*, Pidax, 2015.
The film *Calling Paul Temple* was originally to be called *Paul Temple and the Canterbury Case*, then *Paul Temple – 999*, before the final title was decided. It was released in Germany and Austria as *Wer ist Rex?* and in Sweden as *Kvinnan i grått*.

204. *Paul Temple's Triumph*. Butchers/Nettlefold, 1950. Based on his 1939 radio serial *News of Paul Temple* (**123**). Screenplay: A.R. Rawlinson. Producer: Ernest G. Roy. Director: Maclean Rogers. Original music by Stanley Black.
Cast: John Bentley as Temple, Dinah Sheridan as Steve and Jack Livesey as Sir Graham Forbes, with Beatrice Varley, Barbara Couper, Hugh Dempster, Dino Galvani, Ivan Sampson, Jenny Mathot, Bruce Seton, Andrew Leigh,

Leo de Pokorny, Michael Brennan, Joseph O'Conor, Shaym Bahadur, Gerald Rex, Ben Williams, Anne Hayes, Peter Butterworth, Hamilton Keene, Frederick Morant, Jean Parker, Denis Val Norton and Michael Hogarth.

Plot summary: See **123**.

DVD, Renown Pictures, 2011. Also included in the DVD set marketed as *The Paul Temple Collection Limited Edition*, Renown Pictures, 2011. Also available as one DVD containing the English and German (dubbed) versions – *Jagd auf Z*, Pidax, 2015.

The film *Paul Temple's Triumph* was released in Germany and Austria as *Jagd auf Z* and in Sweden as *Paul Temple och gäckande Z*.

205. *Paul Temple Returns*. Butchers/Nettlefold, 1952. Based on his 1942 radio serial *Paul Temple Intervenes* (**142**). Screenplay: Durbridge. Producer: Ernest G. Roy. Director: Maclean Rogers. Original music by Wilfred Burns.

Cast: John Bentley as Temple, Patricia Dainton as Steve and Peter Gawthorne as Sir Graham Forbes, with Grey Blake, Valentine Dyall, Robert Urquhart, Christopher Lee, Dan Jackson, Ronald Leigh Hunt, Arthur Hill, Andrea Malandrinos, George Patterson, Ben Williams, Gerald Rex, Elizabeth Gilbert, Vi Kaley, Michael Mulcaster, Sylvia Pugh, Dennis Holmes and Margaret Samuel.

Plot summary: See **142**.

DVD as *Bombay Waterfront*, Renown Pictures, 2009. Also included in the DVD set marketed as *The Paul Temple Collection Limited Edition*, Renown Pictures, 2011. Also available as one DVD containing the English and German (dubbed) versions – *Paul Temple und der Fall Marquis*, Pidax, 2015.

The film *Paul Temple Returns* was released in the USA as *Bombay Waterfront* (Bombay being a London dock wharf, not a change of scene to India!) and in Sweden as *Paul Temple i dödsfara*.

206. *The Broken Horseshoe.* Butchers/Nettlefold, 1953. Based on his 1952 television serial (**173**). Screenplay: A.R. Rawlinson. Producer: Ernest G. Roy. Director: Martyn C. Webster. Original music by Wilfred Burns.
Cast: Robert Beatty, Elizabeth Sellars, Peter Coke, Hugh Kelly, Vida Hope, Janet Butler, Ferdy Mayne, James Raglan, Hugh Pryse, George Benson, Roger Delgado, Frank Atkinson, Ronald Leigh-Hunt, Toke Townley, Jean Hardwicke, Robert Raglan and Marc Sheldon.
Plot summary: See **173**.
DVD, Renown Pictures, 2011.
Peter Coke, who played Insp. Bellamy in this film, assumed the mantle of Paul Temple on radio in the following year. The film *The Broken Horseshoe* was released in Finland as *Huumausaineliiga*.

207. *Operation Diplomat.* Butchers/Nettlefold, 1953. Based on his 1952 television serial (**174**). Screenplay: A.R. Rawlinson and John Guillermin. Producer: Ernest G. Roy. Director: John Guillermin. Original music by Wilfred Burns.
Cast: Guy Rolfe, Lisa Daniely, Patricia Dainton, Sydney Tafler, Ballard Berkeley, Anton Diffring, Michael Golden, James Raglan, Avice Landone, Brian Worth, Eric Berry, Edward Dain, Alexis Chesnakov, Ann Bennett, Jean Hardwicke and Derek Aylward.
Plot summary: See **174**.
DVD, Renown Pictures, 2011. This also includes the 1964 non-Durbridge crime film *The Sicilians*.

208. *The Teckman Mystery*. Corona/British Lion, 1954. Based on his 1953/54 television serial *The Teckman Biography* (**175**). Screenplay: Durbridge and James Matthews. Producer: Josef Somlo. Director: Wendy Toye. Musical Director: Muir Mathieson. Theme music: "The Shadow Waltz" by Clive Richardson and Sam Heppner as "Paul Dubois". Original music by Clifton Parker.

Cast: Margaret Leighton, John Justin, Roland Culver, Michael Medwin, Duncan Lamont, Raymond Huntley, Meier Tzelniker, George Coulouris, Jane Wenham, Harry Locke, Frances Rowe, Warwick Ashton, Barbara Murray, Irene Lister, Andrea Malandrinos, Gwen Nelson, Mary Grant, Dan Cressey, Peter Taylor, Ben Williams, Frank Webster, Peter Augustine, Maurice Lane, Mollie Palmer, Bruce Beeby and Gordon Morrison.

Plot summary: See **175**.

DVD, Studiocanal/Network, 2016.

The film *The Teckman Mystery* was released in Denmark as *Den farlige mand* and in Sweden as *Hemligheten F-109*. It was shown on German television on 16 August 1960 as *Der Fall Teckmann*.

209. *Portrait of Alison*. Insignia/Anglo Amalgamated, 1955. Based on his 1955 television serial (**176**). Screenplay: Ken Hughes and Guy Green. Producer: Frank Godwin. Director: Guy Green. Musical Director: Philip Martell. Original music by John Veale.

Cast: Robert Beatty, Terry Moore, William Sylvester, Geoffrey Keen, Josephine Griffin, Allan Cuthbertson, Henry Oscar, William Lucas, Terence Alexander, Stuart Saunders, Bruno Barnabe, Raymond Francis, Marianne Stone, Sam Kydd, Jack McNaughton, Neil Wilson, Andreas Malandrinos, Robert Raglan, Jack Howarth, Frank Thornton, Eric Corrie, Hal Osmond and Reginald Hearne.

Plot summary: See **176**.
DVD as *Postmark for Danger*, RoDon Enterprises (US), 2006. DVD as *Portrait of Alison*, Studiocanal/Network, 2014.
The film *Portrait of Alison* was released in the USA as *Postmark for Danger*, in Italy as *Il segno del pericolo*, in Denmark as *Farlig post*, in Finland as *Kuolema saapuu postitse* and in Brazil as *Carta a um Assassinato*.

210. *Town on Trial*. Marksman/Columbia, 1956. Screenplay: Robert Westerby and Ken Hughes. Producer: Maxwell Setton. Director: John Guillermin. Original music by Tristram Cary and Paul Broussé.
Cast: John Mills, Charles Coburn, Barbara Bates, Derek Farr, Alec McCowen, Fay Compton, Geoffrey Keen, Elizabeth Seal, Margaretta Scott, Meredith Edwards, Harry Locke, Raymond Huntley, Harry Fowler, Maureen Connell, Magda Miller, Newton Blick, Oscar Quitak, Totti Truman Taylor, Grace Arnold, Dandy Nichols, John Warwick, Frank Sieman, Vivienne Martin, Hal Osmond and the Blake Twins.
Plot summary: When a good-time girl is found strangled at an élite sports club, Det. Supt. Mike Halloran is faced with a wall of silence and a formidable list of suspects in London suburbia.
It is arguable that *Town on Trial* should not have been listed in this book, as it is a false entry in Durbridge's filmography. It is included here simply because of the sheer volume of assertions on websites and in newspaper/magazine film listings that it was based on his novel *The Nylon Murders*, which was published as a *Sunday Dispatch* serial in 1952/53 (**9**). This is totally incorrect, as not only does Durbridge's name receive no mention on the credits of *Town on Trial* but also his novel

The Nylon Murders has a plot and characters that bear little resemblance to this film. Having established that, it has to be said that the film admittedly has a sort of Durbridge atmosphere about it and its long-mistaken attribution to Durbridge has probably enhanced its reputation.

211. *The Vicious Circle*. Romulus / Beaconsfield / Independent Film Distributors, 1957. Based on his 1956 television serial *My Friend Charles* (**177**). Screenplay: Durbridge. Producer: Peter Rogers. Director: Gerald Thomas. Original music by Stanley Black.
Cast: John Mills, Derek Farr, Noelle Middleton, Wilfrid Hyde White, Roland Culver, Mervyn Johns, Rene Ray, Lionel Jeffries, Lisa Daniely, David Williams, Diana Lambert, Hal Osmond, Gillian Moran and John Gordon.
Plot summary: See **177**.
Included in the DVD set marketed as *The John Mills Centenary Collection II*, ITV DVD, 2008. Also available as one DVD containing the English and German (dubbed) versions - *Interpol ruft Berlin*, Pidax, 2014.
There are assertions in reference books and on websites that this film was based on a Durbridge television serial called *The Brass Candlestick*, but there is no evidence that he ever used this title in the UK. A brass candlestick as a murder weapon and a motif is central to his television serial *My Friend Charles*, and the film closely follows the characters and plot of that serial. While the film credits Durbridge it fails to name the original television serial. Nevertheless *Variety* reported (30 January 1957) that "last Monday Peter Rogers started filming a screen version of Francis Durbridge's thriller *My Friend Charles* with John Mills." It is also confirmed in production notes

on the 2008 DVD that this film was based on *My Friend Charles*.

The film *The Vicious Circle* was released in the USA as *The Circle*, in Germany as *Interpol ruft Berlin*, in France as *Scotland Yard joue et gagne*, in Italy as *Il cerchio rosso del delitto*, in Spain as *El Circulo Vicioso*, in Portugal as *O Circulo Vicioso*, in Denmark as *Mistaenkt*, in Sweden as *Scotland Yard spelar och vinner*, in Finland as *Näkymätön murhaaja*, in Greece as *I symmoria tou kokkinou kyklou* and in Brazil as *Ardil Diabólico*. Somewhat ironically, however, it was indeed released in some Spanish-speaking countries including Argentina as *El Candelabro de bronce* – which translates as *The Brass Candlestick*!

212. *Piccadilly null Uhr zwölf* (*Piccadilly Zero Hour Twelve*). Divina-Film, 1963. Screenplay: Rudolf Zehetgruber. Producers: Ilse Kubaschewski and Eberhard Meichsner. Director: Rudolf Zehetgruber. Original music by Russell Garcia.

Cast: Helmut Wildt, Hanns Lothar, Ann Smyrner, Klaus Kinski, Pinkas Braun, Karl Lieffen, Ilja Richter, Marlene Warrlich, Camilla Spira, Rudolf Fernau, Stanislav Ledinek, Dieter Eppler, Franz Liefka, Conny Rux, Kurt Zips, Albert Bessler, Herbert Grünbaum, Toni Herbert, Erik Radolf, Artur Schilsky, Peter Hippler and Erhart Stettner.

This German film is stated on several websites (including the usually reliable IMDb) to have been adapted from a Durbridge story called *Twelve Past Twelve*, but there is no trace of anything by Durbridge with this title. The film plot concerns a man released from prison who seeks revenge on those who put him there, but a curiosity is that Ilja Richter appears as "der junge Edgar Wallace". According to Michael R. Pitts in *Famous Movie Detectives III* (Scarecrow Press, 2004) this young Edgar Wallace helps to solve the murders, but this is incorrect as the character only appears in two short scenes. In fact his inclusion and the use of Durbridge's name was, as in the case of the 1964 Austrian film *Tim Frazer jagt den geheimnisvollen Mister X* mentioned above, a ride on the twin bandwagons of Durbridge's enormous popularity in Germany and the cult series of over thirty Edgar Wallace thrillers produced by Rialto Film GmbH at that time. Nevertheless Durbridge's name appeared on the film credits and posters, so it is more than likely that he was persuaded to write *Twelve Past Twelve* as a "treatment" for the film-makers but that it was never published; and the resulting film was something for which, not surprisingly, Durbridge never claimed authorship.

The film *Piccadilly null Uhr zwölf* was released in France as *Piccadilly minuit douze*, in Italy as *Piccadilly ore X missione segreta* and in Greece as *Piccadilly ora miden*.

Finally, and probably just a coincidence, the central character of the film (Mike Hilton) has the same name as the central character in Durbridge's book *The Pig-Tail Murder* (**26**) – but this original novel was not published until 1969, and there is no similarity of plot.

THE PAUL TEMPLE COMIC STRIP

The late 1940s saw the radio exploits of Paul Temple attracting many thousands of listeners, so it is not surprising that Temple was adopted by the London *Evening News* for a new comic strip to be published on six days each week. The first of these appeared on 11 December 1950, and the series was clearly successful as it ran until 1 May 1971. Other newspapers also published the strip, including the *Lancashire Evening Post*, the Hull *Daily Mail*, the *Derby Evening Telegraph*, the *Gloucester Citizen* and the *Lincolnshire Echo*.

From Durbridge's financial records it is clear that in April 1949 he was commissioned to produce this strip for the *Daily Mail*, but at that time the *Daily Mail* already had its long-running strips *Rip Kirby* by Alex Holland and *Rufus* by Trog. Given that a daily newspaper strip must require the author and artist to build up a backlog of instalments before publication, there would have been an accumulation of the Paul Temple strips originally intended for the *Daily Mail* before they eventually launched on 11 December 1950 in the same newspaper group's *Evening News*. This was preceded by widespread announcements that Temple was about to appear in strip form for the very first time, with a publicity campaign featuring newspaper advertisements throughout the south of England and placards on the vast fleet of *Evening News* delivery vans.

It was therefore a very big deal, and it paid off for well over twenty years. Nevertheless it is likely, after the strip had been running for a while and its longevity was assured, that Durbridge left the actual writing to others although he would have retained overall control. Indeed the very fact that the character Paul Temple was his undisputed creation fully justified the newspaper byline "by Francis Durbridge" that appeared throughout the entire life of the strip.

In the complete list below, the break in publication of *Paul Temple and the Dubious Jurors* arose from industrial action by the Society of Lithographic Artists, Designers, Engravers and Process Workers, which affected various newspapers in 1968. The only other breaks were for Sundays and Bank Holidays, when the *Evening News* was not published.

For the first few years, apart from the running title "Paul Temple by Francis Durbridge", most of the strips had no titles given to the individual stories - so appropriate titles in parentheses have been invented below in order to identify and separate them, whereas actual published titles are italicised. The instalments of the first four stories were numbered continuously from 1 to 337, after which each story bore its own inclusive numbering.

The first artist was Alfred Sindall, who also illustrated the three Paul Temple stories that appeared in the early 1950s in the *Daily Mail Annual for Boys and Girls*. The first two strips, called here [The Drake Affair] and [The Frazer Case], were signed by Sindall - which takes us only to 4 July 1951. After this there was a long period in which the identification of the artists becomes a problem, because the newspaper did not acknowledge the artists and no artists' signatures appeared on the strips. In fact the next signed strip was not until 29 August 1958, confirming *Paul Temple and the Limping Baronet* and all the subsequent strips to be by John McNamara. It is generally believed, however, that Sindall continued for some time after his signature disappeared, that McNamara was the artist for a long period before he started signing, and that there were other artists in between.

There has been no agreement on this question among aficionados of the comic strip. Some suggest that Sindall continued until 1954, and as it can be established that from 1 November 1954 he drew the *Tug Transom* strip for the *Daily Sketch* it can reasonably be assumed that his tenure as the Paul Temple artist ended before then. Others claim that in 1954 Sindall was succeeded by Bill Bailey and then fairly rapidly by John McNamara, or indeed that after Bailey and before McNamara there was a period during which Philip Mendoza was the artist.

This question is not easily resolved by simply examining the strips themselves, as all the artists adopted a similar style for the sake of series conformity rather than clearly exhibiting their own individual styles. Most recently, however, members of the Newspaper Strip Collectors Club have put considerable work into trying to identify the dates of the various Paul Temple artists, and their conclusion is that Sindall dates from the outset to 12 January 1952, Bailey from 14 January 1952 to 14 October 1954, Mendoza from 15 October 1954 to 27 August 1956, and McNamara from 28 August 1956 to the end of the series.

Conflicting views about the Paul Temple artists will doubtless continue to appear on the Internet, however, so the following list only confirms the artist with certainty if a strip was signed and states the possibilities in all other cases.

Interestingly John McNamara, from *Paul Temple and the Groomgate Killer* on 23 January 1970, began to depict Temple and Steve as likenesses of Francis Matthews and Ros Drinkwater, the actors who were then appearing in the Anglo-German television films.

<u>11 December 1950 – 4 July 1951. Signed by Alfred Sindall.</u>
[The Drake Affair]. 80 parts (1-80). 11 December 1950 – 15 March 1951.
[The Frazer Case]. 94 parts (81-174). 16 March – 4 July 1951.

<u>5 July 1951 – 12 January 1952. Unsigned, but generally agreed to be by Alfred Sindall.</u>
[The Milroy Diamond Affair]. 94 parts (175-268). 5 July – 22 October 1951.
[The Circus Mystery]. 69 parts (269-337). 23 October 1951 – 12 January 1952.

<u>14 January 1952 – 14 October 1954. Unsigned, but either by Alfred Sindall or Bill Bailey.</u>
The Mystery of Lord Marthing's Folly. 51 parts. 14 January – 13 March 1952.
[The Larry Fry Boxing Mystery]. 46 parts. 14 March – 7 May 1952.
[The TV Hamlet Mystery]. 51 parts. 8 May – 5 July 1952.
[The Luvonian Espionage Plot]. 48 parts. 7 July – 30 August 1952.
[The Dartmoor Enterprises Affair]. 37 parts. 1 September – 13 October 1952.

[The General Julius Affair]. 45 parts. 14 October – 4 December 1952.

[The Chloe Durnley Kidnapping]. 57 parts. 5 December 1952 – 10 February 1953.

[The Hudson Test Pilot Mystery]. 39 parts. 11 February – 27 March 1953.

[The Richworth Diamonds Case]. 43 parts. 28 March – 18 May 1953.

[The "Morocco" Mount Affair]. 51 parts. 19 May – 16 July 1953.

[The "Lardy" Dahl Case]. 40 parts. 17 July – 1 September 1953.

[The Francek Gun Affair]. 52 parts. 2 September – 31 October 1953.

The Debroy Pearls Affair. 55 parts. 2 November 1953 – 6 January 1954.

[Paul Temple and the Rival Gangs]. 53 parts. 7 January – 9 March 1954.

[The Cain Affair]. 94 parts. 10 March – 28 June 1954.

[The Fernand Launoy Case]. 43 parts. 29 June – 17 August 1954.

[The Chaverton Chalice]. 50 parts. 18 August – 14 October 1954.

<u>15 October 1954 – 27 August 1956. Unsigned, but either by Philip Mendoza or John McNamara.</u>

Lader's Diamonds. 60 parts. 15 October – 22 December 1954.

The Varsity Rag Affair. 60 parts. 23 December 1954 – 4 March 1955.

Paul Temple and the Little White Spot. 59 parts. 5 March – 13 May 1955.

Paul Temple and the Sanluzar Affair. 53 parts. 14 May – 14 July 1955.

Paul Temple and the Invisible Crook. 63 parts. 15 July – 26 September 1955.
Paul Temple and the Muravian Assassins. 54 parts. 27 September – 28 November 1955.
Paul Temple and the Secret of Marlesse Castle. 61 parts. 29 November 1955 – 9 February 1956.
The Case of the Silent Witness. 56 parts. 10 February - 16 April 1956.
Paul Temple and Project 'M'. 60 parts. 17 April – 25 June 1956.
Paul Temple and Miss Truelove's Obsession. 54 parts. 26 June – 27 August 1956.

<u>28 August 1956 – 28 August 1958. Unsigned, but generally agreed to be by John McNamara.</u>
The Marsh Curlew Affair. 71 parts. 28 August – 17 November 1956.
The Missing Twin. 80 parts. 19 November 1956 – 21 February 1957.
Operation Shrike. 74 parts. 22 February – 20 May 1957.
Double Event. 62 parts. 21 May – 31 July 1957.
Paul Temple and 'The Magpie'. 64 parts. 1 August – 14 October 1957.
The Phantom Fireman. 60 parts. 15 October – 23 December 1957.
The Safari Mystery. 63 parts. 24 December 1957 - 8 March 1958.
Paul Temple and the Blackmailed Bridegroom. 72 parts. 10 March – 2 June 1958.
The Nerve-Gas Gang. 75 parts. 3 June – 28 August 1958.

<u>29 August 1958 – 1 May 1971. Signed by John McNamara.</u>
Paul Temple and the Limping Baronet. 60 parts. 29 August – 6 November 1958.

The Q.40 Mystery. 60 parts. 7 November 1958 – 17 January 1959.

The Big Lift. 62 parts. 19 January – 1 April 1959.

The Gun Runners. 66 parts. 2 April – 17 June 1959.

The Cordwell Affair. 55 parts. 18 June – 20 August 1959.

The Element X Affair. 68 parts. 21 August – 7 November 1959.

Paul Temple and the Stanyeate Mask. 70 parts. 9 November 1959 – 30 January 1960.

Paul Temple and the Penruan Murder. 82 parts. 1 February – 6 May 1960.

Paul Temple and the April Smith Mystery. 54 parts. 7 May – 8 July 1960.

Paul Temple and the Assassins. 66 parts. 9 July – 23 September 1960.

Paul Temple and the Counter Offensive. 102 parts. 24 September 1960 – 23 January 1961.

Death in the Outback. 63 parts. 24 January – 7 April 1961.

Paul Temple and the Sheikh's Heir. 83 parts. 8 April – 13 July 1961.

Paul Temple and the King of Diamonds. 67 parts. 14 July – 29 September 1961.

Paul Temple and the "Close-Up" Affair. 67 parts. 30 September – 16 December 1961.

Paul Temple and the Deadly Cargo. 76 parts. 18 December 1961 – 17 March 1962.

Paul Temple and the Nemesis Group. 62 parts. 19 March – 30 May 1962.

Paul Temple and the Ulderman Assignment. 61 parts. 31 May – 9 August 1962.

Paul Temple and the Studio Murder. 90 parts. 10 August – 22 November 1962.

Paul Temple and the Ann Peters Case. 55 parts. 23 November 1962 – 28 January 1963.

Paul Temple and the Fortescue Diaries. 86 parts. 29 January – 9 May 1963.

Paul Temple and the A4 Murder. 64 parts. 10 May – 23 July 1963.

Paul Temple and the Missing Twin. 60 parts. 24 July – 1 October 1963.

Paul Temple and the Thalia Affair. 65 parts. 2 October – 16 December 1963.

Paul Temple and the Nevastrian Bombers. 80 parts. 17 December 1963 – 20 March 1964.

Paul Temple and the Red Peppers. 84 parts. 21 March – 27 June 1964.

Paul Temple and the Dancing Dolphin Affair. 76 parts. 29 June – 24 September 1964.

Paul Temple and the Pep-Pill Mystery. 70 parts. 25 September – 15 December 1964.

Paul Temple and the TRX4 Affair. 64 parts. 16 December 1964 – 2 March 1965.

Paul Temple and the Affair of the Tired Tiger. 77 parts. 3 March – 1 June 1965.

Paul Temple and the Great Jewel Robbery. 71 parts. 2 June – 23 August 1965.

Paul Temple and the Au Pair Affair. 86 parts. 24 August – 1 December 1965.

Paul Temple and Project Deep Plunge. 106 parts. 2 December 1965 – 6 April 1966.

Paul Temple and the Khanwada Conspiracy. 84 parts. 7 April – 14 July 1966.

Paul Temple and the Barracombe Boxes. 111 parts. 15 July – 21 November 1966.

Paul Temple and the Erasers. 88 parts. 22 November 1966 – 6 March 1967.

Paul Temple and the Disappearing Destros. 79 parts. 7 March – 7 June 1967.

Paul Temple and the Cabloni Affair. 80 parts. 8 June – 8 September 1967.

Paul Temple and the Circle of Hecate. 64 parts. 9 September – 22 November 1967.

Paul Temple and the Fakers. 83 parts. 23 November 1967 – 29 February 1968.

Paul Temple in Always on a Thursday. 74 parts. 1 March – 28 May 1968.

Paul Temple and the Dubious Jurors. 74 parts. 29 May – 2 August 1968 and 11 September – 30 September 1968.

Paul Temple and the Manhunters of Mahlheim. 83 parts. 1 October 1968 – 7 January 1969.

Paul Temple and the Brain Twisters. 63 parts. 8 January – 21 March 1969.

Paul Temple in Order to View. 61 parts. 22 March – 3 June 1969.

Paul Temple in Death Sitting Down. 72 parts. 4 June – 26 August 1969.

Paul Temple and the Valbury Vandals. 55 parts. 27 August – 29 October 1969.

Paul Temple and the Runaway Knight. 71 parts. 30 October 1969 – 22 January 1970.

Paul Temple and the Groomgate Killer. 81 parts. 23 January – 28 April 1970.

Paul Temple and the Aphrodite Affair. 79 parts. 29 April – 1 August 1970.

Paul Temple and the Big Ear. 65 parts. 3 August – 16 October 1970.

Paul Temple and the Other Paul Temple. 82 parts. 17 October 1970 - 23 January 1971.

Paul Temple and the Puddock Affair. 81 parts. 25 January – 1 May 1971.

A short-lived series of paperbacks, published twice monthly in 1964 by G.M. Smith Publishing Co (Micron Publications) as *The Paul Temple Library*, reprinted ten of the comic strips. Those selected were from early 1957 to mid-1959, but in some cases the titles were either slightly amended or completely changed. They appeared as: *Paul Temple and the Magpie Mystery* (March 1964), *Paul Temple and the Gun Runners* (March 1964), *Paul Temple and the Nerve Gas Gang* (April 1964), *Paul Temple in Operation Shrike* (April 1964), *Paul Temple Plays With Fire* (May 1964, presumably the 1957 *The Phantom Fireman*), *Paul Temple Meets His Double* (May 1964, presumably the 1957 *Double Event*), *Paul Temple and the Safari Mystery* (June 1964), *Paul Temple in The Charge is Murder!* (June 1964, probably the 1958 *Paul Temple and the Blackmailed Bridegroom*), *Paul Temple and the Q.40 Mystery* (July 1964) and *Paul Temple and the Missing Van Gogh* (July 1964, which I cannot trace back accurately to the original).

It is highly likely, irrespective of Francis Durbridge's enormous success as a radio, television and stage dramatist, that his most lucrative project was the Paul Temple comic strip – as witness Nicholas Durbridge's comment in his Introduction to this book. Not only did the Paul Temple strip run for many years in a London and several provincial newspapers, but it continued to be syndicated for at least a decade after its last appearance in the London *Evening News* and was published as far afield as France, Holland, Sweden, Cyprus, Portugal, the USA and the Philippines. After its run of over twenty years in the *Evening News*, its continuation elsewhere presumably consisted of reprinted earlier strips rather than new stories.

FRANCIS DURBRIDGE - SOME OTHER WRITINGS
[This list is almost certainly not complete, as Durbridge probably wrote other stories and articles that have not yet been traced]

First Broadcast: The Moments Before the Half-Hour. A very short story, not involving crime but telling of a young singer trying to control her nerves in the moments before her first live radio performance. Signed only with the initials F.H.D. *Birmingham Post*, No. 23,567, 16 January 1934, p.15.

Writing a Melodrama. A brief article introducing his musical melodrama *Murder in the Embassy*. *Radio Times*, 56 (722), 30 July 1937, p.8.

Meet Paul Temple. A brief article telling how Temple came into existence. *Radio Times*, 59 (760), 22 April 1938, p.10.

The Return of Paul Temple. A full page article commenting on the public reaction to *Send for Paul Temple* and introducing *Paul Temple and the Front Page Men*. *Radio Times*, 61 (787), 28 October 1938, p.7.

Johnny Cordell: The Man from Washington. A brief article introducing his new radio character, whom he describes as "a tall, slim, quiet young man ... gentle, rather shy ... in appearance not unlike the film star James Stewart." *Radio Times*, 71 (920), 16 May 1941, p.4.

Potting Paul Temple. A brief article about the problems of condensing the serial *Send for Paul Temple* into a one-hour radio play. *Radio Times*, 73 (941), 10 October 1941, p.5.

Paul Temple Returns. A brief article introducing his serial *Send for Paul Temple Again*. *Radio Times*, 88 (1145), 7 September 1945, p.4.

Paul Temple's White Christmas. A short story. *Radio Times*, 93 (1212), 20 December 1946, pp.6,19.

A Present for Paul. A short story. *Yorkshire Evening Post*, 24 December 1946, p.4. Also published on the same date in the London *Evening Standard*, p.3.

Paul Temple and the Elusive Mr. Wade. A short story. London *Evening Standard*, 10 January 1947, p.8.

Paul Temple and the Elstree Affair. A short story. London *Evening Standard*, 17 January 1947, p.8. Much later, in 1971, Durbridge re-wrote this as "Coffee Break" and replaced Temple with Det. Supt. Hamer (see below).

Paul Temple and 'The Colonel'. A short story. London *Evening Standard*, 24 January 1947, p.8.

Paul Temple and the Granville Sisters. A short story. London *Evening Standard*, 31 January 1947, p.8

Paul Temple and the Crawford Case. A short story. London *Evening Standard*, 7 February 1947, p.8.

Paul Temple Meets an Old Friend. A short story. London *Evening Standard*, 14 February 1947, p.8.

Paul Temple and the Eccentric Millionairess. A short story. London *Evening Standard*, 21 February 1947, p.6.

Paul Temple and the Girl in Grey. A short story. London *Evening Standard*, 28 February 1947, pp.6,7.

Paul Temple and the Garage Mystery. A short story. London *Evening Standard*, 7 March 1947, p.6.

Paul Temple and the Blonde Cashier. A short story. London *Evening Standard*, 14 March 1947, p.6.

Paul Temple and the Car Robberies. A short story. London *Evening Standard*, 21 March 1947, p.8.

Paul Temple and the Dark Stranger. A short story. London *Evening Standard*, 28 March 1947, p.8.

Paul Temple and a Dr. Belasco. A brief article introducing his serial *Paul Temple and Steve*. *Radio Times*, 94 (1224), 28 March 1947, p.4.

It Began with a Pair of Spectacles. A brief article introducing his serial *Paul Temple and the Sullivan Mystery*. *Radio Times*, 97 (1259), 28 November 1947, p.13.

The Superintendent Convinced Him. A brief article introducing his serial *Paul Temple and the Curzon Case*. *Radio Times*, 101 (1312), 3 December 1948, p.3.

Paul Temple Returns. A full page article, written with Martyn C. Webster, introducing the serial *Paul Temple and the Madison Mystery*, with comments by Webster on making the Temple radio programmes. *Radio Times*, 105 (1356), 7 October 1949, p.7.

This Man Temple. An article including Durbridge's biography of Temple, prompted by the fact that an episode of *Paul Temple and the Vandyke Affair* was to be broadcast that evening. London *Evening News*, 27 November 1950, p.2.

Light-Fingers. An eight-page Paul Temple story in *Daily Mail Annual for Boys and Girls*, Associated Newspapers, [1950, October]. Many years later (15 March 1995) this was read by Sandy Neilson on BBC Radio Scotland.

A Present from Paul Temple. A twelve-page story in *Daily Mail Annual for Boys and Girls*, Associated Newspapers, [1951].

My First Television Serial. A brief article introducing his television serial *The Broken Horseshoe*. *Radio Times*, 114 (1478), 7 March 1952, p.49.

Operation Diplomat. A brief article introducing his second television serial. *Radio Times*, 117 (1510), 17 October 1952, p.49.

The Ventriloquist's Doll. An eight-page Paul Temple story in *Daily Mail Annual for Boys and Girls*, Associated Newspapers, [1952].

Paul Temple and the Nightingale. A three-page story in *Late Extra: a Miscellany by "Evening News" Writers, Artists & Photographers*, edited by John Millard, Associated Newspapers, [1952].

My Friend Charles. A very brief article explaining how the idea for this television serial came to him. *Radio Times*, 130 (1686), 2 March 1956, p.1.

Scripting for Suspense. A three-page article in *TV Mirror Annual 1956*, Amalgamated Press, 1956. The heading reads "Francis Durbridge, creator of Paul Temple and author of 'Portrait of Alison', lets you into a few secrets of Scripting for Suspense."

Talking of Serials. A brief article on the technique of the serial, marking the opening of two Durbridge serials on 13 November 1957 – *Paul Temple and the Spencer Affair* on radio and *A Time of Day* on television. *Radio Times*, 137 (1774), 8 November 1957, p.9.

Speaking for Myself. A brief article about his favourite television programmes. *Radio Times*. 139 (1799), 2 May 1958, p.9.

The World of Tim Frazer. An article introducing his new serial character. *Radio Times*, 149 (1931), 10 November 1960, pp.30-31.

The Desperate People. A full page article introducing his new television serial. *Radio Times*, 158 (2050), 21 February 1963, p.13.

Meet Paul Temple Again. A brief article introducing the new production of *Paul Temple and the Jonathan Mystery* and including Durbridge's biography of Temple. *Radio Times*, 161 (2083), 10 October 1963, p.22.

Paul Temple and the Geneva Mystery. A brief article introducing his new radio serial. *Radio Times*, 167 (2161), 8 April 1965, p.21.

Coffee Break. A two-page story in *Showguide No.6*, Keith Prowse Ltd, Christmas 1971. This was originally published on 17 January 1947 as "Paul Temple and the Elstree Affair" (see above).

The Second Chance. A seven-page story in *The Radio Times Generation Game Christmas Special*, BBC, November 1974. This was originally written in 1956 under the title "Lady at the Villa", and although Durbridge's financial records indicate that it was bought by the *Daily Mail* there is no trace of its publication in that newspaper at the time.

SOME OTHER REFERENCES

ADLEY, Derek. The Paul Temple Saga. *The Armchair Detective*, 9 (4), October 1976, pp.267-269.

ANDREWS, Graham. Francis Durbridge: Creator of Radio Sleuth Paul Temple. *Book and Magazine Collector*, (173), August 1998, pp.18-26.

ASHFORD, David and WRIGHT, Norman. Heroes of the Wireless. *Book and Magazine Collector*, (257), July 2005, pp.56-67.

AYRE, Leslie. The Man Behind Paul Temple. An appreciation of Durbridge by the *Evening News* radio critic, with a portrait of Durbridge by Alfred Sindall. London *Evening News*, 29 November 1950, p.2.

BARNES, Melvyn. Francis Durbridge. Included in *Twentieth-Century Crime and Mystery Writers*, edited by John M. Reilly, Macmillan/St Martin's Press, 1980. Later editions saw some writers removed and others added, but the Durbridge entry remained in all editions as follows. 2nd ed., edited by John M. Reilly, St James Press, 1985; 3rd ed., edited by Lesley Henderson, St James Press, 1991; 4th ed., retitled *St James Guide to Crime and Mystery Writers*, edited by Jay P. Pederson, St James Press, 1996.

BELL, Jack. 25 Years of Being Paul Temple's Steve. An interview with Marjorie Westbury. *Daily Mirror*, 17 May 1965, p.21.

BLEASDALE, Alan. The Heart of a Craftsman. A brief reminiscence by Bleasdale, a longtime admirer who finally met Durbridge to discuss the proposal to re-write the television serial *Melissa* the year before Durbridge died. *The Guardian*, 13 April 1998, p.13.

DE MANIO, Jack. An eight-minute interview with Francis Durbridge, previously broadcast by the BBC in one of De Manio's radio programmes, now included on the fourth of the four CDs of *Paul Temple and the Conrad Case*, BBC Audio, 2004. This interview was early in 1975.

DOWN, Richard and PERRY, Christopher (Eds). *The British Television Drama Research Guide*, 2nd ed. Kaleidoscope, 1997.

EMERSON, Joyce. Steve Temple and her Radio Husbands. A brief article based on an interview with Marjorie Westbury. *Radio Times*, 137 (1775), 15 November 1957, p.6.

EXPLOITS OF A REDBRICK HANNAY. A brief anonymous article prompted by a repeat of *The World of Tim Frazer* on television, this also comments upon Durbridge's work generally. *The Times*, 23 December 1961, p.3.

FOWLER, Christopher. Forgotten Authors No. 39: Francis Durbridge. *Independent on Sunday*, 27 September 2009, p.41.
Also www.christopherfowler.co.uk /blog /2009/10/09

GAISFORD, Sue. Still With Us: Peter Coke. A full page article based on an interview. *The Oldie*, No. 195, June 2005, p.15.

GIFFORD, Denis. *The Golden Age of Radio*. Batsford, 1985.

GLOVER, C. Gordon. Francis Durbridge, the Creator of Paul Temple and the Margo Mystery. A full page interview launching Durbridge's new radio serial. *Radio Times*, 149 (1938), 29 December 1960, p.14.

HADLEY, Katharine. Whatsisname Gets the Paul Temple Image. A brief interview with Francis Matthews, who had secured the role of Temple in the Anglo-German television series. *Daily Express*, 18 July 1969, p.8.

HALL, Craig C. Send for Paul Temple! *ThrillerUK*, (29), April 2005, pp.2-8.

HAMILTON, Fred. Zoom In When You See The Tears: 30 Adventurous Years at the BBC. Fantom, 2011. Autobiography of the cameraman who worked on numerous television series including *Paul Temple*.

HARRISON, Kathleen. "I'm the BBC's Char". A full page article about her role in the radio series *The Daily Dodge*. *Radio Pictorial*, (284), 23 June 1939, p.11.

HATTON, Charles. Return of Paul Temple. A full page article about the success of *Send for Paul Temple* and introducing the second serial, *Paul Temple and the Front Page Men*. *Radio Pictorial*, (250), 28 October 1938, p.14.

HEALD, Tim. Francis Durbridge Enjoying a Life of Crime. *The Times*, 29 April 1981, p.12.

HOUSEHOLD, Nicki. Danger Men. An article introducing Durbridge's last television serial *Breakaway*, with reflections on playing Durbridge protagonists by Gerald Harper (*A Man Called Harry Brent* and *A Game of Murder*), Peter Barkworth (*The Passenger* and *Melissa*), Jack Hedley (*The World of Tim Frazer*) and Martin Jarvis (*Breakaway*). *Radio Times*, 226 (2930), 5 January 1980, pp.4-5.

JOHNSON, Pete. "By Timothy, Steve – we're eighty." *CADS: Crime and Detective Stories*, (77), March 2018, pp.49-50.

KABATCHNIK, Amnon. *Blood on the Stage 1950-1975: Milestone Plays of Crime, Mystery, and Detection*. Scarecrow Press, 2011.

KEATING, H.R.F. Last Seen Approaching the Cliff-Edge. A full page feature to mark the second television production of *Melissa*, with quotes about Durbridge from Michael Gilbert, Dick Francis, Edmund Crispin and Anthony Shaffer. *Radio Times*, 205 (2664), 28 November 1974, p.17.

LIDSTONE, Frederick. Suspense. An article on television crime drama, previewing *Portrait of Alison*. *TV Mirror*, Vol 4 no.8, 19 February 1955, pp.10-11.

MATTHEWS, Francis. Being Paul Temple: An Interview with Francis Matthews. Included on the first of the four DVDs marketed as *Francis Durbridge's The Paul Temple Collection*, BBC/Acorn Media, 2009. A candid interview about the making and ultimate fate of the 1969/71 Anglo-German television series.

NORTON, Charles. *Serial Thrillers: The Adventure Serial on British Radio*. Kaleidoscope, 2012.

OBITUARIES

John Bentley (1916-2009)

By Gavin Gaughan. *The Guardian*, 19 August 2009, p.33.

Peter Coke (1913-2008)

By Jack Adrian. *The Independent*, 13 August 2008, p.36.
(Anonymous). *The Times*, 23 August 2008, p.68.
By Gavin Gaughan. *The Guardian*, 5 September 2008, p.39.

Francis Durbridge (1912-1998)

By Jack Adrian. *The Independent*, 13 April 1998, p.15.
By Dennis Barker. *The Guardian*, 13 April 1998, p.13.
(Anonymous). *The Times*, 13 April 1998, p.23.

Marjorie Westbury (1905-1989)

(Anonymous). *The Times*, 18 December 1989, p.16.

OLD BRADFORDIANS. Books LLC, 2010, printed on demand. A collection of Wikipedia articles about thirty-seven former pupils of Bradford Grammar School, including Francis Durbridge.

PATE, Janet. *The Book of Sleuths*. New English Library, 1977.

PETERS, Pauline. The Mystery of Francis Durbridge. *Sunday Express Colour Magazine*, (33), 22 November 1981, pp.12-13.

PITTS, Michael R. *Famous Movie Detectives III*. Scarecrow Press, 2004.

PUGH, Marshall. Just for a moment the mystery man lifted his mask. A quarter-page article based on an interview with Durbridge. *Daily Mail*, 18 May 1964, p.6.

QUINLAN, David. *British Sound Films: The Studio Years 1928-1959*. Batsford, 1984.

RICHARDS, Jeffrey. An unbroadcast interview with actor Peter Coke, dated 20 March 1998, included on CD10 of the ten-CD set marketed as *Paul Temple : The Complete Radio Collection: The Early Years 1938-1950*, BBC/British Library, 2016.

RICHARDS, Jeffrey. The Radio Detectives (1): Send for Paul Temple. A thirty-minute broadcast on BBC Radio 4 on 20 May 1998, a month after Durbridge died. Now included on the fifth of the five CDs of *Paul Temple and the Vandyke Affair*, BBC Audio, 2004.

SAUNDERS, Michaela. Peter Coke and the Paul Temple Affair. A thirty-minute radio interview with actor Peter Coke, first broadcast on BBC Radio 7 on 31 December 2005 and repeated several times, but particularly on 27 September 2008 as a tribute to Coke who died on 30 July 2008. Now included on CDs 18 and 19 of the nineteen-CD set marketed as *Paul Temple: The Complete Radio Collection: The Sixties 1960-1968*, BBC, 2017.

SNOWDON, Roger. Dick Barton and all that. A forty-five minute radio documentary on 31 October 1982, recalling four popular series of the 1940s and 1950s – *Paul Temple*, *Appointment with Fear*, *P.C. 49* and *Dick Barton* - with participants including Francis Durbridge, Marjorie Westbury, Valentine Dyall, Joy Shelton and Noel Johnson.

TIBBALLS, Geoff. *The Boxtree Encyclopedia of TV Detectives*. Boxtree, 1992.

VAHIMAGI, Tise. Prime Time Suspects: Part 4.1: Themes and Strands (Durbridge Cliffhangers). 2011. Accessible online at: www.mysteryfile.com/blog/?p=11090

WEBSTER, Martyn C. News of Paul Temple. A full page article about the origin of the Temple serials, which also confirms Webster's practice of withholding the solution from the cast until they arrive to rehearse the final episode. *Radio Times*, 65 (841), 10 November 1939, p.8.

WEBSTER, Martyn C. And Now Meet Francis Durbridge. A brief article as *Portrait of Alison* began. *TV Mirror*, Vol 4 no.8, 19 February 1955, pp.11-12.

WEBSTER, Martyn C. Paul Temple and his Creator. A brief article by Durbridge's producer, with insights into their association. *Radio Times*, 142 (1842), 27 February 1959, p.3.

WEBSTER, Martyn C. "An' It Don't Seem A Day Too Much!" A brief article about his association with Durbridge, confirming that the script of *Paul Temple and the Alex Affair* arrived after a hiatus in Temple serials – though failing to acknowledge that it was a re-write of *Send for Paul Temple Again*. *Radio Times*, 178 (2311), 22 February 1968, p.20.

WILTSHIRE, Maurice. Paul Temple's Casebook. A brief article introducing *Paul Temple and the Madison Mystery*. *Daily Mail*, 11 October 1949, p.4.

WINTON, Malcolm. Who is Master-Minding Paul Temple? A brief article introducing the Francis Matthews television series. *Radio Times*, 185 (2402), 20 November 1969, p.16.

WOODWARD, Ian. Man of Mystery: The Elusive Francis Durbridge. *Woman's Journal*, March 1976, pp. 58-59.

WRIGHT, Nicholas. Creator of Paul Temple: Francis Durbridge, TV's most successful mystery writer, talks to Nicholas Wright about his career and methods. *Illustrated London News*, 29 November 1969, pp. 20-21.

WYNN JONES, Michael. Investigating the Mastermind behind 30 Years of Violent Crime. An interview with Francis Durbridge about his television career, launching his serial *The Passenger*. *Radio Times*, 193 (2502), 21 October 1971, pp.66-71.

CHRONOLOGY – PAUL TEMPLE RADIO PRODUCTIONS

(** = Marketed as Audiocassettes and/or CDs)

1938, 8 April – 27 May. *Send for Paul Temple*. [Hugh Morton as Temple, Bernadette Hodgson as Steve, Lester Mudditt as Forbes] **112**. **The 1940 Canadian production [Bernard Braden as Temple, Peggy Hassard as Steve, Earle Grey as Forbes] is available on CDs

1938, 2 November – 21 December. *Paul Temple and the Front Page Men*. [Hugh Morton as Temple, Bernadette Hodgson as Steve, Lester Mudditt as Forbes] **114**

1939, 13 November – 18 December. *News of Paul Temple*. [Hugh Morton as Temple, Bernadette Hodgson as Steve, Lester Mudditt as Forbes] **123**

1941, 13 October. *Send for Paul Temple* (New production, abridged to one hour). [Carl Bernard as Temple, Thea Holme as Steve, Cecil Trouncer as Forbes] **112A**

1942, 30 October – 18 December. *Paul Temple Intervenes*. [Carl Bernard as Temple, Bernadette Hodgson as Steve, Lester Mudditt as Forbes] **142****

1944, 5 July. *News of Paul Temple* (New production, abridged to one hour). [Richard Williams as Temple, Lucille Lisle as Steve, Laidman Browne as Forbes] **123A**

1945, 13 September – 1 November. *Send for Paul Temple Again*. [Barry Morse as Temple, Marjorie Westbury as Steve, Lester Mudditt as Forbes] **151**

1946, 7 February – 28 March. *A Case for Paul Temple*. [Howard Marion-Crawford as Temple, Marjorie Westbury as Steve, Lester Mudditt as Forbes] **152**

1946, 17 October – 19 December. *Paul Temple and the Gregory Affair*. [Kim Peacock as Temple, Marjorie Westbury as Steve, Lester Mudditt as Forbes, Frank Partington / Billy Thatcher as Charlie, Arthur Ridley as Vosper] **154**

1947, 30 March – 18 May. *Paul Temple and Steve*. [Kim Peacock as Temple, Marjorie Westbury as Steve, Lester Mudditt as Forbes, Kenneth Morgan as Charlie] **155**

1947, 21 November. *Mr. and Mrs. Paul Temple* (Forty-five minute play). [Kim Peacock as Temple, Marjorie Westbury as Steve, Lester Mudditt as Forbes] **156**

1947, 1 December – 1948, 19 January. *Paul Temple and the Sullivan Mystery*. [Kim Peacock as Temple, Marjorie Westbury as Steve, Lester Mudditt as Forbes, Kenneth Morgan as Charlie] **157**

1948, 7 December – 1949, 25 January. *Paul Temple and the Curzon Case*. [Kim Peacock as Temple, Marjorie Westbury as Steve, Lester Mudditt as Forbes, Billy Thatcher as Charlie, Arthur Ridley as Vosper] **158**

1949, 12 October – 30 November. *Paul Temple and the Madison Mystery*. [Kim Peacock as Temple, Marjorie Westbury as Steve, Lester Mudditt as Forbes, Desmond Carrington as Charlie, Arthur Ridley as Vosper] **160**

1950, 30 October – 18 December. *Paul Temple and the Vandyke Affair*. [Kim Peacock as Temple, Marjorie Westbury as Steve, Lester Mudditt as Forbes, Michael Harding as Charlie] **162****

1951, 10 May – 28 June. *Paul Temple and the Jonathan Mystery*. [Kim Peacock as Temple, Marjorie Westbury as Steve, Lester Mudditt as Forbes, Frank Partington as Charlie] **163**

1953, 8 April. *Paul Temple and Steve Again* (One-hour play). [Kim Peacock as Temple, Marjorie Westbury as Steve, Lester Mudditt as Forbes, James Beattie as Charlie] **164**

1954, 29 March – 17 May. *Paul Temple and the Gilbert Case*. [Peter Coke as Temple, Marjorie Westbury as Steve, Lester Mudditt as Forbes, James Beattie as Charlie] **165****

1955, 20 June – 8 August. *Paul Temple and the Madison Mystery* (New production). [Peter Coke as Temple, Marjorie Westbury as Steve, Lester Mudditt as Forbes, James Beattie as Charlie, T. St. John Barry as Vosper] **160A**

1956, 11 April – 30 May. *Paul Temple and the Lawrence Affair*. [Peter Coke as Temple, Marjorie Westbury as Steve, Lester Mudditt as Forbes, James Beattie as Charlie, Arthur Ridley as Vosper] **166****

1957, 13 November – 1958, 1 January. *Paul Temple and the Spencer Affair*. [Peter Coke as Temple, Marjorie Westbury as Steve, Lester Mudditt as Forbes, James Beattie as Charlie, Hugh Manning as Vosper] **167****

1959, 1 January – 19 February. *Paul Temple and the Vandyke Affair* (New production). [Peter Coke as Temple, Marjorie Westbury as Steve, Richard Williams as Forbes, James Beattie as Charlie] **162A****

1959, 2 March – 20 April. *Paul Temple and the Conrad Case*. [Peter Coke as Temple, Marjorie Westbury as Steve, Richard Williams as Forbes, James Beattie as Charlie, Hugh Manning as Vosper] **168****

1959, 22 November – 1960, 10 January. *Paul Temple and the Gilbert Case* (New production). [Peter Coke as Temple, Marjorie Westbury as Steve, Richard Williams as Forbes, James Beattie as Charlie] **165A****

1961, 1 January – 19 February. *Paul Temple and the Margo Mystery*. [Peter Coke as Temple, Marjorie Westbury as Steve, James Thomason as Forbes, James Beattie as Charlie] **169****

1963, 14 October – 2 December. *Paul Temple and the Jonathan Mystery* (New production). [Peter Coke as Temple, Marjorie Westbury as Steve, James Thomason as Forbes, James Beattie as Charlie] **163A****

1965, 11 April – 16 May. *Paul Temple and the Geneva Mystery*. [Peter Coke as Temple, Marjorie Westbury as Steve, John Baddeley as Charlie] **171****

1968, 26 February – 21 March. *Paul Temple and the Alex Affair* (New production of *Send for Paul Temple Again*). [Peter Coke as Temple, Marjorie Westbury as Steve, James Thomason as Forbes] **151A****

2006, 7 August – 2 October. *Paul Temple and the Sullivan Mystery* (New production). [Crawford Logan as Temple, Gerda Stevenson as Steve, Gareth Thomas as Forbes, Greg Powrie as Charlie] **157A****

2008, 16 May – 4 July. *Paul Temple and the Madison Mystery* (New production). [Crawford Logan as Temple, Gerda Stevenson as Steve, Gareth Thomas as Forbes, Greg Powrie as Charlie, Michael Mackenzie as Vosper] **160B****

2010, 11 June – 30 July. *Paul Temple and Steve* (New production). [Crawford Logan as Temple, Gerda Stevenson as Steve, Gareth Thomas as Forbes, Greg Powrie as Charlie] **155A****

2011, 24 August – 12 October. *A Case for Paul Temple* (New production). [Crawford Logan as Temple, Gerda Stevenson as Steve, Gareth Thomas as Forbes] **152A****

2013, 3 July – 11 September. *Paul Temple and the Gregory Affair* (New production). [Crawford Logan as Temple, Gerda Stevenson as Steve, Gareth Thomas as Forbes, Greg Powrie as Charlie, Michael Mackenzie as Vosper] **154A****

Printed in Great Britain
by Amazon